I0557586

ANGEL OF DEATH

DONNY HUNT

This is a work of fiction. Names, characters, places, and incidents are products of the author's imagination or are used fictitiously and are not to be construed as real. Any resemblance to actual events, locations, organizations, or persons, living or dead, is entirely coincidental.

World Castle Publishing, LLC
Pensacola, Florida
Copyright © Donny Hunt 2017
Paperback ISBN: 9798891263901
eBook ISBN: 9781629898254
First Edition World Castle Publishing, LLC, November 27, 2017
http://www.worldcastlepublishing.com
Licensing Notes
All rights reserved. No part of this book may be used or reproduced in any manner whatsoever without written permission, except in the case of brief quotations embodied in articles and reviews.
Cover: Karen Fuller
Editor: Maxine Bringenberg

Table of Contents

Chapter 1

The Angel of Death walked unbowed through the night and the pouring rain. Her bright violet eyes were laser-locked on her target and she was a heat-seeking missile, bent on absolute and total destruction.

All around her bodies swirled like a human ocean, ebbing and flowing and then parting as she passed. She sliced through like a knife, barely cognizant of the mass of bodies around her. The only thing that existed in the world at that moment was her target, and there was no force on Earth that would stop her from completing her task.

It was a cool, early spring New Mexican night, warm enough for the attendees of the Greater Southwestern Comic-con to leave their coats at home and come out in all of their fully costumed weirdness. The people flowed in, out, and around Tingley Coliseum, most all of them dressed in the garb of their favorite fictional characters. The coliseum grounds were a wild collection of superheroes, space pirates, feudal knights, robots, and aliens of all kinds. There were tons of women there, almost all of them made up in ways to make them look sexy and showing plenty of skin, even the ones who didn't have the body to pull off the looks they were going for.

All of it went over Angel's head. She'd never had time for comic books or movies, for playing dress up or for imagination. Her life had been the kind of real life horror show that people like this never knew and couldn't understand. Angel felt the resentment percolating deep in her soul as she watched the smiling faces pass by her and heard the laughter carried on the mountain winds.

Angel used that resentment; it fueled her and drove her forward, closer to her target. Angel blended right in with the wildly dressed crowd. No one paid too much attention to the pretty, short girl with the sassy, hip swinging walk, even with the toy six shooters in a plastic holster slung low around her waist, or the repurposed broom handle that served as a home-made staff that hung down the center of her back. She whizzed past people, her long, rainbow-colored hair trailing behind her, face covered in pale white makeup with slut red lipstick and glittery eye shadow. She paid no attention to the admiring looks she got from more than one convention goer as she strutted past in her blood-red, faux leather bustier under a black motorcycle jacket, tiny plaid miniskirt, and knee-high white stockings with low topped black boots. Under her left arm, Angel felt the reassuring weight of the very real Glock nine-millimeter pistol in a shoulder holster, fully loaded and hungry for blood.

Ahead of Angel, two high powered headlights cut through the swirl of humanity as a black limo pulled quickly up to the curb and sat idling, brake lights shading everything behind the limo in bright red as the driver declined to put it in park. Out of the corner of her eye, Angel watched as the first security guard emerged from the front entrance a moment later, a thick Mexican gentleman in a nicely tailored suit and closely cropped black hair. He walked with a sense of urgency and a certain weight that immediately sent a message to anyone around him, and dutifully, if subconsciously, the crowd gave him room. He circled around the rear of the car, passing through the beams of the brake lights, and took up a post just beside the driver's door.

Almost immediately a second guard emerged. He had the same walk and attitude, though this man was taller and leaner than the first. His suit didn't fit as well, and when he took his post ten feet out from the left side passenger door, Angel clearly saw the bump of his gun under the man's suit jacket.

Next came the target, Rafael Baca, the pathetic half-son of a powerful Mexican drug lord. Known derisively as "Reckless Raffy," Baca lived large on his father's money and reputation. Baca existed on a diet of high quality cocaine, expensive liquor, and cheap whores. He was a wash-out; a family embarrassment that was largely unwelcome at home and completely unrelated to the family business.

It was his reckless lifestyle, not his family connections, which had marked Rafael Baca for death. The overgrown fan boy had gotten wasted and stupid and strangled a sixteen-year-old girl dressed as Wonder Woman, and left her body lying in an alley in downtown Minneapolis. He'd left it up to his bulky bodyguards, his expensive attorney, and his family name to keep himself out of jail, and it had worked.

The grieving father, frustrated with the failure of the so-called justice system, had sought relief from other sources. Somehow, he had been put in contact with a man known on the streets as The Thunderbird. For a generous fee, The Thunderbird had agreed to resolve the issue. He had, in turn, dispatched Angel to provide the family with the only kind of justice they would ever get.

The Thunderbird was Angel's master. He had taken her in off the streets and molded her into what she was now: a highly efficient, emotionless killer. The only thing in the world that mattered to Angel was the job in hand, the target, and the successful completion of the mission. Success made Master happy, and when Master was happy, life was good.

Angel had *never* failed Master.

Baca emerged from the front door of the coliseum looking like the cliché that he was. It was the look he aimed for, wearing an expensive tailored suit with the shirt unbuttoned a quarter of the way down, Italian loafers, slicked-back hair that was intentionally ruffled, and lots of jewelry. He was not an attractive man in the least and he knew it, which was why he dripped money everywhere he went. Money was the only thing that could make this mousy, acne-scarred shrimp of man appealing to the beautiful girls that managed to gather at every stop.

Angel had been following Baca for weeks now as he hopped from one convention to another. She had observed his every move, and by now had a detailed understanding not just of how he worked, but how his three-man security detailed operated. She knew how much cocaine they snorted, how much alcohol they drank, and exactly how they moved around each other. She had thrilled when Baca had gotten himself into a scuffle at a Meet-and-Greet for some famous comic book artist in Las Vegas and his bodyguards had left him twisting in the wind for several minutes. Angel had smiled as she watched them taking in the scene with amusement before finally, reluctantly, swooping in to save their charge.

She recognized in each of the three men an air of danger and a certain taste for the rougher aspects of their job. She also noticed their blatant dislike for Baca, and it was that dislike that made them soft and slow. They used their stature as their primary deterrent and that had been more than enough to diffuse any trouble.

It wouldn't be enough to save Reckless Raffy on this night.

Everything about her look was specially tailored to catch Baca's eye. She might have felt foolish in the get-up, if feelings were something she allowed herself, but they were not. The costume was just a tool, the key to get her next to Baca, nice and close, where she could deliver her message intimately and publicly.

Baca strolled out into the night with a girl under each arm; one was a big busted blonde in booty shorts and pigtails, the other a shorter, stouter Asian girl with a teal wig, wearing a tight, black leather bodysuit. Baca was talking a mile a minute and grinning from ear to ear while the girls giggled and hung on his every word. Behind him, the third security guard trailed, holding an umbrella not quite over Baca's head. He was the oldest of three and the one Baca liked the best, so he was always the one that stayed closest and got the embarrassing jobs like holding Baca's umbrella. On this night, there was just enough wind that the guard had to hold the umbrella with both hands to keep the wind from ripping it out of his hands, the guard's gun completely useless under his suit jacket.

Angel had timed her approach perfectly, passing through Baca's line of vision just as he came around the rear of the car. She let her gaze settle on him, making sure that he saw.

"Whoo, wow baby, look at that," he called out loudly. "Look at that strut."

Angel kept walking briskly, but gave him a corner of a smile and slight head nod to acknowledge his comment. Baca couldn't stand for a woman to ignore him once she had caught his eye. He stopped walking and slid his right arm away from the busty blonde's shoulder.

"Hey! Yo! Rainbow! Over here, sweetness."

Angel stopped short and pivoted sharply to face him. She cocked her head to one side, placed one hand on her hip, and

9

leaned forward slightly to give him a glimpse at her cleavage. Angel wasn't particularly endowed by any means, so the outfit that she wore was specifically designed to make her appear much larger, and it worked. Baca's eyes slid down her and back up, like he was eyeing a piece of meat in a steakhouse window. His tongue slithered out of his mouth as he licked his lips.

"Hey baby," he called out again. "You like to party?"

Angel straightened up and shifted her weight from one foot to the other. "Whaddya you think?" she called out in a ridiculous accent that was somewhere between a southern drawl and Brooklyn snark. She never claimed to be an actress.

"I bet you do," Baca muttered with a shake of his head. "Come over here, baby. Let me get a better look at you."

She smiled full, letting him see a mouthful of pretty white teeth as she sauntered towards him. Angel's eyes moved quickly to each of the three bodyguards. She was looking for any sign of recognition, of danger. Instead she saw only complacency and annoyance. They weren't prepared for a fight, weren't ready to act. She passed by the taller guard and gave him a flirty wink. She was inside their triangular perimeter now, and although none of them knew it, Rafael Baca was already a dead man. As she got closer, Angel licked her own lips, slowly, letting him see her tongue make its way around. He smiled bigger. Beside him, the girls were annoyed at Angel's presence and both yapped at him to get in the car, that they didn't need any more company. They didn't want to share their newfound sugar daddy.

Angel stopped her approach an arm's length away and again leaned forward to give him a glimpse. "You like what you see, baby?"

"You know I do, sugar," Baca grinned.

Quick, quicker than Angel expected, he reached out, wrapped his left arm around her waist, and yanked her in close. The move stole Angel's breath for a second, before she rebounded. He was an inch or so taller than she, so she craned her neck slightly to look up into the face of her victim. He reeked of overpriced cologne and booze.

With his left arm still around her waist, he traced the line of Angel's face with his right index finger. "I don't know this character," he whispered. "But I like her." He let his hand fall, brushing over her breast and down her side. Angel feared for one second that he might feel the Glock, but his hand never came near it. Instead, it settled on one of the toy guns in her holster. He pulled it slowly and held it up to the side of her head. "Boom," Baca grinned, and pulled the trigger, and the plastic hammer clicked in her ear.

"Are you playin' with me?" Angel teased, still putting on the silly accent.

"I sure am. I like to play. Do you?"

"You know it." The other girls glared at her and Angel returned the favor. "I can show you things you could only dream of."

"I doubt that," Baca cooed back at her. "But you're welcome to come back to my hotel and try and prove me wrong. You wouldn't mind a little company, would you, girls?" They kept glaring, but as he looked down at each in turn, they grudgingly put on fake smiles and agreed.

"So let's get the party started. What do you say…uh…?"

"Cassie," Angel answered. Cassie was the name of the girl he had killed. Now she searched his eyes for any glimmer of recognition and found none. Angel nuzzled up closer and slowly inched her right arm inside her jacket until her fingers brushed the grip of the Glock. She knew that their bodies were shielding the guard by the door and the one holding the umbrella, so as long as the point man couldn't see what she was doing, this would be

11

easy. "Do you know what she does?" Angel asked eagerly.

Baca rolled his eyes quickly, then down at her with a condescending grin. "What does she do, sweetness?"

Angel smiled back at him. "She avenges murdered girls," she said, dropping the fake accent. In those few seconds, it finally dawned on Rafael Baca what was happening. Only now it was far too late. Angel produced the Glock like magic, pressed it under his chin, and fired two quick rounds directly into his head. The girls screamed and plastered themselves against the limo in terror.

Everything turned to chaos around her as the crowd began screaming and swirling. They were trying to get away, but most people had no idea where the shots had come from so they scattered in all directions at once. As Baca's limp body began collapsing to the ground Angel turned slightly, targeting the guard by the door, who she had assessed to be the most dangerous of the three. As he tried to pull his gun, she shot him in the forehead.

Angel turned, aware that the other two guards would be pulling on her at any second. The one with the umbrella was struggling, momentarily stunned by the speed of Angel's moves. Knowing that the point man was the immediate threat, Angel reached out for the blonde, grabbing her by the arm. She yanked the tall blonde forward and shoved her directly at the point man, who had already cleared his weapon and had Angel dead to rights. Angel moved forward toward the Asian girl, who was finally getting her wits about her. The point man fired, but the blonde stumbled into his line of fire and her head exploded as the bullet slammed into her skull.

The umbrella guard had finally let go of the umbrella and was reaching under his sports coat as the Asian girl started to run. Angel fired a blind shot at the point man to slow him down as she lunged at the Asian girl and shoved her in the direction of the umbrella guard. The girl went sideways and down, her teal wig flying off as she stumbled and rolled into the guard's feet, knocking him off balance just as he was clearing his gun.

Angel continued moving toward the rear of the car. The rear guard was trying to extricate himself from the Asian girl at his feet and never saw Angel target him, never had any clue that death was coming as Angel put in a bullet in the top of his head. The man toppled over the screaming girl.

One guard left. Angel risked a glance over her shoulder as the point man adjusted his aim and she fired another quick shot, not going for a hit but merely trying to make him pause. She was surprised when her shot found home, ripping through the meat on his left side, just above his hip bone. It was enough to make him jerk as he fired, and yet another potentially fatal shot missed her, slamming into the rear quarter panel of the limo. Angel felt a sting as something, probably a sliver of metal, penetrated her leg, but she was moving too fast and far too busy to worry about it. She reached the rear of the car, hurdling the fallen bodies of the guard and the girl, when a second car came tearing through the crowd toward her. Angel stopped in surprise as a huge gold Lincoln Continental screeched to a stop and the doors flew open.

She'd never known that he had a second security team. She'd never caught any wind of them whatsoever.

Angel skidded to a stop, then quickly turned and rounded the rear of the car as three men emerged from the Lincoln, each with a gun in hand. The point man was still firing, but again her change of direction had thrown him off and his shot went into the crowd, where an onlooker fell and a fresh set of screams erupted from the crowd. The limo driver had finally realized what was going on and hammered the gas, causing the limo to lurch forward and fish tail. Angel crouched low and ran alongside, using it for cover.

Someone yelled out in Spanish, which was quickly answered, and then more shots filled the air, many impacting the limo, the pavement, or the walls of the coliseum around her. As the limo turned away from her and towards the street, Angel peeled off the other way, heading for an adjacent parking lot. As she ran she began shouting, "Gun, gun! They're shooting! Call the police!" This sent people skittering in all directions again and gave Angel some cover. The shots were still coming and getting closer, so Angel fired two blind shots over her shoulder with an immediate answer and a new round of screams.

Angel reached the parking lot, still crouched low, and tried to lose herself in the throng of cars. She moved slower now, more carefully. She tried to pick out the sounds of approaching footsteps from those that ran away in terror. She zig-zagged along, sprinting from one row of cars to the next. Sirens fired off somewhere in the distance, but coming closer.

Angel forced the myriad of questions that pounded at the back of her mind to be silent. She needed to concentrate. Without some sort of a break, she would have to shoot her way out, against four-to-one odds with no element of surprise. If this was the end for her, she would go out fighting and she wasn't going alone. Angel kept flexing her fingers around the butt of the pistol, readying herself for the final shootout, when a new sound filled the air: the high-pitched whine of a motorcycle starting up.

Angel risked raising her head, and two rows ahead of her position a brightly colored head in a full-faced motorcycle helmet began moving quickly. Almost instantly the men spotted her. A man yelled "Ahi" and the gunfire started again. Angel immediately ducked and began running, only now she changed her course, angling to intercept the bike. As she ran, Angel stowed the Glock in her holster and slipped the broom-handle staff off her back and into her hands. The men behind her were continuing to yell to each other, their shots coming closer, but Angel only needed a few more seconds now.

She popped out from between two cars seconds before the bike passed her. She took the chance, standing tall and gripping the broom handle with both hands like a baseball bat. The rider's head swiveled toward her but he was too late. Angel hit him across the chest and knocked the rider off the back of the bike, which fishtailed for a few feet then went down on its side and skidded into a parked car.

Angel tossed the broom handle aside and pulled the gun. Two of the newcomers were chasing her, but they were further off her track than she had originally thought. She pulled the gun and fired a quick shot in the general direction of each, just enough to make them duck. Just enough for her to make it to the downed bike and get it back on its wheels. As the fallen rider groaned loudly behind her, she mounted the crotch rocket and screamed off, throwing up a plume of thick, white tire smoke as she did.

Angel screamed out of the parking lot a moment later. Ahead, the interstate and freedom beckoned. She risked a glance over her shoulder to see the Lincoln with its fancy custom paint job glittering under the orange street lights rounding a corner behind her, the two men waiting anxiously at the curb for it to stop.

Good luck, she thought as Angel accelerated, certain that the bulky old car had no chance of keeping up with her. In normal conditions she would have been right, but she hit a puddle on the street and the bike slipped and skidded on the wet pavement, forcing Angel to back off and use her feet to keep the bike upright. Behind her, the Lincoln's tires squealed as the driver floored it, the headlights illuminating her fully in the night.

"Damn it," she muttered as she righted the bike again and started for the interstate. She had gotten cocky and it had almost cost her. It still might. Angel rode low, as close to the motorcycle's body as possible, and she kept zigging, making herself a small target, all the while fully aware of how quickly the powerful bike could get away from her.

That didn't stop the men in the car from firing at her, with a couple of shots whizzing by much closer than she would have liked. Then the on-ramp to the interstate materialized out of the mist. She'd almost run right past it. Angel hit the brakes hard, causing the back tire to lift up, and the bike was dangerously close to nosing over. Angel threw her weight back and the rear tire slammed back down with a jolt that rocked her. Knowing that she had no time to waste, she jerked the bike to the left and took off again, rocketing up the ramp and onto the highway, the Lincoln closing in all the while.

Angel wanted to let the bike out full throttle, but the slippery conditions prevented it. Up here, the puddles were deeper and the traffic was throwing showers of water at her as she passed. All of it allowed the Lincoln to keep in sight of her, the men inside occasionally risking a shot, even in the moderate evening traffic. They were headed east, toward the dark shadows of the Sandia Mountains in front of them. Angel pushed as hard as she could as she tried to build herself a little cushion. She had spent several days driving all over the city, plotting out various escape routes. She knew one would come available to her once they left the city and the darkness swallowed them up. She just needed space and time, two things she was sorely lacking at the moment.

The chase continued, both vehicles weaving dangerously in and out of traffic as innocent commuters narrowly avoided them. The lights of the city thinned out and the highway made a sweeping curve to the left, and just like that the city was gone, obscured completely by the mountains. Angel put the bike in the far inside lane as she readied herself to make her big move, the one that would either secure her freedom or seal her fate. She glanced over her shoulder to see the Lincoln weave over in response as she'd hoped they would. She backed off the throttle and let the Lincoln close the gap. They started shooting again, but Angel held the line for one heartbeat…two…three. Then she wrenched the bike hard right across the other lanes of traffic, angling for an off ramp she'd ridden right up on. Behind her the Lincoln squealed and skidded, but there was no way the driver could replicate her move.

Angel sped down the ramp, where several cars waited at a red light at the base. She piloted the bike between the idling cars, looked once to assess the flow of traffic, then shot into the intersection, braking hard and steering left, accelerating again before the wheels could gain traction, throwing more smoke into the air. Just before the tires bit and the bike lurched forward, she saw the Lincoln barrel down the ramp after her, the chase not yet finished. She poured on as much speed as she dared. Ahead, the mountains rose to greet her, the traffic thinned, and the darkness surrounded her.

Angel relaxed just a bit and sat up straight, giving her back a much-needed break from the uncomfortable position she'd been riding in. It was only a brief respite, because far sooner than she'd expected, headlights swept around a corner and fixed on her. Even as Angel slumped back down and gunned the engine, she had a fleeting moment of respect for whoever was driving the Lincoln. Not many drivers could have stayed with her, especially in an ancient old barge such as that.

The gunfire resumed, only heavier now that there was almost no traffic in the way. Now as she dodged their shots, the realization dawned on Angel. In a night full of uncharacteristic mistakes, she'd just made the fatal one. She'd planned on having enough space and time to just duck off the road and let her pursuers shoot past her in the dark, but they'd stayed close, and now it was only a matter of time before one of those wild shots hit home. The only thing she had left to hope for was that when the bullet did hit, it would be an instant death and not just a wound. She had no desire to be dragged off and tortured by some depraved cartel enforcer.

She kept pushing, kept dodging, hoping for something that could tilt the odds back in her favor. The Lincoln couldn't close on her, but she couldn't lose it either. No matter how small and nimble a target she was, the law of averages told her she was running out of time and luck.

Ahead, yellow reflectors warned her of a coming turn. Angel knew what she had to do. She sped into the coming turn and was thankful for the momentary relief as the Lincoln's headlights disappeared. They were back a moment later, the opposing driver still charging hard in his pursuit. If she could hold off until the next curve, Angel could simply put the bike down in a controlled skid and skid right off the road and into the woods. She would probably fly into a tree trunk and snap her back, or scoot right off the edge of a cliff, but both of those outcomes were preferable to torture. More reflectors appeared in front of her and Angel prepared herself mentally for what was to come. No matter what happened next, she knew it was going to hurt like hell.

The curve approached rapidly and Angel sat upright on the bike, preparing to force the skid, when a bullet slammed into her left shoulder. The impact threw her forward. The bike danced on the wet pavement and then went over on its side. Angel flew off, landing hard on her right side, and went skidding across the pavement, then into the dirt and off the side of the road. She went airborne again for a moment before landing hard on her back.

She was on a steep incline, first sliding, and then rolling down the hill. Above her, the bike hit a tree and the darkness lit up as it burst into flames. Angel saw the light of the fire for just a moment before she was absorbed by the dark. Her descent continued, her body skewered by sharp rocks and twigs and brush. Angel tried to stop her slide by digging her feet into the soft ground, but she was going too fast. Her ankle buckled and she cried out in pain, only to be rewarded with a mouthful of sod for her trouble. The move had sent her tumbling off to the side for several feet before slamming into a tree stump. The impact knocked all of the air out of her lungs and sent her tumbling off in a different direction, flipping over onto her stomach. Her body was burning everywhere, her mind swimming, almost overcome by pain. Instinctively, Angel dug her nails into the ground and finally, mercifully, she slowed, and came to a halt.

Angel spat out a mouthful of moist earth and managed to look back up the mountain that she'd just slid down. There was but a faint glow of orange high above her. Angel managed a faint, exhausted smile before the pain overcame her and she passed out.

CHAPTER 2

Case Talley walked unbowed through the rain because he didn't give a damn. In fact, it had been a long time since he'd given a damn about anything. He had built himself a nice little cabin in the wilderness, far from prying eyes, and disappeared from the world. He only stuck his head up once a month, after his check was deposited in his bank account. He often drove hundreds of miles out of his way to withdrawal the funds from a different ATM in a different city. From there, everything he did was with cash so as not to leave a trail. Case Talley was a ghost.

On this night, he had settled in front of his fireplace with a copy of *Sports Illustrated* and a cup of coffee. He had a static-filled feed of the Rockies game on his radio and a pot of chili on the stove. He was content.

The commotion outside got his attention. Immediately Case's instincts kicked in. He shot up out of his ratty old garage sale recliner and threw on his boots and a camo parka. He pulled the shotgun off the wall over the fireplace, grabbed a metal flashlight off a table, and set out into the night. Case immediately smelled smoke in the air from a nearby fire, which added to his concern. Forest fires had long been Case's biggest fear, the only kind of monster that could drive him out of his cozy hiding place.

Case walked a wide circle around the cabin, training his flashlight into the darkest reaches of the woods, and saw nothing. He was ready to write it off as nothing more than his mind playing tricks on him. Case had always been keenly aware of the risks his isolation posed. He feared the onset of some sort of loneliness-induced hysteria. Was this the beginning?

Just as he switched the flashlight off, the beam flashed across something unnaturally white in the trees. Case flicked the beam back on and soon found the item in question…a white stocking, torn and stained black with mud and red with blood, attached to a black boot. He approached carefully, shotgun ready in one hand. With each step, more of the figure was revealed. When he was standing over her, he could tell it was a girl.

She was a curious sight there in the mud and the leaves. Her legs were cut up and bleeding, her plaid skirt pushed up over white cotton panties that were similarly stained. A leather motorcycle jacket had bunched up around her shoulders, and her hair was dyed the colors of the rainbow. The left side of her face was exposed to him and she appeared to be pretty, but was wearing ridiculous make up that was smeared all over her face.

Case had read all about this new trend. Cosplaying, where grown adults dressed as movie characters and made fools of themselves. It made him sick to think that half a world way, young men were dying, or worse, in the asshole of the world so that grown people could play make believe without a care in the world.

At first Case feared the girl was dead, but as he knelt beside her body, he detected light but troubled breathing. Case knew what to do…he'd had years of training and even more experience. Yet in that moment he hesitated, rocking back onto his haunches as he stared down at the young woman and debated. They were miles away from a hospital, far off any main roads. It would take forever for an ambulance to get to them, and that was after he went miles looking for a phone.

Case had no choice. He cradled the woman's head and rolled her over gently. His eyes immediately fixed on the nasty exit wound on her left shoulder, just below the clavicle. He'd seen enough gunshot wounds to recognize it immediately. Who was this strange girl, and why was she out here? Had someone dumped her body here, thinking her dead?

This was no time for wondering. Case scolded himself and went back to assessing the girl. He pried the girl's eyes open and found violet eyes staring lifelessly back at him. "What the…?" he muttered. Case let her eyes close.

Case stood and hurried back to his cabin. He had a long folding table that he used as a kitchen counter. He cleared it, wiped it down, and folded the legs up underneath it. In a box in his coat closet he found a pair of ratchet-downs, gathered them with one hand, and carried the table back to the girl.

When Case got back she was moaning softly, her red lips making a perfect little O as she did. She was so young. What could she have possibly done to have deserved this? Case shook his head. He should know better than to ask that question. He'd seen enough to know that life didn't much care what you did or didn't deserve. Bad things happened to people all the time, often for no reason.

He placed the table on the ground next to the girl and prepared to transition her to it when his hands brushed against something hard under her jacket. Case's mind told him instantly what it was, but he couldn't believe it. He reached under her coat and pulled the pistol out. Case chuckled at the thought of this tiny girl running around with a hand cannon under her arm. He clicked the safety on and tossed the gun to the side. He would come back for it later.

Carefully he edged the young woman onto the table, then secured her using one ratchet strap across her forehead and another just below her knees. Then he began to drag the table back to his cabin. The trip was rougher than it he would have liked and with each bump he feared that he could be doing more damage if the girl had sustained a neck or spinal injury. Still, he knew he had no choice but to move her. He couldn't leave her, and help was too far away.

The table bumped over the entryway to his little cabin, and Case slowly and carefully negotiated the table through the living room, down a narrow hallway, and into his cramped bedroom. He angled the table against the foot of the bed, undid the ratchet straps, and carefully slid the girl onto the bed. Case took a few moments to arrange her, then tied her with the straps so that she wouldn't roll off the bed while he was gone.

Case was on automatic pilot now. On a shelf in the bedroom closet was the bag of doctor tools he'd never been able to part with, some part of his brain knowing that, sooner or later, his skills would be needed again. He gathered clean towels and a bottle of hydrogen peroxide from the bathroom, and two mixing bowls and a clean sponge from the kitchen. Once he had everything he needed, he set the table up beside the bed, again wiped it down with Lysol, set up his workstation, and began tending to the girl.

He stripped her first, carefully removing what he could, and then cutting away the rest. He found hundreds of cuts, scrapes, and bruises, as well as scars from several old wounds; wounds that Case recognized easily enough. She had been abused, probably for years. There was a nasty, dark purple bruise under her left arm, and he quickly reasoned that she'd broken several ribs. He removed her boots and found her right ankle discolored and badly bruised. He was thankful for the girl's unconsciousness as he reset the dislocated joint. She called out in discomfort, but the pain wasn't enough to fully wake her.

Case carefully cleaned the gunshot wound. The bullet appeared to have missed doing any serious damage, so he stitched it up and bandaged it. Then Case set about tending to the less serious wounds, picking concrete and gravel and splinters out of the cuts. He cleaned a nasty case of road rash that ran from her right buttock midway up her back and side.

Once Case was done with all of that and confident that he'd done everything he could in the moment, he went to his medicine cabinet, took out one hydrocodone and one amoxicillin, ground them up, dissolved them in a salt water solution, and injected the concoction into her arm.

Once he was finished with the girl, Case walked back outside to find the gun. The rain had slowed to a mist and the slight smell of smoke that he'd noticed earlier was gone. The night was peaceful and still now, no hint whatsoever of the strange goings on that had resulted in a woman being dumped on his doorstep. It took some searching but Case finally located the gun. He started back inside when he noticed the drag marks on the ground from the table. He was instantly beset by a nagging thought in the back of his mind. Case tucked the pistol into his waistband and set about obscuring the trail. On his hands and knees in the dark, more than once Case felt foolish. Who was going to come traipsing through this part of the woods looking at the ground? Instantly the response was: the kind of people who would shoot a girl and dump her over a cliff.

Once Case was done obscuring his trail he sat down and inspected the pistol. The girl wasn't just carrying it as a deterrent, she'd fired it. He counted six shots left in the fifteen-bullet clip. That single piece of information bothered Case more than the rest. Up until that point, he'd been convinced the girl was on the run, a victim. Now it seemed that she might be complicit in something, something likely to be illegal, and Case might have unknowingly brought a felon into his home. He studied the gun in his lap with a heavy heart. He was right back in the shit now, with not even an inkling of just how deep it went.

Finally, Case managed to gather the energy to get up. He carried the gun into the bedroom, pulled a locked box out from under the bed, entered a four-digit code on the keypad, and popped the box. Inside was his old service pistol, three fully loaded clips, a loaded .22 revolver, two boxes of shells for each, and a cleaning kit. He disassembled the Glock and gave it a thorough cleaning. When he was done with that, he tossed it and the clip inside, slammed the box shut, and slid it back under the bed.

After that he cleaned up his impromptu work station. He threw the bloodied towels in the wash. He took her tattered clothes outside, threw them in a metal barrel and burned them. When all of that was done, he checked on the girl, who seemed to be sleeping fine. He covered her with a heavy quilt and trudged back to his recliner.

Case was jacked up with adrenaline so much that his hands were shaking. He was silently impressed with himself, though. Even after all the years, he hadn't lost his touch. He wondered some more about the girl as well. She was obviously mixed up in something very bad. By bringing her into his home, had he unwittingly put himself in harm's way?

With worries preying heavily on his mind, Case Talley plopped down in his seat and eventually fell asleep.

Chapter 3

Slowly, Angel returned to the world.

The first thing she noticed was the sound of the rain falling hard on a roof. The knowledge that she had been brought indoors stirred her and she began to move. Each movement brought fresh waves of pain from fresh places. Before she opened her eyes, she began to make a mental checklist. Her left shoulder was killing her, as was her right ankle. She had a pounding headache and her entire body felt raw, like all the skin had been peeled away.

With a deep breath, Angel opened her eyes and found herself lying on her back in a soft, warm bed. She was nude, but covered to her chin with a heavy quilt. The room was dark, but as she waited, her eyes began to pick out tiny details. There was a small window high on the opposite wall that was covered with dark curtains, green perhaps, that had some sort of tiny design on them. The walls were plain sheetrock, no pictures hanging, and the room was small. Underneath the window was a long, squatty piece of furniture that looked like a dresser with no mirror.

She turned her head, getting the best look she could, but the movement caused a nasty wave of nausea. She closed her eyes and breathed deep and slow, a relaxation technique she'd picked

26

up somewhere. When Angel opened them again, she noted a small nightstand on her left side with two amber pill bottles, a glass of water, and a small lamp. Just inside the door, a portable table leaned up against the wall with the legs folded underneath.

Slowly, she turned her head all the way to the right and willed away the nausea. There was another door that looked like a closet on the right wall, and that was it. She turned her head back to center and stared at the ceiling. Someone had found her and brought her in and, best of all, had not called the cops. That was a stroke of luck.

Angel tried to push herself up, but her left shoulder immediately protested. With a growl, she wiggled her butt and slowly inched her way up. The bed had no headboard, but she pushed herself up far enough to lean her head on the wall. The exertion was painful and her lungs felt like they were on fire. She struggled to catch her breath from such a simple task.

She had really messed up, and now she was at the mercy of whoever had taken her in. For all she knew, this stranger might have already taken advantage. She didn't feel as though he had, but as much as she hurt she couldn't be sure.

The thought didn't really bother Angel, not anymore. She'd been through the ringer often enough that she was numb to the entire process. Master had been using her for his personal pleasure for years. For Angel, unwanted sex was merely part of the job.

Her mysterious host knocked quietly on the door. Angel straightened herself up and the pulled the quilt back up over her. "Yes," she said hoarsely.

The door cracked open and a face appeared in the crack. "How are you feeling?" a man asked in an almost fatherly tone.

"I guess I'll survive," Angel answered. "I feel like shit warmed over."

The man pushed the rest of the way into the room and closed the door quietly behind him. He walked down the side of the bed and flicked on the bedside lamp, which cast a soft yellow glow around the room, before sitting softly on the edge of the bed.

He looked like a lumberjack in faded blue jeans and a flannel shirt. His hair was cut military short and he had a rugged face with a dark, brushy beard. He had two noticeable scars…one a thin, white line just below his right eye, and the second was a big, gnarly scar that ran along the right side of his neck. Yet his demeanor didn't match his appearance at all. He moved more like…like what? She couldn't put her finger on it.

"Well," he said in a deep, soothing voice. "That's a fairly accurate description. That tumble you took down the hill really did a number on you. That, and most people who have been shot and lived to tell the tale usually don't feel so hot afterwards."

Angel looked hard into the man's soft brown eyes, her face utterly emotionless. "Did you call the cops?"

The man seemed taken aback. "No, I haven't. I'm not a doctor."

Angel looked down at her bandaged shoulder, then up at the man. "Looks like it to me," she answered. "You brought me in, bandaged me up. You know something."

"I do," he said calmly. He clearly wasn't in the mood to give anything away. "Would you mind telling me what happened to you? Did someone dump you out there?"

Angel's eyes bored into the man's as she thought about her answer. "No, I wasn't dumped." Best not to give away anything more than necessary, she reasoned.

"That's it? You don't have anything more to say?"

Angel shrugged. "Look. You found me, so I'm sure you found the gun. You know I've been shot. I take it that if I tell you that you're better off not knowing, then you're smart enough to put two and two together and realize that what happened isn't something you want to be involved in."

She waited for him to respond, and eventually he did. "I get that."

"Good. So for your own sake and mine, I suggest you drop it. I appreciate what you did for me, but the sooner I can get out of here the better it will be for both of us. If I could please have my clothes—"

"I can't do that," the man answered firmly. "You are in no condition to be moving around. I should call an ambulance and have you transported to the nearest hospital because I'm sure that you have a concussion, but I'm going to assume that you don't want me to do that."

"You assume right," Angel said. "And though I appreciate the concern, I've got to go." She started to sit up, but more dizziness and nausea swept over her and she slumped backwards.

"No, you don't. Your ankle is all busted up, so you can't walk. Your ribs are probably broken, so you can't breathe. Trying to get up and leave right now would be extremely foolish."

"And the men who shot me are going to come looking for me. They may already be on the way."

The man chuckled. "I doubt it. It's been raining off and on all night, very hard at times. I doubt anyone would be foolish enough to try to hike down that mountain in the dark and the rain without proper gear. By now the rain has been hard and steady enough to obliterate any marks you left on the way down. Plus, this is a big forest with lots of area to cover, and the people who live in these woods are very distrustful of strangers. More likely, they assumed you were dead and left you."

"You know a lot about drug-runners, do you?"

"More than I care to," he answered. He leaned down and tucked the blankets in around her. "Please, just stay here and rest. I will take care of you, and when you're good enough to go, I'll even give you a ride somewhere. I promise that I won't hurt you. You're my patient now and I have an obligation to you. I don't care what you did. And if anyone comes looking…." Angel waited for him to finish. She was curious as to what he had to say. "Let's just say that I can take care of myself. You'll be safe here."

Angel continued studying the man's eyes, but they never wavered and she finally decided that she had no reason to doubt him. Nothing about the man fired her instincts, and she always trusted her instincts. "Fine. For what it's worth, when I do get out of here, I'll make it worth your while. Money isn't a problem."

"I'm not concerned with money. There is just one thing I want from you."

"What would that be?" Angel asked suspiciously.

"Your name. If we're going to be spending the next few weeks together, I don't want to be saying 'Hey you' every time I address you."

Angel kept her face expressionless despite his request. Her name, her real name, was something that she never gave. "You can call me Angel. That's what Master calls me."

"Master?" He seemed disgusted at the word. "You call someone Master?"

"Careful," Angel warned. "Don't start thinking too much about things that don't concern you."

"Okay, fine," he said, though he didn't sound pleased. "It doesn't sound like you care for the name."

Angel shrugged. "It's just a name. Doesn't matter much."

"Then pick another one," the man said. "Choose any name you want. It doesn't have to be your real one. Whatever you are out there, you don't have to be here."

Angel thought about it, reaching back through the fog of years and memories better forgotten to come up with a new name. One of her own choosing. It was a foreign thought for a woman who had always been someone else's property. After a long minute, she looked back at the man. "Mara. Call me Mara."

He smiled at her, and it was a friendly smile. "Mara. All right, Mara. I'm Case. Like, I'm on the Case." He waited for her to laugh or smile, but that wasn't something she did. "Sorry," he finally said, once he saw that he would get no reaction. "That's just something I used to say to…people." He seemed to drift off for a moment, and Angel could tell the brief flash across his face that Case also had a past he didn't care to relive. "Anyway," he said as the moment passed. "I have to admit that I'm not really prepared for company, so I'll have to run into town for some supplies."

She fidgeted in the bed and Case quickly read her discomfort.

"I promise, I won't say a word about you. I don't particularly want people poking their nose into my business any more than you do. I just need some more food and some medical supplies. There's a general store in the next town that has everything I need. I'll be back in an hour."

Case started to leave, then stopped and turned around. He picked up one of the pill bottles, then the other, twisted the top, and dropped two pills into his hand. He put the bottle back down and held his hand in front of her. "For the pain. It'll probably help you sleep." He held out his fist, palm down, and waited for her to open her hand to take them. She refused. "You don't have to take them," Case said. He laid them on the table beside the glass of water, and then pulled the table forward so that it was easier for her to reach. "You can take 'em if you want." He popped the other bottle and took out one pill. "This one you have to take. It's an antibiotic. Infection is a big concern with that gunshot."

When Angel wouldn't hold out her hand, Case physically turned her hand over and dropped it in her palm. "It's an antibiotic," he repeated. "It won't make you loopy or knock you out. You need it. Take it."

She hesitated but Case wouldn't quit hovering, so she finally tossed it in her mouth. Clearly pleased, Case handed her the glass of water and she swallowed. "Ugh. Could I maybe have some cold water?"

"Thirsty?"

"Very," she answered.

"Let me get you some." Case took the glass and left the room. She could hear water running further into the house, much longer than what was needed to fill up a glass. When he came back, he was carrying a red plastic pitcher and the glass, which was filled with ice. "Here you go." He poured her a glass and handed it over. Angel drank it greedily, like she'd spent a month in the desert. Before she could ask, Case took the glass from her and filled it again. "Slow down on this one. You don't want to waterlog yourself." He placed the pitcher on the table. "Consider the pain pills."

Angel sipped at the water as Case left the room. He seemed like a nice guy, from what she'd heard of nice guys. She'd never had an actual experience with one. Still, how far could you really trust a stranger living in the woods? Angel looked around the room again, hoping to see her clothes or her gun. She'd feel so much better if she could have the gun handy. There was nothing.

From somewhere inside the house, Angel heard Case say "Oh." She heard his heavy footsteps coming and he popped into the room a second later. "I almost forgot." He opened one of the drawers on the dresser and pulled out a pair of plaid boxers, and out of another pulled a purple T shirt, then tossed them gently on the bed by her hands. "You might want to get dressed. Your clothes were ruined."

Angel gathered them with her right hand. She recognized

the logo of some sports team on the T shirt. Case noticed her studying the logo.

"You like the Rockies?"

"I have no clue who that is," she said coldly.

"Oh," he said sheepishly. "Do you need help with that, or can you manage it on your own?"

"I can handle it," Angel answered. She slipped her right arm into one sleeve and pulled the T shirt over her head with a considerable amount of effort. Case was leaning on the dresser, watching her. "I've got it," Angel said again, a little more forcefully.

"Whatever you say," he told her, looking somewhat amused. "I'll be back in an hour or less. Don't worry."

Angel waited until she heard him leave, and then counted to a hundred in her head to give him time to get down the road. She had no intention of still being there when the man got back. He might have seemed like a nice guy, but she had no reason to believe the he wouldn't come back with an army of cops. Angel pushed the quilt off her, gathered her strength and her resolve, and quickly swung her legs off the bed. The dizziness washed over her quickly and Angel had to close her eyes until it passed. Once it did, Angel slipped on the boxers and forced her left arm into the T shirt. It hurt like hell, but it was done.

Angel noticed the pain pills on the table and thought about taking them, but remembered that they would make her sleepy and passed. She would have to fight through the pain. Gingerly, Angel touched her left foot to the floor, which was covered in a thick brown carpet, then her right. She paused again, then pushed up off the bed...and promptly crumbled to the floor.

Angel cried out in pain and grabbed for her ankle. For the first time since she was a little girl, she cried. As she lay fetal on the ground, praying for the pain to go away, a part of her brain was still screaming at her to move, to get out.

Doing the best she could to ignore the pain, Angel got to her hands and knees and crawled across the floor to the dresser. Bracing herself against it, she rifled through the drawers and found a pair of sweat pants and some socks and tossed them on the floor. With tears streaming down her cheeks, she crawled to the closet, slid open the door, and found a pair of hiking boots on the floor. Angel drug them over to where she had thrown the pants and socks, turned herself around, and began dressing.

It was a painful process, but she managed to get the pants and socks on and spread the boots out as wide as she could to push her feet into them. The left shoe went on easily and she tied it up; the right one she dreaded. Her ankle was still throbbing from her earlier attempt to stand, and putting on the sock hadn't been much easier. Finally, Angel convinced herself to just do it, and shoved the foot into the boot. She cried out in pain, but it was done.

She gave herself a minute to rest, then using the bed as a base, struggled to her feet, keeping as much weight as possible off her right foot. She had made it this far, now what? There was nothing more of value to her in the bedroom, so it was time to explore.

Angel hopped to the door on one foot and leaned against the door frame once she made it. Her head was swimming, her ankle was screaming, her lungs burning, but she would make it. Outside the bedroom was a narrow hallway that opened into the living room. Angel could see an old TV on a stand and a ratty recliner. Better still, she saw the front door.

Angel placed one hand on the wall of either side of the hallway and began hopping towards the door. With each jump her head seemed to swim even more. She felt like someone had stuffed cotton balls behind her eyes. At the end of the hall she

Nollie's General Store was just that, an old fashioned general store with creaky hardwood floors and a lunch counter in the back. On most visits, Case would find several of the townsfolk sitting around the counter drinking coffee and talking about disaster prepping, the NRA, and godless Democrats, mostly in that order. Today, however, the only patron was a rough looking Mexican man, tall and thin as a rail, with long straight hair and a brushy Fu Manchu mustache. He wore khaki slacks and a white dress shirt under a thin beige sports coat. Case could clearly make out the bump of a gun in a shoulder rig through the back of the jacket. He wasn't trying to hide it.

The tall man stalked through the aisles, not really shopping but instead keeping a casual eye on Case. At the checkout, Bill Holland stood stiffly at his register, wearing the black Viet Nam Vet baseball cap that he never left the house without. He was keeping a careful eye on the stranger. In the back, he could hear Nollie himself kicking around in the kitchen.

"How's it going, Bill?" Case called out casually as he walked in. He and Bill exchanged a knowing glance.

"Loving this rain," he said. "Keeps the damn fire hazard down."

"Right on that," Case responded as he grabbed a shopping cart and pushed past the register and started down the aisles. As Case shopped he was keenly aware of the Mexican. He was keeping a discreet distance and trying to look casual, but Case knew that he was being tracked.

Case felt a finger of fear crawling up his spine and fought hard to suppress it. It wasn't fear like he'd felt in Iraq, but a more personal fear. It was one thing waiting for a bomb to blow you to bits; it was quite another knowing that someone might intentionally finger you for death.

Case hurried through the aisles, stocking up on medical

supplies and food. He was incredibly anxious to get out of the watchful eye of the stranger. As he finished his shopping and headed for the checkout, he was relieved that the man was still lingering around the back of the store. Relief that quickly faded as the man started quickly up the aisle toward him. As Bill began scanning items, the man nudged up behind Case and ducked his hands into his pockets.

"Interesting shopping list you got there," he said. He had just the slightest hint of an Americanized Mexican accent, and his voice was deep and gruff.

"Yeah?"

"Yeah. What do you need all those bandages and stuff for? You got somebody hurt?"

Case tried to pass it off as casual. "Always do," he said, trying to sound friendly. His heart was racing and he feared that the man was going to see through his lie. "There's no hospital or clinic anywhere near here and I used to be a doctor, so when somebody gets hurt, they come to me."

The stranger grunted. "Somebody hurt now?"

"The Fleming boy, ain't it?" Bill said, jumping in to help Case. "I heard that damn fool fell through the roof of his shack."

Case turned his attention from the stranger to Bill. "Yes, that idiot. I told him after the last time to hire someone, but he thinks he knows everything. I'm a little tired of patching that boy up."

"You feeding him too?" The Mexican cast a suspicious eye at them both.

Case turned his glare to the stranger and summoned up some indignation. "You sure are interested in what I'm buying. Who are you again?"

The man took his hands out of his pockets and turned them over. "Just a stranger passing through town, making polite conversation with the locals," he said with a sneer. "I just find your basket a bit…odd."

"Not that it's any of your business, but my son is coming. I get him over spring break, so I'm stocking up." He turned back to Bill. "Thank God he doesn't live with me. That boy would eat me out of house and home. All he does is play video games and shove food in his face."

"I hear ya," Bill answered. "Raised three boys myself. Eating is about all they're good for. And don't even get me started on those stupid ass games. Downfall of western civilization is what they are."

The stranger reached into his jacket and pulled a folded paper from his breast pocket, unfolded it, and slapped it down on the counter in front of Case. "You seen this woman running around anywhere?"

Case looked down at the paper, which was a crudely drawn portrait of a woman, though whoever drew it did have some skill. The drawing was done with colored pencils, and the girl had purple eyes, red lips, and rainbow hair. It was undoubtedly Mara.

"Can't say that I have," Case said, injecting a bit of humor in his voice. "But if I see Rainbow Bright skipping through the woods I'll be sure to let you know." He laughed and Bill laughed with him.

The Mexican reached out for Case's arm, spun him around, and bent him over the counter. Suddenly there was a very large knife in his hand and he was pressing it against Case's throat. "You think I'm joking?" he snarled at Case. "That woman killed my friends, and she's around here somewhere. We're going to find her, and anybody who's helping her."

The fear Case had been trying to hide boiled to the surface. "No," he said, his voice wavering. "I haven't seen anybody like that around here, and believe me, somebody like that would be noticed."

Whether it was his words or the obvious fear in his voice, the Mexican seemed appeased and let up. Just as suddenly as it appeared, the knife disappeared. "Thank you," he said as he straightened his jacket.

His casual manner turned Case off and he felt his own rage building. "Now," Case said as he tried to compose himself. "Let me tell you something, pal. The people around here don't much care for strangers poking around, and everybody around here has guns and they're not afraid to use them. You go wandering around these woods looking for trouble, somebody is sure as hell going to give you some. There are plenty of places to bury a body around here where it won't be found, and local authorities aren't going to be too concerned over a missing thug. Do you understand?"

Behind him, Bill chuckled as the Mexican and Case sized each other up. Slowly, the corner of the Mexican's mouth turned up into a smile. "I understand well. I think that trouble is already here. I will find that girl. I don't care what I have to do, and anyone who gets in my way…." He smiled bigger. "Will wish that they didn't." He pushed past Case and strode out the door.

Case let out a deep breath and turned to Bill, hoping to hide his shaking hands. Bill laughed at him and took his hands out from beneath the counter to reveal the sawed-off shotgun he'd been holding the whole time. "You're okay, Doc. I had your back. I like the way you talked to that guy though. I didn't know you had that in you."

Case looked up at Bill and forced a weak smile. "I didn't either."

#

Feeling paranoid after his encounter with the Mexican, Case took a roundabout way home. He watched his mirrors carefully, turned down some wrong roads, turned around a few times, and passed the turnoff to his home more than once. Only when he was convinced that no one was following him did he finally complete the trip.

The rain had begun falling heavily again, so he jumped out of the truck and ran to the front door of the cabin to unlock the front door before getting the groceries out. As he pushed the door open, he saw Mara curled up on his living room floor, whimpering.

"Goddamn you," he spat out before he raced inside and scooped her up in his arms. He was amazed at how light she was, and quickly carried her back to the bedroom. "What the hell are you doing? I told you that you couldn't get up, damn it."

"I have to," she mumbled. "I have to get out." When they'd spoken earlier, Mara had sounded tough, but now her voice was a mere whine.

"No, what you have to do is be smart," Case grumbled. He yanked the boots off her feet, which elicited a cry of pain from her. "Sorry," he muttered, but he wasn't really all that sorry. He stripped off the sweat pants and then covered her up. "This time, I'm insisting that you take the pain pills." Case scooped the oblong white pills off the nightstand and pushed them into her hands.

"All right," she said. She popped the pills and Case handed her the water and watched as she washed them down. "Thank you," she finally said, though with a hint of attitude.

Case settled on the edge of the bed. "What you did was very foolish. In your condition, you could have made your injuries worse. That's not to mention the concussion. Do you know how serious concussions can be? The permanent damage you could do?"

Mara's purple eyes settled on his. "It doesn't matter. If I stay here, a concussion is nothing. If they find me —"

"They're already looking," he snapped. Her eyes got wide. "I bumped into a tall, nasty looking Mexican in town driving a gold Lincoln. I'm assuming that's who you're referring to?"

Mara pushed herself up, but the dizziness pushed her back down. "I've got to go. I've got to get to Master. Once I get to him, they won't find me."

Case looked at her sadly and shook his head. "I can't even begin…so many questions. Listen. Nobody knows that you're here, and nobody is just going to stumble over us out here. They're going to have to look long and hard, and if they come…." He paused, causing Mara to look up at him in anticipation. "I know a few things. I can take care of myself if I need to. There is one thing though."

"What?" Mara had stopped whimpering and was already showing signs of getting loopy.

"We need to change your appearance. They've got a drawing of you, but it's crude. Without the makeup and the hair, it wouldn't look much like you at all."

"That's why I wear the disguise," she said, her voice flighty. "People focus on the disguise and they don't see the details." She smiled slightly. "No tats, no piercings. No distinguishing marks at all. I was taught well. He…taught me well." She was fading by the moment, causing Case to worry that two hydrocodone were too much for the slight girl.

Case stayed with her until he was sure that she was in a deep sleep before going back for the groceries. His mind was already racing. He would have to be careful, watch his back, and cover his tracks well. Despite his assurance to Mara, he knew eventually they would find his cabin, and he had to be prepared.

He moved quickly. First he cut up paper bags and taped them over all the windows. Then he doused the fire in the fireplace. He had no shortage of blankets and jackets if things got too cold.

After that he walked all around his place, making sure that there was no metal lying around, nothing that could reflect light if someone came through with a flashlight or they rented a plane and started doing flyovers.

Once all of that was done, Case checked on Mara again and left her a quick note. For the rest, he had to go to town, but he didn't dare go back to Springer. He'd have to go into the city and watch his back very carefully. He had to hope that if she woke before he returned that Mara would be smart enough to stay in bed.

He took the drive into the city slowly, working his way in from the northeast and avoiding the interstate, because it would be harder to watch his mirrors. Case didn't believe that anyone was following him, but if the person following him knew what they were doing, he wasn't supposed to know.

He stopped first at a sporting goods store on the edge of town that was the favored shopping place for all the survivalists he knew. He stocked up on ammo for his guns, a high-dollar hunting knife, a laser scope for one of his rifles, camping equipment in case they had to make a run for it, and a camo-cover for his truck. After leaving the sporting goods store, he stopped by a health care supply store and picked up more supplies for Mara, including a pair of crutches, and then a beauty supply store. The girl at the beauty shop sold him a ridiculously priced bottle of stripper that she swore would take the dye out of Mara's hair.

On the way out, he stopped and grabbed a fried chicken meal and headed back to the cabin. He was careful the whole time, meandering his way about and watching his mirrors. By the time he made it back to the cabin, darkness was beginning to creep in. He parked the truck as close to the house as possible, unloaded, and then threw the cover over the truck. His hope was that if they started doing flyovers, the house and the truck would blend into the countryside.

He was finally done, but his nerves were shot. For the hundredth time in the last eighteen hours Case asked himself why he was doing this. There was no reason in the world for him to stick his neck out for this strange girl, especially one that was apparently a killer. It would have been so much easier to bring the local sheriff and just be done with her. He wanted to believe that it was the last lingering vestiges of his old life, the Hippocratic oath he had sworn, that was driving him.

Yet in his darkest heart he knew better. It was her. It was her beauty and her vulnerability that had roped him in. He wanted to protect her. He wanted to save her. He *desired* her.

The thought scared him to the core.

CHAPTER 5

Mara was just starting to wake up when Case brought her a plate with two pieces of chicken, cole slaw, potato salad, and a biscuit. "Thought you might be hungry," he said, holding up the plate for her to see.

Mara let out a heavy yawn and pushed herself up with her right arm. "Starving," she answered in the emotionless way that she always spoke. She took the plate with her right hand and set it on the bed beside her. She was blinking like crazy.

"Eyes bothering you?"

"Yes," she answered. Mara struggled, but managed to get her left hand up to her right eye, held the eye open, and with her right hand, pulled out a contact and tossed it on the bed. She then did the same with her left eye.

Case felt stupid for never having realized that she was wearing contacts. He scooped them up off the bed, hurried to the bathroom, and flushed them. When he came back, Mara was watching him quizzically.

"I don't want to leave anything lying around, in case those guys do happen upon us." He looked at Mara again. "Your eyes are blue."

"They are?" Mara responded sarcastically.

"I just didn't know," Case said, feeling embarrassed. Mara was still blinking. "Do you need some drops?"

"That would be nice," Mara said. "I kept those in for too long."

Case excused himself back to the bathroom, found the eye drops, and hurried back. Mara had begun tearing into a chicken leg and ate like a prisoner. "I am so hungry," she said around a mouthful of food. "This is good. I haven't had fried chicken… ever, I don't guess."

Case set the eye drops on the night stand and sat down. "Ever? How could you have never had fried chicken?"

Mara fixed her blue eyes on him, and they were as cold as an Arctic frost. "If you had lived my life, you'd know how. There's lots of things I've never done, and lots of things I did that I never should have done." She held that gaze for a moment before going back to her plate.

Case watched her eat, debating if he dared ask the question that was burning in his mind. He finally decided to go ahead. "The man in town, the Mexican, he said that you killed his friend."

Mara shoved a plastic spoonful of potato salad into her mouth and snorted. "Friend my ass," she snapped, showing the first real flash of emotion. "Boss. I killed his boss. Put two hollow point nine millimeters through the top of his skull at point blank range. Sorry piece of shit."

With one paragraph, Mara had changed in his eyes. She was suddenly no longer a victim, the helpless girl tossed aside and left to die in the mountains. She said the words with such venom, such ferocity, that he could no longer see her as some helpless victim. God help him, he thought it made her seem sexy.

"Is that what you do for a living?"

"Yep."

"And this master fellow you keep talking about...."

Mara stopped with another bite inches from her mouth. "You don't want to know Master. If you know Master, if you see Master, you die. There are three people in this world who know Master. We work for him. To everybody else, Master is a myth."

She said it with such sincerity that it made the hair on Case's neck stand up. He suppressed a shudder. "Is that what he goes by? Master?"

"No. He goes by another name. We call him Master, because that is what he is. He owns us. He takes care of us, but he also controls us. We don't displease Master." She went back to shoveling food in her face.

"So you're scared of him. Is that why you are so desperate to leave?"

Mara shrugged. "I can talk my way out of it. I can explain, but I can't let the Mexicans catch me. They'll do things to me...." She shivered. "I'll die first." She started to take another bite, then stopped and put her spoon back down on her plate. "Why are you helping me?"

Case studied her, really took her in for the first time. She had the tiny features of a young girl, but the wicked stare of a much older person. He realized that she was a Venus flytrap, alluring on the outside but with a deadly intent. "You need help, so I'm helping. It's what I do." He stopped and shrugged. "Well, it's what I used to do."

Mara glared back at him with those cold eyes. Case feared that she was seeing through him, that she was ripping the cold, dark truth out of his soul. "Well, you shouldn't," she finally said. "It'll bring you nothing but trouble in the end."

Case knew she was right. The rational part of him wanted to throw her in the truck and take her to the nearest Greyhound station immediately. He had come to these mountains to get away from people, not to get mixed up with hoods and assassins.

"You're thinking about it," Mara said without looking at him. "I scare you."

Case tried to shrug it off. "I've never met a professional killer before. It's a little disconcerting. But I won't turn you in. I give you my word on that. When you're healthy enough to leave, I'll take you somewhere; but you don't scare me."

"I should," Mara grunted and finished eating. She then washed it all down with two glasses of water. "Thank you," she said again, sounding satisfied.

Case picked up her plate and carried it away and tossed it in the kitchen trash. He took a minute to straighten up the kitchen and put the leftovers away before he went for the supplies he had bought. He carried a bath seat and the bottle of stripper into the bathroom and set them next to the claw foot tub. Then he went back for Mara.

"What's up, Doc?" she asked flatly. If she was trying to be funny it didn't show.

"There's something I have to do," Case said. "That *we* have to do. I don't want to. I'm afraid it's too soon, but we don't have a choice."

Mara looked at him with interest. "What would that be?"

"I have to wash your hair." Mara responded with a curious glance. "We need to get that dye out of your hair. Once we clean you up, I don't think they'd recognize you even if they did come here."

"Do what you've gotta do," she answered. "It's just a disguise anyway."

"All right then," Case said.

He scooped her up and Mara wrapped her arms around his neck. As Case carried her to the bathroom he tried not to think about how good it felt to hold a woman again. "Out of curiosity, why don't you just wear a wig? Seems like it would be a lot easier."

"I tried that, on my first job," Angel said. Her soft voice in Case's ear, her breath against his skin, threatened to ignite him. "All I did was wear a wig, nothing else to change my appearance at all. I got close to the mark, but he realized what I was there to do. We struggled, he grabbed my hair, and when I pulled away, he got the wig and a handful of my natural hair as well. Lots of people saw me leaving the scene, so there was a good description of me out. I vowed never to make that mistake again. So now, I go all out."

Case was amazed by her story. She told it like a teacher would tell a horror story about a student, like murder was the most natural thing in the world.

Once they reached the bathroom he sat her gently on the bath seat with her back to the tub, started the water running, and let it get lukewarm before he tilted her head back over the edge of the tub and started.

As Case wet her hair, Mara asked, "So what's your story, Doc?" She gasped for breath after asking the question. This wasn't a good position for her to be in, so he had to work fast. He poured a handful of the stripper into his palm and started working it into Mara's hair.

"Why do you keep calling me Doc?"

"Well," she gasped. "You bandaged me up...sewed up my arm...fixed my ankle—"

"Right," he interrupted so she would quit talking. "Well, I am...was...a doctor. Now I write stories for a living."

She gasped again, and then asked, "You write books?"

"No," Case answered. "I write for this underground magazine, *The Unblinking Eye*. It caters to survivalists, gun lovers, far right wingnuts, anarchists, and general weirdoes. I write under the byline Fallujah Frankie. I type up a couple of stories a week and mail them off, and I get a direct deposit once a month for my trouble."

"What kind of stories...do you write?"

Case finished working the stripper into Mara's hair, rinsed his hands, and turned off the water. "We need to let that sit for a few minutes." Case eased her back into an upright position. "Sit tight," he said before hurrying out of the room.

He returned with a bottle of astringent, some nail polish remover, and a large bag of cotton balls. "Let's get that make-up off, shall we?" He went to work removing the rest of her disguise and eventually returned to his story. "Mostly what I write is bullshit. Conspiracy theory stuff. I take what little I know about the military and the government, mix it with some popular hot button topics, and pass it off as thoughtful commentary. The yahoos eat it up."

Mara tilted her head back up and took three deep breaths. "If it's bullshit then why do you write it?"

"It's not all bullshit. Only about ninety percent." He smirked at her as he finished taking the nail polish off one hand, tossed the cotton ball, and moved to the next. "That's the thing about conspiracies. Only ten percent of it *needs* to be true. The other ninety gives you reasonable deniability. If you can reasonably deny ninety percent, no one will pay any attention to the other ten no matter how compelling the evidence to the contrary."

Mara was watching him intently, studying his every movement with a predatory intensity. "You believe in all of that stuff? Government conspiracies and all of that?"

"Shit no," Case answered. "When you work for the government you quickly realize that there's no way any of those big government conspiracies could ever work. One, there's so much bureaucracy that it's not even feasible. Second, a lot of government departments are staffed by people who couldn't find their own ass with a flashlight and a diagram, and third, the government is just people, and people talk. People are always looking for a way to cash in, get famous, or sometimes, heaven forbid, do the right thing. I don't worry about big government at all."

"Something worries you," Mara said after she took another deep breath. "Or you wouldn't be hiding out here in the wilderness."

Case tossed another cotton ball in the toilet, soaked another in astringent, and went to work on Mara's face. "I don't fear big government. What I do fear are small groups of like-minded people in positions of power. I don't think the Chairman of the Joint Chiefs is going to activate some Navy Seal hit team to hunt me down for what I write. I do fear that something I write might strike too close to home, and that someone in a position of authority can call someone else, who calls someone else, and suddenly there's a rainbow-haired girl with a Glock full of hollow points standing on my porch."

Mara snuffed. "I wouldn't have rainbow hair," she said. "This was a special look. I usually wear much different war paint." Case stopped dabbing at her face and Mara smirked at him. "Actually, with a guy like you, I wouldn't bother with the war paint. I'd just walk up to you in the store. I'd look like some girl on a snack run. You wouldn't even think twice about me. Or maybe you'd think 'she's pretty,' and then I'd put a bullet in your head and that would be it. By the time people figured out what was going on, I'd be around the corner and gone. Luckily for you, I don't think that there are many like me out there anyway."

"You mean assassins?" Case asked.

"I mean people like me." She was totally serious, not even the slightest hint of humor in her voice or face.

51

"I don't suppose there are," Case said as he finished wiping the ridiculous make up off her face. "Let's see how that stripper is doing. The girl at the beauty shop said it might take multiple applications."

"You told someone about me?" There was the slightest hint of a threat in her voice.

"No," Case laughed. "I told her that my daughter got drunk and came home with a ridiculous dye job, and we wanted it gone, pronto. I told her that I couldn't take my daughter to church looking like a box of crayons had melted on her head." Mara giggled, and it sounded like music in Case's ears. "She laughs," he said. "She may be human after all."

"Never have had much reason to laugh," Mara answered, her cold demeanor snapping back into place like a steel door. "Emotions get in the way of my work. I've found that hating the world and everything and everyone in it makes my job much easier."

Case put his hand under her chin, tilted her head back, and began rinsing Mara's hair. "That's terrible to think that way."

"Why?" Mara gasped. "It sounds like…you've seen how bad the world…can be. Or are you going to tell me…that in spite of everything…that drove you into hiding… you're still hopeful?"

"I just mean that it's terrible for someone to be so young and so jaded," Cade answered as he vigorously worked his fingers through her hair. "Yeah, I've had plenty of experience with how brutal the world can be, and no, I'm not overly optimistic for the future."

"I'm probably…not as young…as you think," Mara answered. "Don't let…the looks fool you. That's part…of the lure. My looks…are what gave…Master the idea."

"Really?" Case asked rhetorically. He finished rinsing her hair, and then carefully towel dried it and pulled Mara up. "I don't guess we'll know for sure if it got it all out until it dries, huh?"

"Guess not."

Case stored his materials and then carried Mara back to bed. "While we wait," he said, "I want to change out your bandage and unwrap your ankle. It needs to get some air. By then, maybe we'll be able to tell if you need another round."

"Whatever you say Doc."

Case carefully worked to remove the bandage from her shoulder and cleaned the wound. He kept a careful watch on Mara, who clearly hurt but tried her best not to show it. Case had been around a lot of injured people, and he was certain that Mara had to be among the toughest he'd ever worked on. After he finished replacing the bandage, he moved to her ankle. Again, he worked slowly and carefully. When he finished removing the wrap, Mara choked off a gasp.

"That looks horrible," she said. She sounded like she might throw up. The ankle was badly bruised dark purple and green, and extremely swollen.

"That stunt you pulled earlier didn't help matters much," Case reprimanded her. "You're lucky you didn't break it."

"How do you know I didn't?" Mara asked, still sounding a bit queasy.

"I can tell the difference between a break and a dislocation," he said, sounding insulted. "Mild dislocation at that. Once the swelling goes down, you can probably start to hobble around, though I'd advise against it." He looked up from her ankle, and whatever he had planned on saying next floated away. "Wow."

"What?"

Case shook his head. "You look completely different." Her hair had dried to a dark blonde with some natural gold highlights, and without the tacky make up she looked more like

53

a fresh-faced college coed than a heartless killer. "I don't think that they'd recognize you." Case found it difficult to tear his eyes off her.

"You like what you see," Mara said with that predatory stare of hers.

"No, not at all," Case said awkwardly, and he began shuffling around to keep from looking at her. "I mean, you're very cute, but I'm just surprised because how you looked before…and now…."

"Uh huh," she answered.

Case knew she wasn't buying it, and it made him feel like a pervert. "You should get some rest. I'll get you another antibiotic. Do you need any more pain pills?"

"I'm good," she snapped.

Case hurried to the bathroom for the pill, and when he came back, he actively avoided looking directly at her. He put the pill in her hand and filled up her water glass again. "I'll be in the living room. If you need me, just yell."

Mara took the pill quickly. "Could you kill the light on the way out?" It came out more as an order than a request.

"Sure," Case answered.

He turned off the light and softly closed the door behind him. In the living room, he turned on the radio and surfed the dial until he found a Nuggets broadcast coming out of Denver. He settled into his recliner and tried to immerse himself in the game. He was desperately hoping that the excited tones of the play-by-play announcer would somehow silence the voices in the head. The ones that wouldn't quit talking about how pretty she was.

The ones that kept wanting him to go back into the bedroom and do what he knew he shouldn't.

CHAPTER 6

Case was lying on his side, balled up in a fetal position, when the pounding on the front door startled him awake. He jerked and tumbled out of the recliner and onto the dusty carpet. The radio was still on, but the previous night's basketball game had been replaced by two annoying guys talking about the upcoming NFL draft. He reached up and turned off the radio as the person at the front door pounded again.

Case tried to rub the sleep out of his eyes as he went to the door. He peered through the peep hole to find the tall Mexican from the day before standing on his doorstep, only this time he was flanked by two other men.

"Fuck," he muttered to himself. He needed to act, to wake Mara, to move her or at least warn her, but he didn't have time. The doorknob was starting to rattle. Case knew he had to do what he could to keep them out of the bedroom. As someone outside picked at the lock, Case yanked the door open.

"What the fuck do you think you're doing?" Case barked as he flung open the door.

Another Hispanic man was kneeling in front of the door with a set of lock picking tools in his hands. He looked up in surprise, then smiled at Case with a mouthful of crooked teeth.

The tall man from the store looked over his left shoulder at a blond man with gages in both ears and a ratty goatee. "Look who I just found."

"Get off my property," Case snapped. "You're trespassing." Case was secretly wishing that he'd had the presence of mind to at least grab the shotgun off the mantel. Instead he'd have to make due with balls and nothing more.

"The tough talker, the doctor," the tall man said, ignoring Case's impotent talk of trespassing. "We need to look inside your house."

"Are you cops? If you are, then you'd know you need a warrant. So, until you come back with a warrant, shove it up your ass." He started to slam the door, but the tall man blocked him with the palm of his hand.

"You want a warrant?" He turned to the blond guy. "He wants a warrant. Rooney, show him our warrant."

The blond guy named Rooney said, "Sure, Estavio," reached under his jacket, and pulled out a small cannon. "Here's your warrant, tough guy." A perverse satisfaction glimmered in his eyes.

In all his years and experiences, Case had never had a loaded gun pointed directly at him before. It was an experience he could have done without. He tried to hold on to his composure and not show his fear. "Who the hell are you guys?"

Estavio said, "You don't want to know. Are you gonna let us in or is this going to get ugly?"

Case knew when he was beat. He pushed the door open wider and stepped aside. "When you put it that way...."

Estavio stepped inside and slapped Case lightly on the cheek. "Good decision." Rooney and the stocky man followed him in. Case positioned himself between the intruders and the hallway, and watched as the three men strolled through his living room and kitchen.

The one named Rooney spotted the shotgun over the fireplace and pulled it down. "Hey, Cairo," he called to the stocky one. "Check this out." Rooney checked the shells and saw the gun was loaded. "This dude's ready to throw down."

"You should keep it, might come in handy," Cairo said with no hint of an accent at all.

Rooney said, "I think I will." He then pointed the gun at Case's face. "You don't mind if I keep this, do you?" Case glared back at the man but made no attempt to stop him. "No? Didn't think so," Rooney laughed.

Estavio strolled through the two rooms, then back out. "Nice place. What's down there?" Estavio asked, looking over Case's shoulder and down the hall.

"Just the bathroom and my bedroom. Nothing much to see." Case started backing down the hall, keeping his body between them and the bedroom door.

"I think I'll just look for myself," Estavio said.

"Be my guest," he said, swinging his arm towards the bathroom. He kept backing until he banged up against the bedroom door, and hoped like hell that Mara had something up her sleeve.

Estavio peeked his head into the bathroom, gave a casual glance, and moved on. "Gonna need to see in that bedroom."

"Or course," Case said. He fumbled for the door knob and tried to play off the nervousness. He finally got his hands on it and wiggled it as he turned it. "You're not going to find any mad dog killers or cartoon characters in there, but go ahead." He pushed the door open, but before he could glance inside, Estavio put a hand on his chest and pushed him out of the way.

As Estavio started inside, Case began saying a silent prayer in the hopes that they would kill him quickly.

#

Mara woke up with a start when she heard the pounding on the door. Moments later she heard Case yell at someone, and she knew instantly what had happened. As she'd feared, the cartel men had tracked her down.

Panic started to set in, but she pushed it back. Now was no time for panic. She had to think. Mara looked around the room, but saw no acceptable hiding place. They would surely look under the bed and in the closet. She saw nothing she could use as a weapon either.

The voices on the other side of the door kept bantering. She imagined that Case was doing what he could to stall, but that would only buy them minutes at most. Then an idea came to her all at once. Mara remembered Case's shock after seeing her cleaned up. She had to gamble that the change would be enough.

She pushed the quilt and sheets off her, grabbed the bedsheet, and began pulling up. It took some effort and killed her injured shoulder, but she managed to get one end pulled free, then the other. The voices outside were getting closer, coming down the hall. Mara had seconds left now.

She wrapped the sheets around her arm to make a ball. Then she lifted her shirt, pulled down her boxers, and stuffed the wadded up sheet inside. Pulling up the shorts and pulling down the shirt, she did the best she could to straighten it out and make it look natural.

The door rattled. They were coming in. She quickly pulled the quilt up partway over her makeshift baby bump and rested both hands on top, careful not to press down. It had to look solid, at least from a distance.

The door pushed open and a tall, rough looking Mexican pushed into the room. Case, his face as white as a ghost, stood behind him.

"Honey," Mara said, affecting what, in her ears, sounded like a hillbilly accent. She tried to look scared. "What's goin' on, sweetie? Who is this?"

The Mexican glared daggers at her. He studied her face carefully, and Mara watched as his eyes moved down and settled on her stomach. She began rubbing the bump the way she'd seen so many other women do it.

"Baby, what's goin' on?" she asked again. She put more fear in her voice and made her lip tremble. She felt a tear gather in the corner of one eye. "Baby, I'm scared. What's going on?"

Case looked totally stunned and lost, but he rallied quickly and pushed into the room next to Estavio. "Well, honey, these men are…U.S. Marshals." As he talked, Case started to gain confidence. "Apparently there's a dangerous killer running around the mountains, and these men are looking for him."

"Oh," she said. Mara let her eyes get wide, so he could get a good look at her baby blues. "How exciting." He'd also let her know that there was more than one man, though she could see no one else in the hallway.

"It sure is dark in here," Estavio said. He started circling the room, no longer looking at Mara.

"The light bothers me," Mara said. "I get the horrible migraines since our little bundle of joy came along." She rubbed her belly more, making it look good. "Poor Casey here had to darken all the windows in the house. He's gonna look like an albino by the time this kid is born." She let out a ditzy laugh.

The other two thugs appeared at the door as Estavio opened the closet door and looked inside. They both looked at her not like a suspect, but like a piece of meat. She hoped they wouldn't pull the clichéd bad guy move and decide that raping the pregnant lady would be a fun way to spend the morning. She noted that one of them, a tall blonde white boy, had a shotgun perched on one shoulder.

Estavio slid the closet door shut and turned quickly on his heels, glaring at Case. "I thought you were doctoring somebody up."

"The Fleming boy? Oh hell, I patched him up and sent him home. They live way on the other side of the big mountain."

Estavio stalked over to Case while the other two kept eyeballing Mara. "Long way to go for a make believe doctor."

Case backed up two steps. "Not when you don't have insurance and can't afford a proper doctor," he retorted.

"And what about your son? Thought you said your son was visiting."

"Coming," Case corrected. "He's coming next week. I was just trying to stock up in advance."

Estavio was huffing like an angered bull. He glanced quickly back over at Mara, who kept rubbing her belly and trying to look confused. He looked back at Case and stuck a finger in his face. "I don't like you. We're going to be around for a while. I suggest you keep a low profile. I might be motivated to kill you, and your little lady there, just for the fun of it."

Case, wisely, didn't answer. He just stepped aside and let Estavio pass. Cairo stood in the door, staring at Mara and licking his lips. "Come on, boys," Estavio said. "Let's keep looking."

Rooney pointed the shotgun at Case. "Thanks again for the gun, brah." Cairo took one last lustful look and moved on. They both held their breath until they heard the front door slam shut. As soon as it did, Case hurried to the door and locked it. Mara was pulling the rolled up sheet out of her shorts when he came back into the room. "I was wondering how you did that."

"Best thing I had available," she said nonchalantly.

"That was close," Case said. His hands were shaking badly. "I thought that we were dead for sure." He noticed Mara watching his hands, so he tucked them in the front pockets of his jeans. "Those guys...?"

"Mexican drug cartel," she said. "The guy I killed was the son of a kingpin."

"You took out the son of a drug kingpin?" Case's voice rose into a near yell.

"Keep your voice down," Mara scolded. "They might still be out there. And for the record, I took out the panty waste stepson of a drug kingpin for a completely unrelated reason. But I made a mistake. He had a second security team watching him. One that I'd never picked up. If it hadn't been for them, I would have gotten away and been safe back with Master before anyone knew anything."

"Jesus Christ," Case muttered. He took his shaking hands out of his pockets and rubbed his head. "This just keeps getting worse all the time."

Mara watched Case teetering on the brink of a full-on meltdown, and actually felt a smattering of guilt. "I told you that I would bring you nothing but trouble. Tonight I want you to take me out of here. You can drop me at a bus station and let me do the rest. Do it before I get you killed."

Case started pacing. "And what if those guys come back and suddenly my very pregnant, bed-ridden wife is nowhere to be found? They'll know I was lying and they'll—"

"They'll carve you up like a Thanksgiving turkey."

Case stopped his pacing at stared at her. "That doesn't help me."

"But it's true."

They exchanged glances and then Case went back to pacing. "No. I need you to sit tight. At least for a couple of days. Hopefully when they don't find anything, they'll move on. Then I can sneak you out. But I want you here just in case they come back. Besides, if I put you on a bus in your current condition, something worse might happen to you."

"Worse than getting caught by a Mexican drug gang? I've been raped before, and trust me, the drug gang would be worse."

Case looked at Mara like she was insane. "How could anything be worse?"

"Because they'd rape me with a dull machete." She said it coldly, like telling him about the weather. "You know that you'll have to leave here, right? It doesn't matter if they come back in a few days or a few weeks. When they don't find the girl they're looking for, they'll double back around. They'll find you with no son and no pregnant wife, and then they'll take you apart."

"Damn it," Case barked. He stopped pacing and sat heavily on the foot of the bed, grazing her injured ankle and causing Mara to wince. "Sorry," he said awkwardly. "I came here to get away from this shit."

"Nothing but trouble," Mara said in her trademark monotone. "I told you that I'm nothing but trouble."

"There has to be some way out of this," he said as he ran his fingers through his hair. "There has to be."

"There is," Mara responded after a short silence. "But you wouldn't like it."

Case shifted so that he could look at Mara. There was a slight glimmer of hope in his eyes. "I'm willing to listen to anything."

"Okay," Mara said. "We'd have to go back to the city. Then we cruise the streets until we find a hooker or a runaway, someone with my rough build. We lure her to a hotel room, knock her out, and make her up to look like I did. Then we take her out somewhere where she'll be found, but not too quickly, and I put a bullet in the back of her head." Absolute disgust crossed Case's face then. "It gives the Mexicans a body. Then there's no reason for them to come back here."

"That's just…," Case pushed up off the bed and began pacing and rubbing his head again. "That's…." He stopped and rested his hands on the top of the dresser with his back to Mara as he digested the idea. Finally, he turned back to her. "That's the most cold-blooded goddamn thing I've ever heard."

Sitting comfortably in bed, Mara shrugged at him. "But it will work. If you want to do it…."

"No, I don't want to do it. You'd kill an innocent person?"

"There's no such thing as an innocent person," Mara said. "The type of girl I'm thinking of, we'd be doing her a favor. Your doctor's mentality may not see it this way, but there are a lot of people out there that have no chance. Their lives are just one long nightmare right up until the day they die. There are people out there that are better off dead. I know this, because I was almost one of them."

Case's face softened. He came around the side of the bed, sat gingerly, and patted Mara's arm. "That's how you wound up like you are now?"

Mara slipped her arm out from under his hand. "That's all you get from me, Doc. Are we going to do it or not?"

"No, we're not going to do it." Case stood up quickly and stomped to the bedroom door. "There's got to be another way. Let me think." He stormed out, slamming the door behind him.

Mara stared at the back of the closed door and whispered, "Good luck with that."

CHAPTER 7

Case sat in his recliner and stewed the rest of the morning. The very thought of plucking an innocent person off the streets and killing them just to save their own necks was disturbing on multiple levels. Again, the rational side of him started screaming to be done with the woman. Despite what Mara said, he did believe that there were innocent people in the world, and the mere fact that their lives hadn't turned out well didn't mean that they weren't innocent. Or that they deserved to have that life snuffed out.

Yet he couldn't think of a better way to get out of their current predicament. Case couldn't help but think that she was right about the cartel men. They would continue to hunt for her as long as they had her boxed up in the mountains. It was only a matter of time before they worked their way back to him. Simply getting her out of his house wasn't going to be enough.

Frustrated, Case stomped back down to the bedroom and cracked the door open. Mara was splayed across the bed and sound asleep. He pushed the door open further and leaned on the door frame as he watched her sleep. To see her like this, it was hard to believe that she was a cold-blooded killer. In her sleep, with her walls down, Mara seemed fragile, and that urge to take care of her, to protect her and love her, came creeping back into his mind.

Case completely entered the room and stood over Mara. He gently probed at her ankle. The swelling was beginning to subside slightly, thanks to a constant regimen of ibuprofen and ice. He pushed the sleeve of her shirt out of the way and peeked behind the bandage on her shoulder. He was looking for irritation or infection, but found no signs of either. She was healing as well as could be expected given all circumstances. If he gave her another twenty-four hours she should be good enough to go, though he'd want her on her feet. The concussion was still a concern, though she seemed to be recovering well.

Case hovered over her a minute longer, not as a doctor but as a man, looking down on the beautiful, damaged thing in his bed. He found it so hard not to look at her that way, despite what he knew about her. He wanted so much to touch her, hold her.

Case started thinking that together, they could be happy. He had plenty of money saved back, enough to hop a flight to somewhere warm and start over. It was already Friday afternoon, so he'd have to wait until Monday, but if they could avoid detection until then….

Case shook his head, hoping to drive the thoughts out of his head. He left Mara's bedside and went back to the living room. This was foolish. He was dreaming of running off to paradise with an assassin. For all he knew, Mara might well kill him and take off with the money herself. The smart answer was obvious: dump Mara as soon as possible, cash out, and start over again someplace new. His experience with Mara had taught Case that medicine was still his calling. Perhaps he could disappear in some South American country and work in a small village far from prying eyes.

Or they could give the Mexicans the body they wanted and he wouldn't have to leave at all.

Case plopped down in his recliner and buried his face in his hands. This strange girl had him all twisted in knots. The worst part was she hadn't done anything at all. It was all on Case. Something about her had set his mind on fire and he was burning up. He lusted after her, yet he knew she was poison.

Case forced himself up and into the kitchen, where he reheated a plate of chicken and then sat down at his computer to try and write a new story. He couldn't stop thinking about the girl in his bed. Case wondered if it was just the years of isolation, that the loneliness had simply become unbearable and that any female companionship would have set him off. Maybe, once he dumped Mara, he could ease back into civilization and find a normal woman.

What if it wasn't that at all? What if it *was* her? Was he drawn to her *because* she was poison? He feared that he was falling prey to the hero complex and that it was the opportunity to save her that was fueling this angst. Or maybe it was his self-loathing, and he felt that he only deserved someone that would bring destruction into his life. Maybe he was bored and looking for an adventure.

Maybe, maybe, maybe.

Case was a mess. He couldn't focus on his work, so he put it aside. He tried to watch TV or listen to the radio. He tried reading. Yet every other thought led him back to Mara. He found that he wasn't even thinking about how to get out of the mess he was in, he just thought about her.

The day slipped away to night, but Case was still a nervous wreck. He was so turned around that he had no idea that Mara was standing in the hallway watching him until she spoke.

"Hey, Doc."

Chase jumped up out of his recliner, startled by her sudden appearance. Mara cracked a tiny smile.

"You think it's safe for me to take a shower? I feel gross."

Case instantly switched into doctor mode. "How's the dizziness? The nausea?"

"Not too bad," she said. She was leaning against one wall, her right foot dangling in the air behind her. How had she hopped down the hall without him hearing her?

"I don't have a shower, but you can take a bath. You know where the bathroom is." Mara turned and started towards the bathroom. "Do you need me to take your bandages off before you jump in?"

Without turning, Mara called out over her shoulder. "I think I can manage."

Case heard the water go on a few minutes later and tried not to think of Mara slipping into that tub. He had to focus on the problem at hand. Then suddenly, he had the answer. Excited, he nearly ran down the hall and knocked on the bathroom door. "I think I've got it." Mara said something that Case couldn't make out over the running water and through the door. "I think I've got it," he said again, louder.

He still couldn't hear her response. He cracked the door and stuck his face in the crack. "I said I think I've got it."

Mara turned off the water. "I heard you the first time," she said.

"Sorry," Case said, feeling silly.

"Well, come in here and tell me your grand plan," Mara said with a touch of annoyance.

"But you're in the tub and I don't want to—"

"You've already seen everything I have to offer anyway," Mara said. "I'm curious as to what brilliant scheme you've concocted."

Case reluctantly stepped through the door and maneuvered his way to the toilet, doing his best not to look at Mara but not being able to resist a couple of sideways peeks. He put the seat down on the toilet and sat, staring down at the floor so he wouldn't look directly at her.

"I think that you were on the right track, but we don't need to kill anyone. If we could just arrange for someone who looks like you to be seen somewhere else, and to get that word to the Mexicans, then they'd leave and start following a new trail."

"And how are you going to do that? Are you gonna call 1-800-GOON and report a rainbow-haired girl traipsing around Tuscon and hope for the best?"

Embarrassed, Case muttered, "I don't know."

"Uh huh." Mara lifted her left leg up out of the tub and slathered it with shaving cream. "I hope you don't mind," she said, though she didn't sound as if she really cared if he did. "I've let my grooming go these past couple of days."

"Well, there have been extenuating circumstances...." Against his will, Case found his eyes following the long, slender line of her leg as she gently drew the razor across it. He could almost feel her skin under his fingers....

"Excuses aren't accepted," Mara said. She sounded like she was reading off a card. "There's no excuse for not doing what needs to be done." She caught Case watching her and he quickly turned his head away.

"What if...," he started as he looked back at the floor, "We found a girl that's built like you and we gave her a couple of thousand dollars and made her up, and just asked her to walk around and be seen?"

Mara dropped her now shaved leg and let it hang over the edge of the tub. "One, you still have to make sure that the cartel guys find out about her. Two, you're still setting the girl up to be killed. If the Mexicans get the memo, they'll find the girl and then they'll torture her, and she'll tell them that this blonde gimpy chick and a weird bearded guy paid her. And guess where they're going to come next?"

"Well, shit."

"I told you. The trail *has to* end at the girl. It can't go any further than her. There's only one way to assure that." Case looked over at Mara, who held her hand up in the shape of a gun, held it to her head, and made a shooting noise. "That's the only way."

"Can't be," Case muttered. "Just can't be."

"The only other ways I can think of are what we talked about. You get me to Master and then disappear. You'll spend the rest of your life running. I'd advise not going to South America. Go to Canada or Greenland or something like that. Someplace strange Mexicans would stand out."

"Or?" Case asked. Mara looked at him curiously. "You said other ways. What's the other way?"

"Oh," Mara said simply. "I kill them all. I have no problem with that, but the big boss will just send another team and they'll come here first, and someone will point them at you."

Case studied her as she lay in the bathtub, her body submerged in warm, soapy water, her eyes twinkling in the soft yellow light, when a realization struck him. Mara was concerned about him. She tried not to show it, but everything always came back to the Mexicans finding him. "I'm touched that you're thinking of me. I didn't think you'd care."

This time it was Mara that looked away. "I wouldn't...I don't," she said. "But you've helped me out so I'm trying to help you. If worse comes to worse and I have to make a decision...." She looked back at him and waited for Case to return her stare. "I'd shoot you before I let them get their hands on you."

"That's sweet," he said sarcastically.

Mara drew her leg back into the tub and sat up. Case tried not to ogle as the top of her breasts bobbed precariously at the water line, the suds in the tub just barely enough to cover her. She patted the side of the tub. "Come sit over here."

Case couldn't help but feel a tingle of excitement as he got up and sat on the edge of the tub. It appeared that her walls were cracking and she was beginning to warm up to him. She took his face in both hands and moved it side to side, studying his features carefully. Then she let go, filled her hands with shaving cream, and rubbed it all over his face. Without asking for his consent, she began to shave him, using the same quick, sweeping strokes. When she was done, Mara used a washcloth to wipe the remaining cream away from Case's face, and then looked again.

"Huh."

"What?" Case asked. His face felt raw. It had been years since his cheeks had last touched the air.

"You looked better with the beard," she said coldly as she dropped the razor, picked up the can of shaving cream, and began to lather her right leg.

"Thanks," Case said, and he couldn't help but be a little angry. He liked his beard, and to have her shave it off and then insult him was a violation.

"But you look younger now," Mara said. "That's what I wanted to see. The beard adds ten years. You've got a baby face. We might be able to work with that."

Case wasn't sure what overcame him in that moment. One second she was talking, and the next he snatched her face up in his hands and started kissing her. It had been ages since he'd kissed a woman at all, but he had never kissed one like this. He kissed her with every ounce of fire and passion he had, but when he realized that she was just sitting there and not returning the kiss, he broke it off. Ashamed of his loss of control, he shot up and darted out of the room, unable to look at her.

He stopped at the mouth of the hallway and ran his hands over his now bare face. "Jesus Christ, what are you doing?" Case was breathing heavy, his hands shaking. Behind him he could hear Mara getting out of the tub, and he braced himself for what was to come. Would she snap his neck like a twig? Case heard her hobble out of the bathroom and turned.

She had the same emotionless stare as she limped down the hallway, totally naked and sopping wet. Case held up his hands and stammered. "I'm sorry. Please don't—"

Then she was on him. She put both hands on his chest and shoved him. Case, surprised by the strength of the move, stumbled, and then fell. He landed hard on his back, and the impact knocked the breath out of him.

He braced himself for the end, but instead of killing him, Mara dropped to her knees and began tearing at his clothes. In utter shock he watched as she stripped him and mounted him. She rode him like a beast, bucking and thrashing, screaming out with each move. Somewhere in the back of his mind, Case had the distinct impression that she was putting on a performance, but he was powerless to resist her as years of pent up frustration were released and he screamed out in ecstasy.

As soon as it was over, Case lay back and gasped for air while Mara casually got up and hobbled back to the bathroom without a word. There was something not right in the way she did it. It was inconceivable to him that someone could be so wildly passionate one moment and so utterly flat the next.

Case cleaned up and headed for the bedroom, where he changed clothes. Mara's demeanor was bothering him the entire time. As he started back down the hall, Mara hobbled out of the bathroom, now wrapped in a towel. "Do you think I could have some fresh clothes?"

"Sure," Case said. He turned and headed back into the bedroom, Mara limping along behind. "I see you're starting to put weight on the ankle. That's good." She didn't respond, but he heard the bed springs squeak as she sat down. He dug her out another T shirt, another pair of boxers, and some athletic shorts. He handed them to Mara, who took them casually.

"Was that sufficient?"

"Sufficient?" Case asked, confused. He pointed back towards the living room. "The sex?"

Mara nodded. "The payment. Was it sufficient? That's what it was, wasn't it? A trade for services rendered? I don't have any money on me at the moment...."

"I didn't...." Case was dumbstruck. It was like she was negotiating the price on a picture frame at a garage sale. "That wasn't...." She seemed even stranger now than she had before. She peered up at him with something that looked like either childlike innocence or a completely batshit crazy lack of emotion. "Did you feel anything at all?"

"It hurts."

"Oh," Case stammered. "I'm not...it's normally not that rough."

Mara patted her right leg. "The ankle. It hurts. That's what I feel. As far as that," she said with a nod of her head. "I never feel. Master says that is what makes me deadly. He's very proud of me for that."

"That's just...sick," Case spat out. "How could you be like... that? And then be so cold? You can't tell me that you weren't feeling something in there. I don't believe it. You were so... energetic."

"It's what is expected. That's all." Mara stood and removed her towel and dressed as Case watched in stunned silence. When she was done dressing, Mara sat back down. "Is there anything else? If not, I'm hungry and would like to eat."

"You are so weird," Case said. He left her there, steamed into the living room, and plopped down in his recliner. His mind just couldn't wrap itself around the peculiarities of this woman.

Mara limped slowly after him and gently trailed one finger along his shoulder as she came around. Case was scowling as Mara straddled him, resting her knees on either side of his legs. With that same finger, Mara lifted his chin until Case's eyes met hers. "Do you know what your problem is?"

"What," he asked in annoyance.

"You think of me as a person," Mara said. "You shouldn't do that. I'm a weapon, and I destroy whatever I'm aimed at. Make no mistake, if I were aimed at you...." She looked deep into Case's eyes and waited for the connection. Then she snapped her fingers. "Like that. I'd step over your dead body on my way out and not lose a minute's sleep. That's what I am. You should remember that." She slithered out of his lap. "Now. When do we eat?"

CHAPTER 8

They ate dinner in silence. Case watched Mara carefully, but she showed no sign of giving a second thought to their earlier tryst. When they were done, Mara helped him straighten up. The two moved around each other and complimented each other with the type of easy familiarity he had witnessed in long time couples. He took it as a sign.

After dinner, Case sat her in his recliner and changed out the dressing on her shoulder. Mara sat stock still as always while he worked. Case decided to take a chance.

"I was a battlefield doctor in the army," he said conversationally as he cleaned her wound. "Iraq. I enlisted straight out of med school."

Mara kept her eyes straight ahead. "Is this the part where you try to open up about your past in an effort to connect with me?"

"No," Case stammered. "I just—"

"You don't need to do that. You don't need to feel guilty. I knew what I was doing and I knew that you wanted it. I've known it from the start. It was the least I could do to thank you for bringing me in and taking care of me."

Case dropped his hands from her wound. "But you shouldn't do that. Sex isn't something you trade for services rendered. You don't have sex with someone to say thank you."

She finally focused on him, looking up at him like a specimen in a science experiment. "In my life, sex is either given or taken. I prefer not to have it taken. So I give it when I feel it is necessary. You should be happy that I did. I see what's behind your eyes when you look at me. I see the lust."

"There's no…." Case started to protest, and then stopped. There was no sense in lying to her, especially since she already knew it was a lie. Instead, he went back to cleaning the gunshot. "Anyway," he said, wishing that he could go back and erase the last few seconds. "I spent four years over there. I went because I wanted to help, and I know that I did. I know that I saved some lives, but I saw so many people just…shattered. I couldn't deal any more. Those last six months were brutal. I couldn't wait to get out,"

"And that's why you now live in the woods writing conspiracy theory stories for right wing wackos," Mara said sarcastically. "I get it."

"No, you don't," Case said, feeling angry and a little hurt. He roughly finished replacing her bandage. He left her hanging while he cleaned up. When he came back he sat cross-legged on the floor in front of the recliner. Mara stretched her legs out in front of her and studied him intently as he began again.

"After I got out, I still believed in what I was doing. I still wanted to help, so I went to work as an ER doctor in Detroit. I just traded one war zone for another. I knew that I'd see my share of gunshot wounds, gang violence, and all of that. But I saw other things there. Things that were so much worse than what I'd seen in Iraq. The final straw came one night when this couple rushed their three-month old in."

75

Case felt the emotion coming and dropped his head, trying to hide from Mara the tears that were gathering in his eyes. Mara sat patiently while Case gathered himself the best he could. "This kid, this poor baby, had been raped repeatedly. She was a goner, I knew it immediately, but I tried." The tears began to fall this time and he did nothing to stop them. "Oh, I tried," he said, his voice cracking from the emotion of it. "I tried so hard, but the whole time there was this voice in the back of my head saying let her go, that she'd be better off dead."

He forced himself to look up and found Mara's icy blue eyes locked onto him. Her face was a blank slate, but he caught the slight glimmer of connection behind her eyes.

Case continued. "I was so angry. I went out to tell the mother and I saw her in the waiting room arguing with the cops. She's *defending* her boyfriend. She knows that he did it, but she's defending him. And when I tell her that the baby's gone, she's more upset that the cops are arresting her boyfriend than she is about her baby dying. That was it for me. To see someone so... that was just the single most fucked up thing I've ever witnessed. I walked out that night when my shift was over and never looked back. That was when I lost my faith in humanity."

"You do understand," Mara said coldly. "You see how horrible and cold the world is."

"I do," Case admitted. "I didn't come up here because I was afraid of big government. I came up here to get away from people. To get away from a society so sick and depraved that a mother could defend her baby's murderer."

"Yet you still don't want to do the one thing that would make this all go away."

Case stared hard at Mara. Her idea, while repulsive, did have its merits. He also knew that Mara was right. For the type of women Mara was talking about, death was probably a better alternative to the lives they were living.

"I'm still a doctor. I still took an oath. Even if I agree with you that death might be a better alternative for some of these women, to be the actual cause of their death, to pick someone out…that goes against everything I believe in. Any of those women could actually turn their lives around."

"But most of them won't," she countered. "Most of them will die of a drug overdose, or an STD, or get killed by a john in a back alley somewhere. That's the reality and you know it."

Case stood up, shaking his head. "I can't. I won't do it. We'll find another way." He stripped off his shirt and tossed it in the floor. "I'm going to take a bath now. Make yourself at home."

"Haven't I already?"

Case shrugged and headed off to the bathroom. His mind was flooded with images that he'd locked away years before. Images of war and disfigurement and death. Mara had opened his personal Pandora's Box and released the darkness Case had tried so hard to run from. The darkness that now had him thinking about killing an innocent girl in order to set a killer free. The darkness that thought it might be worth it if they wound up together. As he turned on the water, he could see the two of them putting the plan in action: baiting the girl, knocking her out, making her up. Mara would be the one to do the actual killing. All he had to do was set the stage. It wouldn't be that difficult.

"Jesus Christ," he muttered, He turned his face away from the steaming water and caught his reflection in the medicine cabinet mirror. "What the fuck is wrong with you?"

\#

Mara watched Case disappear into the back, and waited patiently until she heard him shut off the water before she moved. She stretched her legs, and flexed and rolled her damaged right ankle. It still hurt like hell and she was doing herself no favors

77

by constantly trying to walk on it. The ankle was still too tender, she decided, to make a break for it yet. Angel noticed the pair of crutches lying on the floor. She slid out of the chair and crawled over to them, then forced herself up. It took her a few moments to adjust them, and then she started down the hallway to the bedroom.

Mara was thankful for Case's help, but she knew that she would have to leave him soon. She hated being a sitting duck, hated feeling helpless. Case, with his moral code, was holding her back. He would have to be dealt with. If she couldn't find a way to throw the cartel men off his scent, she would have to take him out. She just couldn't risk the Mexicans getting a hold of him.

Mara made her way to the bedroom and rifled through everything again, hoping that in her pain and disorientation she had missed something the first time. Still she found nothing of use in the closet or the dresser. Frustrated, she plopped down on the bed and let the crutches clatter to the floor. It would be just her luck to find the only guy in the mountains that didn't have a small arsenal at his disposal.

As Mara sat and thought about what to do, she saw a finger of yellow light seeping quickly from the edges of the blocked-out window and heard the familiar sound of wheels crunching on rocks outside. She jumped up and hobbled to the window. Using her fingernails, Mara peeled enough of the cardboard away from the window to make out the taillights of the car as it pulled to a stop in front of the cabin.

She pulled back quickly and fell to her knees, reaching for the crutches. As she did, she caught sight of a lockbox and several long bags sitting under the bed. She'd never even thought to look under there.

Mara knew that she didn't have time to mess with it now, though. She grabbed the crutches, hurried to the bathroom door, and threw it open. Case had been reclining in the tub; his head leaned against the wall. The water was still hot enough she could see the steam coming up off the water. He shot up when Mara stormed in.

"Someone's here," she said quickly. Her voice sounded panicked in her ears. "Someone just pulled up in front."

"Shit," Case muttered. He shot up out of the tub and fumbled for a worn out green towel that was sitting, folded up, on the toilet. Mara backed out of his way as Case stepped out of the tub and covered himself up.

"I'll be in the bedroom," she said. Their mystery guest began knocking on the front door as she beat a quick retreat. Case was right behind her, headed for the front door. Mara pushed the bedroom door shut and collapsed against it. She would feel so much better if she had something to defend herself with.

She heard Case open the door and begin talking to someone. It wasn't the Mexicans. They would have just burst in. Mara opened her eyes and found herself staring into the open closet, and several bare wire hangers still swinging lightly from her hurried search. Whoever was at the door was coming in. Afraid of making too much noise, Mara carefully tossed the crutches on the bed, one at a time so that they wouldn't clink together. Then she very carefully hobbled over to the closet and took out a hanger. It wasn't a gun, but it would have to do.

#

Case waited until he heard the bedroom door close before he cracked open the front door. Sheriff Jake Charles was standing on the outside in full uniform, his thumbs tucked into his belt but his right hand resting over his holstered weapon. Behind him, his patrol car idled in front of the house.

"Sheriff," Case acknowledged through the crack. "What can I do for you?"

He nodded his head slightly. "I was wonderin' if I could talk to you for a minute about some things that have been going on. Mind if I come in?"

Case felt the shakes coming on and tried to force them down. "Sure," he said, and he opened the door fully. Sheriff Charles stepped inside quickly, but his hand never moved away from his gun. Once he was in, Case pushed the door shut.

Charles was a still a youthful looking man with a powerful build, a face full of dark stubble, and clear blue eyes that could be friendly or intimidating depending upon what kind of mood he was in. The residents of the county respected him because he was a former marine who wore his patriotism on his sleeve and had zero tolerance for anyone who dared question him.

His mouth turned up into an amused smirk as he took Case in. "Interrupt something, Mr. Talley?"

Case looked down to make sure his towel was still secured, then shrugged and forced a weak smile. "Just taking a bath," he said. Over the sheriff's shoulder he saw Mara peek out of the bedroom door, then quickly push it shut again. "What's going on, Sheriff?"

Apparently sensing no threat, Charles took his right hand away from his gun and rubbed his chin. "There have been some incidents around town the last couple of days, and people are thinking that you're involved."

"What kind of incidents?"

Charles's eyes were boring into Case. He could almost feel the confession trying to worm its way out of his mouth as Charles eyed him. It took all the resolve Case had to keep himself calm as he tried to project ignorance.

"There are some guys running around the area, asking about a girl. They're not very friendly guys, and earlier today they got a little rough with the Wagners. Scared the holy shit out of them,

80

and you know the Wagners. Billy is a big ole boy and not scared of anything, but when I went over there, he was about to piss himself. They're loading up their RV and heading out of town for a while."

"I hate to hear that," Case said. "I don't see what that has to do with me."

"Well, I talked to old Bill Holland, and he told me that you ran into these guys at the store the other day. He said that you were buying an unusual amount of stuff, medicine and food mainly, and that you were lyin' your face off. Bill thinks that you've got someone stashed away up here. Someone that these guys are lookin' for." As Charles talked, he was very deliberately looking around the house, obviously looking for signs that anyone else was around. He pushed past Case and started for the kitchen.

"What? Just because I decided to come into town and stock up on some things? Bill Holland's a sweet guy, but he's a bit of a town gossip."

Charles just grunted as he sauntered into the kitchen. The sink was full of dirty dishes he hadn't gotten around to washing yet. Case started thinking. He had tried to be careful about leaving no traces of Mara's presence, but he couldn't remember if she'd used anything before he'd cleaned the ridiculous make up off her face. Had she left lipstick stains on a glass? The panic was welling up inside of him.

"Lot of dishes," Charles said.

"I've been a little lazy lately."

"Uh huh." Charles popped open the door to the tiny utility room that sat just off the kitchen and flipped on the light.

"Have you talked to these guys? Seems to me that you should do that instead of coming down here and bugging me." Case tried to put some indignation in his voice.

"Oh, I talked to them," Charles said over his shoulder as he stepped into the utility room. He emerged a minute later carrying Mara's leather jacket in his hands. He approached Case, and then held the jacket up to him. "Seems a little small for you."

Case's heart dropped but he tried to maintain a stone face. He stepped back and to the side, getting away from the jacket. "What did these men say when you talked to them?"

Charles snickered and folded the jacket over his right arm. "They weren't too scared of me. I get the feeling these boys don't care much for cops," he said. "Now why don't you tell me who belongs to this jacket?" Charles started back toward the hallway.

"Well," Case said, still trying to sound put out. "It's really not—"

"Hey, Casey, hurry up," Mara called out suddenly from the bedroom. She was making her voice deeper. "I'm gonna lose my hard on, and I desperately want another piece of that sweet little ass of yours."

Case felt the blood rush from his face as Charles stopped cold in his tracks. He slowly turned his head toward Case. "Oh. Well...hmm." The sheriff let the coat slide off his arm and onto the floor. "I didn't know...."

Case giggled nervously. "Um, yeah Mark, hang on," he called out for Mara's benefit. "You know," he said, turning back to Charles. "I kind of keep to myself for a reason."

From down the hall Mara called out again. "Hey dude, this lube is tingly. And I want you to tell me if it really tastes like peppermint."

"All right then." Sheriff Charles, the rough and tumble former marine, blushed and turned for the front door. He refused to look back at Case as he opened the door and hurried outside. Case went to close the door behind him, but Charles stopped a few steps from his cruiser and turned around.

"You know, I'm not sure how the community is going to feel

about this."

"Why should the community even know? What I do in my home is my business."

"Yeah," Charles said. "But people look at you as the area doctor and…." He made a face. "Could pose a public health risk. I think that it's in the public's best interest to know what they're getting into if they come here."

"That's bullshit," Case snapped, and this time the anger was real.

"Call it what you want," the sheriff responded as he opened his car door. "Still, I don't know that I'd be expecting too many visitors from now on." He ducked into his car and drove off. Case stood in the doorway glaring after him until the taillights disappeared in the darkness before he slammed the door shut.

#

Mara stood against the wall, just to the right of the door, tightly gripping the unwound wire hanger in her hands. She could feel the wire pressing into the soft skin of her palm. She was breathing slow and deep, picturing the moment in her mind, preparing herself to do what she had to do.

In the living room Case slammed the door shut and screamed out, "Asshole" as he did. Mara relaxed a little as Case stormed down the hall. A moment later he threw the bedroom door open and charged through it.

Mara knew well the anger of a man, and for a fleeting moment, she felt the old fear crawling up her spine. She inhaled sharply, and it caught Case's attention. He spun around, looking like a wild-eyed lunatic. Mara retightened her grip on the wire.

"Thank you," he growled. "You just ruined my reputation."

Mara felt the fear abate, replaced by a genuine curiosity. "How?"

"That was the county sheriff, and now he thinks I'm a fag.

83

And he's going to run all over town telling everybody else that I'm a fag. I'll be an outcast." Case circled the bed, knocked the crutches onto the floor, and sat heavily, his back to Mara.

"Why should that even matter?" Mara haphazardly tossed the unwound hanger on the bed beside Case, hopped over to the bed, and climbed up on it.

"It shouldn't," he said with clear frustration. "But it does. People up here aren't the most socially liberal people in the world."

Mara crawled up behind Case, slipped her arms around his waist, and rested her chin on his shoulder. The move felt so natural, like a comfortable action between two lovers. "Well," she said. "You don't like people hanging around anyway."

"By choice," he said, trying to look over his shoulder at her. "Not by force. And besides...." Case saw the hanger lying on the bed and chuckled. "What did you think that you were going to do with that?"

Mara glanced over at the hanger, then back at Case. "When he came in the room I was going to trip him. Then I was going to climb up on his back and wrap it around his throat, like this." She reached out, plucked the hanger off the bed, and slipped it around Case's neck so quickly and easily. Then she pulled back on it a little. Case reached up for the hanger, trying to relieve the pressure. "When he reached for it like that, I would have reached around, taken out his gun, and done what I do best."

Mara let go of the hanger and it fell to the floor. "Oh," Case said as he rubbed his neck.

"Of course, by killing a cop I would have committed myself, so I would have been forced to make a decision on you." Mara wrapped her arms back around his waist and put her head back on his shoulder. "So I would have shot you too. Then I would have ransacked the cabin and the cop car for anything of use,

84

loaded it all up in your truck, and torched the cabin and the cop car. From there, it would have just been a matter of driving carefully and slowly, making my way back home." Case again turned his head to look at her, his expression one of shock. "You asked," she said defensively.

"My God," Case said, and he slumped over and buried his face in his hands. She thought that he might have started sobbing.

Mara let go of him and lay on the bed, propping herself up on one elbow. "Can you feel it?"

"Feel what?" he said through his hands.

"The noose around your neck. The walls closing in. The air being sucked out of the room. The panic. The fear." Mara waited for Case to look at her. "It short circuits your brain, makes you sloppy. I told you all along, but you still don't believe me. There's only one way out of this for you. Or at least only one that leaves you still breathing."

"We're not killing anybody," he barked. He shot up off the bed, rubbed his head, and then spun around. "Why don't we just run away? We could go into the city tonight and lay low in some cheap hotel. Monday morning when the banks open I'll get my cash, and by Monday night we can be on a plane to somewhere exotic. We couldn't live like kings, but we could live."

Mara shook her head sadly. "Even if the Mexicans eventually give up and stop looking, which is unlikely, Master never will. I'm his prized possession. He would scour the ends of the earth looking for me, and when he found us he'd cut off your dick and make you eat it. Then he'd set you on fire, just for the entertainment value. And he'd get really nasty with me."

Case stood shocked, stammering, looking for something to say. "This man—"

"He's only a man in the most basic of terms," Mara said. "Out of curiosity," she finally said after an elongated silence. "What if

I agreed to run away with you, but only on the condition that we leave everyone a body? Would you do it then? Would you kill the girl to get me?"

"What the fuck?" Case turned a circle, rubbing his face and trying to wrap his mind around it all. Mara continued to recline on the bed and watched, getting a slight kick out of seeing how tangled up he was. "Are you seriously sitting there and telling me that you'll run away with me if I kill someone?"

"No," Mara answered. "I'm asking you to set her up. I do the dirty work. And I'm not saying that I will run away with you. I'm just asking what if. You understand the concept of a rhetorical question?" She sat up on her knees and fixed Case with a somber stare. "How desperately do you want me, Doc? Are you willing to go all the way? Are you willing to take it to the extreme?"

Case returned her stare and she saw something flicker across his face. He slowly walked back to the bed and sat gingerly. Case then reached out and took her face in both of his hands. "If you tell me that you'll run away with me, then yes, I'll help you kill someone."

Mara was genuinely surprised. She realized in that moment just how hard he had fallen for her. The thought was somewhat frightening, but it also stirred something inside of her. Master would kill to protect what he saw as his. Case would kill for her, and that was something completely foreign to Mara.

Case was staring deeply, lovingly into her eyes, tenderly rubbing her face. Her mind was racing and she felt confused. She saw him moving in slowly, going for a kiss. "You want another round already?" she whispered.

Case stopped, and then recoiled in anger. "What? No. Not like that." The air hissed out of his lungs slowly as he shook his head at her. "I want to make love to you, Mara. Soft and slow, the way it's supposed to be."

Mara felt that tingle of fear again, but this was a vastly different fear than she'd ever felt before. "I don't know how to do that."

Case's features softened and he reached out for her hands. "I'll show you."

Mara immediately pulled away from him and scrambled off the bed. "I don't want to know how."

Chapter 9

Mara turned and stormed out of the room as best she could on one leg. She could hear Case jump off the bed and follow after her. By the time she hopped to the end of the hallway he was at her heels. Case reached out and grabbed at her wrist once, twice, and missed. The third time he managed to grab her and spin her around. The grab and spin knocked Mara off balance. She stumbled, flailed for something to grab onto, and started to fall. Case snatched her arm and held her tight, keeping her from falling.

"Would you please stop?"

Mara glared up at Case, feeling full of righteous anger. "Let go of me."

"Okay, fine."

Case let go and Mara fell hard to the ground. The impact knocked the air out of her lungs and set her ribs on fire.

"Ow."

"You asked," Case said. He stood over her, smirking. "Now can we talk about this?"

Mara pushed herself up with some effort. "There's nothing to talk about. You want something from me that I can't give you."

He started to protest, but she cut him off. "And I don't want to give it to you."

"I don't believe you. I saw the look in your eyes when I said I'd kill for you. I can give you a life, Mara. I can take you away from all of this."

Mara stared up at Case in disbelief. "You still don't get it. There is nothing here for you except a warm body. I have nothing to give you except sex." She crawled to his desk and used it to pull herself back to her feet. Case stayed a healthy distance away. "You're a lonely guy who's shut himself away from the world too long. You need to go somewhere and find a woman who can love you, because I can't."

Case continued to shake his head. "You can learn. I'll be patient. I know that it will take time. Just believe in me."

"You're an idiot," Mara snapped.

"Oh, okay. I'm an idiot, huh? Let's see about that," Case said. He turned and hurried out of the room and back to the bedroom. Mara sat on the edge of the desk favoring her throbbing ribs, and wondered what he was up to. She could hear him kicking around, and soon he came storming back out.

Case walked up to her and pushed her Glock into her right hand. "If you really are the monster you claim to be, if you really don't feel anything for me at all, then shoot me now and put me out of my misery. Go ahead. Do it."

Mara looked down at the gun in her hand. Holding it again made her feel instantly powerful. Mara flexed her hand around the butt of the gun as she slowly moved her eyes from the piece to Case, who stood in front of her breathing heavily. Then she pushed herself up off the corner of the desk, pressed the muzzle of the Glock to Case's forehead, and pulled the trigger.

There was a loud click and a terrified Case stumbled backwards. Mara flipped the gun in her hand and shoved the butt end back at him. "It's useless without a clip," she said. "You honestly think I can't tell a loaded gun from an empty one?"

Case's terror quickly faded to anger. He reached out for the gun, but Mara twirled it again and pulled the gun away. "I want the clip back too. With the bullets in it. It's mine."

"You gonna shoot me if I give it to you?"

"Not if you don't make me," Mara said. "I don't want to kill you, Case. I want to help you get out of this. But you keep making things difficult for me. I need to be able to do what I've got to do."

Case smirked at her. "I'm making things difficult for you? So I'm getting in? You do feel something for me."

Mara tucked the gun in the waistband of her shorts. "I feel a smidge of loyalty to you. Don't confuse that with love."

"Duly noted," Case said. He was trying to be casual, but Mara noticed his trembling hands. "I need a drink, how about you?" Case stepped quickly past her and headed for the kitchen. Mara settled back down on the corner of his desk and watched as he opened the freezer and pulled out a bottle of vodka. He twisted the lid and took a long drink, then held it out for her. "Want one?"

"I never drink," she answered. "No smoking, no drinking, no drugs. Master is very clear on these things."

Case laughed and took another long drink before replacing the cap and putting the bottle back in the freezer. "You're missing some good stuff."

"Doubt it."

Case picked Mara up and carried her over to his recliner, then pulled his computer chair over and sat in front of her. "This Master guy, he sounds like a real piece of work."

"One of his men got into cocaine once," Mara said. "He hid it for a while, but eventually he got in too deep. He made a mistake and Master found out. So, Master cut off his nose with a rotary saw. He had the skin made into a necklace and made the guy wear it everywhere he went. Master teaches the kinds of lessons that only need to be taught once."

Case looked like he was about to vomit. "This guy sounds like a complete lunatic."

"He's not," Mara answered. "He could sit next to you in church or strike up a conversation with you in a supermarket, and you wouldn't even remember him five minutes later. He's the most unextraordinary man in the world. He's a piece of plain paper, a wisp of smoke. He's not insane. He is very, very smart."

"You can be smart and still be insane."

Mara ignored Case's argument. "He's not insane. He knows exactly what he is doing and he knows that it is wrong. He's depraved."

"You don't sound like you like him at all."

This time it was Mara who chuckled. "He's not a likeable guy. And he's going to be royally pissed at me when I get back. I made a huge mistake and it's causing problems. I've been gone too long. I roped a stranger into it." Her eyes dropped to the floor and her voice got soft. "He's going to punish me severely when I get back."

Case put a finger under her chin and lifted her head. "Don't go back. I thought we decided that we're running away."

"*You* decided that," Mara said. She pulled away from his touch. "I was asking a hypothetical question. I just wanted to see how far you'd be willing to go. I never consented to anything. I might have, but you started talking foolishness."

Case sat back in his chair and laced his fingers behind his head. "How was it foolish?"

Mara leaned forward in her seat. "It's foolish to think that the Angel of Death can fall in love with you."

Case leaned forward in his seat. Their noses were just inches apart. "You're not the Angel of Death. You're just a girl with a gun. You can be whoever you want to be. You can leave all of this behind."

Mara gently pushed him back and stood up. "You're deluding yourself." She inched her way past Case and started back down the hall toward the bedroom. "What other cool toys do you have back here?"

Case called out after her, but Mara beat him to the bedroom door, where she saw the now open lockbox on the bed. "Bam. I knew you had some goodies around here." She hopped over and dumped the contents of the box out. Immediately she seized upon the clip for her gun. "Mine," she said as she snatched it up.

"Mara, you don't need this stuff," Case implored.

Mara picked up the .22 revolver and pointed it at Case's face. "Nice balance," she said. "The barrel's a little long, so it would be hard to conceal. Feels nice though."

Case froze in his tracks. "Mara, would you please not point the loaded pistol at my face?"

Maya glared at him over the sight at the end of the gun barrel. "Scared? If you are, then you're learning." She tossed the gun on a pillow and picked up the other gun. "What is this, a Desert Eagle? .45 caliber?" Case had just relaxed when she pointed the new gun at his head. "Heavy sucker. I don't like it." She tossed it aside as well.

"If you're finished playing...," Case started, but never got to finish. Mara slipped off the bed and onto the floor. "What are you doing?"

Mara laid flat on her stomach and wiggled far enough under the bed to get her hands on the three long bags she had noticed earlier. When she scooted back out, Case was leaning over the side of the bed watching her. She pulled the long bags out and then looked up at him. "Rifles."

She unzipped the first bag and took out the rifle, which had a large scope attached to the top. Mara let out a long whistle. "Sniper rifle, no less. I thought you were a doctor."

"I was," Case protested. "A guy I served with gave that to me for saving his life. It was right before he got discharged. He swore he'd never pick up another gun. Please put it down."

Mara held the gun up to her face, peering through the scope. "If you had told me about these I wouldn't have needed to make that cop think you were gay. I could have just poked my head out into the hall and…." Mara took the gun down from her face. "Would have been a lot easier. Could have taken out those Mexicans and we could have buried them in the forest somewhere."

"That's why I didn't tell you," Case said. "Please put them back.

Mara noticed that he had put the other guns and ammo back in the box and shut it. She sighed and held the rifle back up. "No. I like this one. It's lighter than it looks. I can use this."

"Come on, Mara, stop. Besides, that one guy already took my shotgun."

Mara dropped the gun into her lap. "The goofy white guy with the big holes in his ears? Don't worry about that. I'll get it back for you. Consider it a going away present."

"A going away present? What are you talking about?" Case reached down for the gun, but she pulled it away from him. He did manage to gather the other two bags and pull them up off the floor.

"Listen Case, if today hasn't taught you anything else, you have to at least know that you have to leave. It's only a matter of time before someone comes for you now. I was thinking about running, but now that I have all of this, I don't have to. If I take out the cartel guys and send the big one's head back to the old man in a box, he'll get the message." She smiled a vicious little smile. "And I owe them one."

Case was still busy trying to gather up the rest of his guns. "Mara, you know if you keep on this path you'll wind up dead, right? If I hadn't found you, you probably already would be."

Mara kept aiming the rifle and peering through the scope. She swept the room until Case's face appeared in it. "I don't fear death," she said calmly. "As long as I have a fighting chance. Sitting in this bed helpless was about the worst thing I can imagine. Now, if I go down, I go down shooting. Can't ask for much more than that."

The worry on Case's face was even more evident through the power scope. "Please put that thing down."

Mara lowered the rifle and put it in her lap. "You have some place I could sight this in?"

Case shrugged. "You could do it here. There's nobody around for several miles. People shoot their guns in the woods all the time. What are you thinking?"

She was stroking the barrel of the rifle like one might pet a puppy. "Once I've gotten familiar with this, we find a nice little sniper's nest for me and then you go to town. You find the Mexicans and you tell them that I'm here. We'll make up some story, something they'll believe. They come out here to get me, and I pick them off." She glared up at Case. "You have a moral problem with me taking them out?"

"As a doctor I can't condone the taking of any life," he answered.

"But you're not a doctor, are you? Not anymore."

"I still took an oath," he said, unconvincingly. "I would prefer to avoid killing anyone if it were at all possible. There's got to be a way."

Mara smirked and went back to fiddling with the sniper rifle. "A few minutes ago you were ready to kill a girl off the street if I was willing to run away with you."

Case sighed and started pacing around the room. "That was…I shouldn't have said that. That was wrong. It's just that I…." He stopped pacing and stared down at Mara, who looked back up at him expectantly. "When it comes to you I'm willing to do almost anything. I know it's wrong." He let out a deep breath and plopped down on the bed. "You make me think crazy thoughts."

Mara again peered through the scope of the rifle and pulled the trigger. The unloaded gun made a click. "Just another reason for me to get out of your life as soon as possible." Satisfied with the gun's action, she laid it on the floor beside her and got up on her knees. As Case stared up at the ceiling, Mara crawled over to the bed and put her chin on the mattress next to Case's head. "You're a good man. You don't need someone like me coming in here and screwing you up."

"Maybe you're right," Case sighed.

"I know I'm right," Mara responded. "How much longer do you think it will take for this ankle to heal up?"

Case rolled his head toward her. "If you'll stay off it, four or five more days maybe."

Mara clicked her tongue against the roof of her mouth and thought it over. "I can't sit here for another week. We don't have that long."

"Well, I could go into town and buy you a brace, a really good one, and tape you up. You'll limp and it'll be uncomfortable, but you can walk."

"That sounds like a plan," Mara said. Grudgingly, she packed the sniper rifle back into the bag and handed it up to Case. "Do you have 9 millimeter shells lying around here? I only have seven shots left."

"No I don't," Case said. "And I don't want to take the chance that someone will see me buying ammunition in town, so I'd have to run into the city."

"Why don't we both go?" Mara asked. She was excited by the thought of getting out of the stuffy cabin. "I'll need some other things before I'm ready to go, and it would be nice to get some fresh air."

"What else are you going to need?"

"Some new clothes, some make up, hair dye, that sort of thing. I want to look like I did the night you found me. I'll make sure that they see me, that they know I'm not around here. That way they'll leave you alone." Case was looking at her with a hangdog look on his face. "What?"

"I know it's for the best," Case muttered. "I just hate to see you go."

Mara shook her head. "After I'm gone, you need to leave here. You need to get back into society and live a normal life. You'll find someone much better than me. You just gotta do one thing first."

"What's that?"

Mara smiled at him, a warm smile that immediately melted his heart. "Grow back the beard."

Chapter 10

Sunday morning Mara woke up to the smell of bacon and eggs. As she struggled up out of the best sleep she'd had in days, she could pick out the sounds of the bacon sizzling in a skillet and Case setting dishes out on the table. She took things slowly, stretching out her muscles and checking her wounds. Her ribs still hurt like hell, but the deep purple bruise was turning green now. The wound in her shoulder was showing no sign of infection, and her ankle, while still swollen, was regaining its natural color.

Satisfied with her progress, Mara got up. Case had left the crutches propped up on the night stand within easy reach, and she easily made her way down the hall. Case was caught up in making breakfast and didn't notice her at first. She stood at the mouth of the hallway and watched him. Mara was well studied enough in human behavior to tell that he was trying to hide his nervousness.

He was headed to the table with a plate of bacon when he finally saw her watching. "Hey," he called out sheepishly as he tried to hide a thin smile. Case plopped the plate down on the table and wiped his hands on his shirt. "I was just coming to wake you up."

"Smells good," Mara said as she made her way over to the table. Deep in her soul there was a stirring, however faint, that this was the way life was supposed to be. This was what normal people did. They cooked breakfast and made small talk and smiled at their loves when they first saw them in the morning. There was a time when Mara had dreamed of a life like this.

She awkwardly made her way into a chair, propped the crutches on the table next to her, and tried to dismiss the feeling. This wasn't reality, not for her anyway. She wasn't meant for a normal life and she knew it. Just as she knew that every moment she spent with Case increased the likelihood that he would meet a very painful end. Mara scolded herself for letting the stray thought enter her head at all. Case was a tool and nothing more. He was a means to an end.

Case slid a tall glass of orange juice to Mara and fixed her a plate of scrambled eggs, bacon, and a biscuit before making his own plate and taking a seat across from her. "So, I'll need to go into town and gas up the truck before we leave," he said. It was casual, so easy. "I figure you can stay here and get ready while I do that. I'll swing by and pick you up, and we'll head into the city."

Mara nodded her head in agreement and took a bite of egg. "One thing," she said. "Let's go to different places than you went last time. Go to a completely different part of town. We want to avoid anything familiar."

"Right," he said, jabbing his fork toward Mara. "Good idea. What all do we need? An ankle brace, a wrap, some athletic tape—"

"Two sets of clothes," Mara picked up. "One casual and one for work. Make up, hair dye, box of 9 millimeters, a knife." Case laughed, causing Mara to glare across the table at him. "What's so funny?"

"Just listening to you. You're talking about work like you're going off to the bank in the morning, but you kill people. Just seems strange."

"Only to you," she said as she picked up a piece of bacon and took a bite. "To me, it's as normal as going off to a bank. It's routine. This," she said as she waved her bacon around the room, "This has been hard."

"I'm going to miss you," Case said softly, looking away from her.

"Don't do that," Mara warned. She glared across the table at Case, who peeked up once and immediately looked away again. "You're only making this worse. You should be happy to be rid of me. You have to start telling yourself that, over and over, until you start to believe it."

"And if I can't believe it?" He finally managed to look up and meet Mara's stare.

"You make yourself believe it. You can, believe me. You tell yourself something long enough and you'll believe it. Whether you want to or not."

#

They finished breakfast, and then Case got dressed in his standard flannel shirt, blue jeans, and work boots and headed into town. Immediately upon stepping outside he caught the faint smell of smoke in the air, and thought of how pleasant it smelled. It seemed odd to him that someone still had their fireplace going, but the mornings were still cool so it wasn't completely unheard of.

As Case drove away from the cabin, he dialed up a local all-news station on the radio. The droning sounds of the deep voiced men debating the hot button issues of the day helped to calm Case and give him focus. He concentrated as he drove on, telling himself that being rid of Mara was the right thing to do.

He repeated the mantra over and over in his head, and even went so far as to start saying it out loud.

He had almost convinced himself when he flashed upon their sexual escapade on the living room floor. The memory of her on top of him, their bodies grinding together, the look of ecstasy on her face, eradicated all of that in a flash. Even if she had been putting on a show for him, and he wasn't sure she was, that one moment ranked extremely high on the relatively short list of great moments in Case's life.

Case slapped himself lightly on the forehead. "Stop it," he growled at himself. "Stop thinking like that. She's a monster." He started repeating it. "She's a monster she's a monster she's a monster." Then he flashed on Mara in the tub, shaving him, her soft skin on his face, the water beading on her arms and her wet hair slicked back.

"Jesus, stop it," Case scolded himself again. She was a killer. She'd pointed a gun at his head and pulled the trigger. She would kill him if she had to, and he knew it.

But she'd only pulled the trigger because she knew the gun wasn't loaded. If Mara's wild thrashing about during sex was a performance, how much else was a performance as well? Was she really the stone-cold killer she claimed to be? Maybe, he thought, she was just a scared young woman playing a role as some sort of defense mechanism.

By the time he pulled into the convenience store on the edge of town, Case was a mess. He simply couldn't reconcile her claims of being a heartless killer with what he had experienced firsthand. Case pulled into the gas pumps nearest the highway and hopped out. As he approached the building, he was calculating in his mind exactly how much gas he'd need to buy to fill the truck up.

The sudden sound of car tires crunching on gravel made him look up, and saved Case from behind run down by a faded yellow

Dodge pickup with a topper on the back. The driver of the truck flew past him, kicking a spray of dust and gravel into Case's face before he skidded to a stop in front of the door and jumped out.

Case stopped and waited for the dust to settle before he started trying to wipe the dirt out of his eyes. "Asshole," he muttered as he started walking again, this time carefully checking for any other cars before he did.

The convenience store was one of the popular local gathering places, so Case wasn't the least bit surprised to see a handful of people sitting around, drinking coffee and eating day old donuts. However, when he walked in, those handfuls of people were standing around a panicked man in overalls and a mesh-backed baseball cap, who was breathlessly relating some sort of tall tale.

"Said it went up like a fireball," said the man, whom Case did not recognize. "Dispatcher said that the firefighters were hearing screams from inside. No doubt it's arson."

Case approached the register, where a washed out, middle aged blonde, who'd enjoyed a few too many day-old donuts, was listening to the man's story with rapt attention. Case had to clear his throat twice to get her attention.

"What?" she finally snapped at him. "Don't you see I'm listening to something here?"

An embarrassed Case glanced over his shoulder to see the rest of the store's patrons staring at him. A couple of them began whispering in each other's ears. No doubt, he thought, the sheriff had already started spreading the word.

"I just need thirty on pump four."

The woman rolled her eyes and snatched two twenties out of Case's hand, punched the buttons on the register hard, and shoved a ten back in his hand. "Here. Now shut up." She looked past Case at the man in the overalls and said, "Go on, Earl."

Earl nodded and picked up right where he'd left off. "They're

101

calling in volunteer units from all the surrounding counties and got a helicopter coming in. But from what I saw, if anybody was in there, they'll be well done before anybody gets to 'em."

Case stopped with his hand on the front door and turned to Earl. "Where is this?"

"Weren't you listening?" Earl said.

"I came in in the middle," Case snapped back. "Some lunatic nearly ran me down in the parking lot."

Earl grinned at him. "Yeah, sorry 'bout that. You should watch where you're going."

Case ignored him. "What's going on? Where's this fire?"

"Out at the Fleming place, man. You could see the flames from the highway. It's insane."

"The Fleming place," Case muttered to himself. "Huh." He shuffled out the front door, certain that he heard snickering from behind him. He walked back out to the car and started pumping the gas, thinking the entire time that he was missing something. There was something pounding at the back of his mind that he just couldn't grab a hold of.

Right about the time the counter on the gas pump hit twenty dollars, the realization finally struck Case. Fleming had been the name he'd given Estavio the first time they'd run into each other. He'd told the hulking Mexican that he'd been doctoring up the Fleming boy. Now someone had burned the place down, apparently with people inside.

"Shit," he muttered. "Shit, shit, shit." He wanted to jump in the truck and go, but he'd paid for the gas and didn't want to waste the money, so he tried to will the pump to run faster. The whole time he kept watching the highway, expecting to see a gold Lincoln come barreling around the curve at any minute. He had no cellphone, no way to alert Mara that danger was coming, if it wasn't already there. He had to hurry back and get Mara out of the house.

Or, he could just sit tight and wait. The thought seemed to materialize out of nowhere, like a devil whispering in his ear. He could go inside and have a cup of coffee and just wait. If Estavio and his men caught Mara at his house, they would take care of each other and Case would be free.

"Shut up," he barked out loud.

The pump finally hit thirty and stopped. Case didn't bother to hang the pump back up, he just tossed it aside, hurriedly put the gas cap back, and jumped in the truck. He peeled out of the gas station, fishtailed when he hit the asphalt, then gunned it for home.

Case knew as he drove that if he were too late, if they were already at the house, or if they came before he could get Mara and get away, that he was a dead man. Internally, he was still debating whether this strange girl was worth the risk. She'd given every indication that she would kill him if she had to, so why risk his neck? Whether it was his heart or something else, he just knew that he couldn't leave her to die.

Case was so caught up with his warring feelings that he almost overshot his turn. He slammed on his brakes and yanked the wheel, and for a moment feared the Blazer might go over. It held and he quickly started off down the dirt trail that led to his cabin. The clock in his head was ticking, running down fast. The Flemings lived on the other side of the mountain, past Springer. If he were in front of them and if they were running the speed limit, he should have time, but not much time. With a sick feeling in his stomach, Case realized that they could come sweeping down on him at any moment.

He drove too hard and too fast down the trail, the truck bumping along the rutted road, jostling Case in the driver's seat as he went. He struggled to keep some semblance of control as the truck bounced along the trail.

Case came up over a hill and saw the cabin down below. With a sigh of relief, he noted no cars or people hanging around. Unless they had already come and gone, he still had time. Of course, if they had already come and gone, his problems were over anyway. Case instantly felt guilty for thinking that way, but it would make his life a lot easier.

He slammed on the brakes and skidded to a stop in front of the cabin. He didn't bother turning off the ignition as he threw the driver's side door open and raced inside. The second he opened the door Case yelled out. "They're coming. They know. We've gotta move."

Mara appeared at the bedroom door a second later, balancing on her crutches. "How do you know?"

Case ran down the hall to her. "The big one, he cornered me in the store that first day and I told him that I was patching up a boy named Fleming who lives on the other side of the mountain. Well, someone just torched the Fleming place, and apparently there were people inside when they did."

"That would be our boys," Mara said coldly. "There are a couple of bags by the front door. Get those." She turned and headed for the bed, where Case saw the lockbox and the rifle bags resting on the bed. "I've got these," she called without looking back at Case. "Just go."

Case ran back to the front door, where Mara had packed up two duffel bags full of supplies. He scooped them up, ran outside, and threw them in the back seat of the Blazer. By the time he got back inside, Mara was limping down the hall, the lockbox in one hand and the three rifle bags slung over her shoulders. She was grimacing with each step, but walking nonetheless. Case ran to her and took the box and two of the rifle bags from her. "Get your crutches," he snarled at her.

"No time for that now. Get those in the truck."

Mara's face had gone cold and hard. He saw her blue eyes frost over. She looked like the same girl, but something had taken hold of her, something that twisted her in ways Case didn't understand and didn't have time to think about. He did as he was told and hurried back to the truck. As he ran, he cast a quick glance to his right and saw the faint hints of dust being thrown into the sky. Was that the lingering effects of his mad drive down the trail, or was someone coming?

Case hurried back inside and caught Mara just short of the front door. "I think someone's coming."

"Probably," she said. "I hope you don't have anything of value left in here."

"Why's that?"

Mara ignored him, hobbled over to the end table, and took a plastic milk jug that was filled with a curious dark concoction. She twisted the lid off, poured some of the liquid around, and then tossed the jug deeper into the room.

"What are you—?"

Before Case could finish, Mara picked up a book of matches, lit one, and tossed it on the ground at her feet. Immediately there was a whoosh and the liquid caught fire, moving quickly toward the jug. "Let's move," Mara said, pushing past him.

Case watched the fire slither and spread, and felt a tinge of anger and sadness as it began to destroy the life he'd carved out here.

"No time for sentiment," Mara said with some effort. "It's gonna get you killed."

Case took one last look before forcing himself to move. He scooped up Mara and raced for the Blazer. No question someone was coming...the dust cloud was getting more pronounced now, and he could hear a vehicle bumping along the road.

"Is there another way out of here?" Mara asked.

"Nope. One road in, one road out," he answered her. He moved to the passenger side and tossed Mara into the seat. She immediately pulled the Glock out of her waistband and stared at it with more affection than she'd ever shown him.

Case was around the truck and into the seat in a moment. "Did you have to burn my place?" he asked as he dropped the truck in gear and peeled out.

"Can't leave anything behind that can be used to find you. I tried to pack anything that looked that it might be important."

"I didn't have much," he said, sounding almost like a whine in his ears. He spun the Blazer in a tight circle and headed back the way he had come, straight at whoever was approaching. Mara was a ball of nervous energy beside him, flicking the safety on and off her gun. Her eyes were trained on the road ahead. "Drive hard and fast, go right at them. You should be able to catch them off guard."

Case pushed the Blazer harder as he started back up the hill. The Blazer went slightly airborne as Case topped the rise, and there was the gold Lincoln making its way up the hill on the other side. Rooney, the gangly white guy with the gauges in both ears, looked shocked as he saw the truck top the hill in front of him, and he jerked the wheel hard right, causing the Lincoln to skitter out of the path of the oncoming Blazer.

As they passed, Case shot a quick look over his shoulder. The Lincoln was coming around to give chase. Beside him, Mara ejected the clip, checked it, and put it back in. "Seven shots," she muttered. "Gotta make 'em count."

She cranked the window down. Behind them, the goons in the Lincoln were rolling their own windows down, getting ready to fire. "Keep driving," Mara told Case. "Move, swerve, don't give them an easy shot."

Case responded by jerking the wheel right, just as their pursuers began firing. Cairo was leaning out of the passenger side window while Estavio was leaning out of the back window behind the driver. Mara pushed herself up on the door and out the window. She held the pistol in her left hand, and with her right she grabbed the luggage rack on the roof of the Blazer. "If I fall out, just keep driving."

"I couldn't—"

"Just do it," Mara snapped at him. "Swerve."

Case shut up, nodded, and swerved back to the left. The Mexicans were firing wildly and missing badly. The terrain was doing them no favors and allowing Case to open a nice gap.

"Put them on my side," Mara ordered calmly. Case acknowledged and went further left. As he did, one of the back windows exploded and a second later the plastic dashboard in front of Mara shattered from the impact of a bullet.

"Whoa," Case called out. "That was close."

"Put 'em on my side," Mara barked louder. "Get me a shot."

Case complied, and as he went further left, the Lincoln appeared from behind the back gate of the Blazer. Mara wrapped her legs around the passenger seat head rest, let go of the luggage rack, and bent over as far as she could, arching her back and bending until she was upside down and almost parallel to the door.

The gunners began to target her. Mara could hear the bullets whizzing through the air. Carefully she sighted the pistol, looking for just the right spot. She found it and fired, and a moment later the Lincoln's front grill was smashed and white smoke started to pour from the radiator.

Case swerved again just as Mara was lining up her next shot, forcing her to pass on a shot. She heard two shots hit the back gate, and reasoned that they must have come from Estavio in the back seat. He didn't have good angle to shoot at her. Cairo, on the other hand, was tightening his shots. One smashed into the back door, causing Mara to flinch away from the impact.

"We're coming up on the highway," Case yelled out and swerved again, this time back to the right. Mara brought the pistol up quickly, shot, and saw the front windshield shatter on the Lincoln. Cairo yelled out, dropped his gun, and ducked back inside the car.

"Go back left," Mara ordered, and the Lincoln disappeared from her view. Case went back left, and as soon as she saw the Lincoln she fired again into the cabin of the car.

"Highway," Case called out again. "Hold on."

Mara felt the Blazer lurch and saw the dirt disappear from behind her, replaced by black asphalt. The Blazer fishtailed as it hit the blacktop at high speed. Case went right and Mara had a brief, clear shot at the passenger side of the Lincoln. She fired twice and put one shot into each of the tires before the Lincoln also hit the highway and fell in behind them.

Mara pulled herself up and slid back in the window. "Floor it. I hit their tires; they won't be able to keep up." The Blazer rocketed forward as Case dropped it into high gear. Mara looked through the rear window as the Lincoln fell hopelessly behind. Rooney was struggling to hold the car straight as the Lincoln threw up a shower of shredded rubber. The chase was over.

Mara sat back heavily in the seat and exhaled. "That was close," she said, only showing a slight hint of emotion. "We probably won't get that lucky again."

Case held on to the wheel tighter, his knuckles white from the death grip he had on the wheel. "You're probably right," he said. "Where to?"

Mara stared out the window and chewed her lip as she thought. Finally she said, "Back to the city. I'd rather head the other way, but we need to ditch this car ASAP and get out of sight. We need a crowded area…a mall, an airport, something like that. We can park the truck, catch a cab, and find a place to hide out from there."

"I know a place," Case said intently. "There's an Indian casino a few miles south of the interstate. There are always cabs waiting to take the drunks home, and the parking lot is always full."

"Sounds like a good place," Mara agreed. "Once we get settled we can plot our next move. We should have a decent enough head start."

Case's eyes wandered up to the rearview mirror. In the distance he could still see a tendril of black smoke from his burning cabin. "I thought I was free up here."

Mara looked over at him with a stone cold stare. "Nobody's free." She looked away again. "Nobody."

CHAPTER 11

They made it to the casino with no problems. Case kept an iron grip on the wheel while Mara watched for police or the gold Lincoln. They crossed under the interstate and continued southwest until the casino rose out of the desert in front of them. As promised, the parking lot was already full, even late on a Sunday morning.

Case cruised the parking lot until he found the perfect spot, sandwiched between two trucks and in front of a conversion van. The truck wouldn't be easily seen, not in the amount of time they would be there.

Mara limped up to the front, where several cabs from various companies waited for a fare. At Mara's direction, Case took a screwdriver out of the glove box and quickly removed the license plates and the VIN badge from the dashboard. He then gathered anything of value from the car and stuffed it all into one of the bags.

He waited by the Blazer's back gate until the cab pulled up. Quickly Case gathered their belongings. Mara leaned over the seat of the cab and asked the Somali cab driver to pop the trunk. He did so, paying no attention to Case and the three long rifle bags he was carrying. While Case put the bags in the trunk, Mara slid out of the cab. She hobbled to the passenger side door of the Blazer and yanked it open. Checking to make sure Case wasn't looking, she quickly pulled the book of matches, lit one, and used it to light an old receipt that was lying on the floorboard, then piled some other discarded papers on the passenger seat and put the burning receipt on top. She hurriedly locked and closed the door and limped back to the cab. Mara wasn't sure if the little pile would be enough to catch the entire car on fire, but it was all she had time for.

Mara ducked in the passenger side door, keeping herself between Case and the Blazer. Case jumped in on the other side and the cabbie sped off. They both kept their eyes open, but saw nothing suspicious, and soon they were pulling into the southeastern edge of the city, easily falling into post-church traffic.

Case spotted a Traveler's Inn and told the driver to pull in. The area was perfect. There were multiple hotels in the area, along with a dozen fast food joints, a convenience store, and a Walmart; everything they needed in one spot. Mara jumped out as Case paid the cabbie, and they both unloaded the trunk.

As the cabbie pulled away, Mara swatted Case on the arm. "What?" he asked.

She pointed across the busy street at a Motel 6 on the other side, one block further down. "Let's go over there."

"Well, if we were going to do that, I could've just had the cabbie drop us."

Mara looked up at Case with exasperation. "I don't want the cabbie knowing where we're staying. If, heaven forbid, they find him, he's going to point the cartel guys here."

"Oh, gotcha," Case answered sheepishly. They lugged the bags to the corner and waited for the opportunity to cross the busy street.

"We need to ditch these bags," Mara said as she hobbled along. Her voice betrayed the pain that she refused to openly acknowledge. "We're so conspicuous. We're also going to need to find some cheap wheels. How much money do you have?"

"Not enough for a car," Case said. "Not on me. I can get more in the morning. I've got money stashed at several banks here, and more stashed in some other cities."

"We should get a paper and check the classifieds," Mara said. They got the light to cross and began lugging their bags across the street. Mara was struggling badly, her ankle clearly bothering her.

When they reached the other side, Case and Mara both dropped their bags while they caught their breath. "You need to get off that foot. Once we get settled I'll walk over to the Walmart and get some more supplies."

Mara shook him off, picked up one duffle bag and two rifle bags, and started down the street. "No. I need to go with you. I need clothes." Then she changed the subject back to the car. "You can buy a car from an individual with cash and won't need to fill out any paperwork. It will be months before the old owner realizes that you never filed the title. By which point, we'll either be long gone or dead."

"Such an optimist," Case said as he caught up to Mara. He took one of the rifle bags off her shoulder and threw it over his shoulder instead. The day was turning into a scorcher, made worse by the steady stream of cars passing so close. They were both thankful to reach the lobby of the motel. Exhausted, they dropped their bags at the front desk.

"Can I help you?" The desk clerk was a thick young woman with long, thick black hair, wearing a navy blouse with a blood red tie. She viewed them both with cautious eyes.

"We need a room," Case said, trying to be casual.

The desk clerk's eyes moved to the pile of bags on the floor. "Are those guns?"

"No," Mara said with a laugh. "Everybody thinks that. We're painters, these are our supplies," she said, picking up one of the bags and giving it a pat. "These are our easels."

"They look like gun bags," the clerk said. There was a silent challenge in her eyes as she stared them both down.

Mara felt the hardness settle over her again. The Glock was pressing into the small of her back, begging to be used. She sighed heavily as she stretched and feigned rubbing her back, her hand moving slowly toward the gun.

Case saw the movement and must have anticipated her next move. "They are," he said affably to the clerk. "We've found that gun bags have extra padding, which is why we use them." The clerk's suspicious eyes moved from Mara to Case, who met them with a goofy grin. "Do you know how much one of these things cost?" He paused for a moment but didn't wait for her to answer. "Well I'll tell ya, they ain't cheap."

Beside him Mara had her hand on the butt of the pistol. The clerk's eyes slid back to Mara, who met the clerk's gaze with one of her own. They stared each other down for three heartbeats, and then the girl gave up.

"Very well," she said with a sigh. "How many nights?"

#

"That was close," Case said once they finally made it to their room on the second floor and on the other side of the building. "I thought she had us made."

"I would have dealt with it," Mara answered. She dropped her bags and collapsed in a heap on one of the two twin beds in the room.

"What were you going to do, blow her away right there in

113

the lobby in broad daylight?" Case asked as he checked out their sparse room.

"If I had to," Mara responded. "Had that bitch kept glaring at me like that, I might have done it on pure principle alone."

Case was appalled. "She was just doing her job."

"So am I," Mara responded. "I keep telling you and you still don't believe me. I do what I have to. I don't think about it, I just do it."

"Yeah, well," Case said, but he had no suitable retort. He finished checking out the room and circled back, scooped up the plastic ice tub, and opened the door. "I'm going to go get some ice and a paper. Do you need anything?"

Mara pushed up on her elbows. "A box of nine millimeters?"

Case rolled his eyes. "Maybe later. I was thinking more along the lines of a soda or some chips. Stuff like that."

"I'm good," she said. Mara fell back on the bed. "I'm just going to rest for a bit."

"Good idea," Case said, sounding very doctoral. "Keep off that foot. I'll be back." He closed the door behind him and wound his way back to the lobby. The clerk glared at him silently as he walked in. Case held up the bucket. "Just getting some ice." She shrugged but kept a careful eye on him.

When Case was done filling the bucket, he swung by the desk and picked up one of a stack of local papers. "How much for the paper?"

"Complimentary for guests," she hissed.

"Great," Case said, careful to remain cheerful. He set the ice bucket on the counter and thumbed through the paper to make sure the classifieds were included. They were. He folded the paper under his arm, gathered the ice bucket, and shuffled on out the front door. The clerk's continued cold demeanor bothered him. He was sure the woman suspected something.

Case was debating packing up and finding another hotel when he got back to the room. He knocked, hoping Mara would open the door for him, but she didn't answer. He knocked again, louder this time, but there was still no response. Case began to feel sick. He put down the bucket and the paper so he could dig the key card out of his back pocket. On the verge of panic, he slipped the card in the slot, but tried to open the door too fast and it locked. Case took a deep breath and did it again, slower this time. The lock buzzed and he pushed into the room.

And heard the faint sound of the shower running from behind the closed bathroom door.

Immediately Case felt foolish. He picked up the bucket and the paper and pushed the door shut. He carried his load over to the built in desk by the window and sat down to look at the paper. Yet his mind wandered, filling with visions of Mara in the shower. He thought of the steamy room, the water beading on her perfect skin, her hair slicked back. He remembered the night she had attacked him on the living room floor.

The paper would wait. Case pushed away from the desk. He couldn't remember a time in his life he had been so aroused. As he made his way to the bathroom he began peeling away his clothes. This time, he would be in control and he would do it right. He would teach her what it was like to make love.

Case pushed the bathroom door open, stepped inside, and pushed it shut quietly. Through the thin shower curtain he saw Mara's silhouette under the showerhead. Carefully he slid into the back of the shower. Mara's back was turned to him, and if she felt his entrance she made no indication. He noticed that she was standing on one foot and using the toe of her right foot to balance herself. The ankle was swollen again.

Case edged up behind her and quickly slid his arms around her stomach. He felt her tighten up but pressed on. As the water began hitting him in the face, Case began lightly kissing Mara's neck. He moved down her neck and out across her shoulder and back again. He pushed her hair out of the way so that he could kiss the back of her neck. The entire time she stood stock still, breathing slowly. She said nothing as he slid his hands up and began to caress her breasts.

Then like a flash she turned. Mara put her hands flush against Case's chest and drove him back until he slammed into the wall. Case gasped as his illusion of control vanished. Mara engulfed him. She kissed him roughly, biting his lips as she did. She barred her left arm across his neck, pushing hard and depriving Case of air as her right hand found his erection and pulled hard. He wasn't sure he'd last long but Mara let go. With her injured right foot, she forced his legs farther apart. Engulfed in passion, desperate for air and utterly helpless, Case looked into Mara's face but saw nothing of the girl he craved. Her eyes were vacant, almost animalistic, her mouth drawn into a tight scowl. Case wriggled under her pressure, trying to get enough air to say something to her. He wanted to snap her out of whatever trance she was in, but then she was on him. Mara ravished him in every way she could. She was a monster, writhing and scratching at him. She finally took her arm away from his neck and drug her nails down his chest, sending fine lines of blood running down his body. As Case reached the breaking point, Mara pulled his hair and screamed in his ear, controlling him every second of their encounter.

When it was over, Case slumped to the floor of the tub in exhaustion, while Mara calmly turned and finished her shower. When she was done, she looked over her shoulder at Case, still slumped in the tub, and said "All yours."

She stepped out of the shower and was gone, leaving Case to attempt to gather himself. He took his time, feeling weak in the knees as he cleaned up.

When Case finally stepped out of the bathroom, Mara was laying on her stomach on her bed, her feet in the air. She was wearing the same T-shirt and shorts she had been wearing for days, and was reading through the ads while chewing on the end of a motel pen. "I need clothes," she said without looking at him at all.

Case, still dripping wet and wearing nothing but a towel, felt a fresh round of arousal sweeping over him. Maybe the third time….

"Not now," Mara said with indifference. "Maybe later if you really want. Now we need to think and plan, and I need some clothes that fit, and I'm hungry."

"How did you…?"

"I have peripheral vision, you know," Mara said. "I can see you getting turned on. If it's that bad I suggest you go take care of yourself. My generosity has its limits."

"Generosity? You sound like you're buying me dinner or something," Case spat out.

Mara sighed and dropped the pen. When she turned, Mara fixed him with a gaze of Arctic proportions. "Are we really going to go over this again?"

She waited for his response and wouldn't break the gaze until Case lowered his head and muttered, "No."

"Good," she said, turning her attention back to the paper. "I've got some possibilities on the car here, but I don't know what kind of money you have." She put the classifieds aside and pulled a full color Walmart ad out and tossed it on Case's bed. "There are some things in there that I need. I marked what I want and wrote my sizes down. Nothing extravagant. I would go with you, but the ankle is killing me." Again she looked away from the ad to glare at Case. "Wonder why that is?" He started to answer but

Mara cut him off. "I need you to find those pain pills of yours."

"As you wish," Case said sarcastically. "Just let me get dressed and I'll get started."

"No hurry on the pills," Mara said as Case began pulling a fresh set of clothes out of his bag. "I want to eat first, and I need some time to think."

"Whatever," Case mumbled as he gathered his clothes and moved back to the bathroom. He was hurt. It was foolish, he knew, but he couldn't help it. The harder he tried to worm his way into Mara's heart, the colder and more distant she seemed to get. The sex was amazing, she knew all the tricks, but without some sort of emotional connection, Case was always left feeling dirty. Maybe, he thought, that was the point all along.

He dressed quickly in a pair of lightweight khaki slacks and a short sleeved red polo shirt. Case wiped the steam off the mirror and glanced at himself. He looked like a car salesman, but at least he had a couple of day's stubble on his face now. A few more and he'd begin to look like himself again.

Case stomped out of the bathroom, quickly put on his work boots, and scooped up the Walmart ad. "What do you want to eat?"

"Whatever you want," Mara said. She had gone back to studying the classifieds. "There's plenty to choose from around here."

"Fine," Case said coldly. He was hoping Mara was hearing anger and not hurt in his voice. "I'll be back in a little bit." He had one foot out the door when Mara called his name. Case turned, suddenly hopeful for some sort of revelation from her.

"Keep your eyes open."

"Sure thing," Case growled, and then he slammed the door shut.

#

Mara was aware of Case's annoyance with her. It didn't bother her. She had been clear with him all along. The fact that he kept insisting that she should feel something was Case's problem, not hers.

She finished going through the ads and then made a list on hotel stationary of her top choices. It would be up to Case to determine which one to get. He was paying.

Done with that and certain that Case would be gone for a while, Mara slid into a pair of oversized sneakers she had been wearing and made her way down to the lobby. The snobby girl from earlier had been replaced with an older, plump red head with a grandmotherly quality. She was chatting up a tourist at the desk and paid no attention as Mara slipped past. She found a payphone down a narrow hallway just off the lobby, across from two darkened meeting rooms.

She dug a handful of change she had liberated from Case's house out of her pocket, dropped some coins in the slot, and called a number she knew by memory. A number she knew would go to a "burner" phone that could not be traced. A number only she had. The phone clicked on the other end.

"Angel?" The voice on the other side was flat, completely devoid of any inflection or accent at all. The mere sound of it sent shivers racing up Mara's spine. In that one word, she was convinced that Master had already looked into her soul and seen all of the wrong she had done.

"Master," she said, trying and failing to keep her voice as even as his.

"It's about time you called," Master answered. "I was beginning to worry."

"I know, Master. I'm sorry." He was the only person in the world that could strike fear in Mara. He always made her feel like the little girl she used to be, begging on the streets for loose change. "I haven't been able to get to a phone before. There were some complications."

"I see," Master answered. Mara was amazed at how his voice could be so unemotional and yet drip with venom the way his did. "And have these complications been cleared up?"

"No, sir," she whispered.

"Excuse me?"

"No, sir," Mara said louder. She was shaking all over. "They will be. Soon. I've been healing."

"You're injured?" There was a slight hint of something. Humor, maybe? Certainly not concern. Master never worried, never concerned himself about anything. "Is it bad?"

"No, sir," Mara repeated. "It's just slowed me down. I'm getting better. I'm up and around now." She glanced quickly over her shoulder to make sure that she was still alone. "I will finish things up in the next few days. I'm planning."

Master stayed silent on the other end for a moment. Finally, he said, "Maybe I should just bring you in. Where are you? I will send Raven and Locke to get you."

This time it was Mara who paused. That was not the way things worked. Master never sent one of his children to help the others, and he never asked for a location. There was too much of a chance someone could be watching or listening, and that could lead to exposing the entire family.

"You don't need to do that, Master. I've got things under control here. I just need a few more days to wrap things up." There was a voice in her head screaming to hang up, that something wasn't right, but you didn't hang up on Master.

"Angel," he said again, and this time there was no mistaking the menace in his voice. "Tell me where you are. We need to talk. You've gotten sloppy."

He knew. He knew it all. The realization buckled Mara's

knees. She nearly fell, slumping against the wall. She turned her head quickly, like a frightened animal. Almost immediately the red-haired desk clerk peeked around the corner.

Mara held the phone away from her ear and faked a laugh. "Clumsy me," she said. "Nearly fell flat on my face." The woman appraised her for a second and then went back to chatting up the tourist. Mara quickly put the phone back to her ear.

"Are you using a public phone?"

Mara felt tears gathering in her eyes. She never should have called him. Maybe he would have thought that she was dead and left it at that. Instead she had just doubled down on her mistakes. "It was the only one I could get too. I'm moving. No one will track me."

"Come in, Angel," Master said again, smoothing his voice back out. "I think you need some refresher training."

Mara inhaled sharply and the tears broke loose and began streaming down her face. She had angered him. She had to get control. If he heard her crying it would only make things worse.

"Angel?"

Mara found that hard edge she relied on and pulled it close. She pushed back the tears and swallowed the fear. "I'm fine," she said, just as coldly as she could as she wiped away the tears with the palm of her free hand "I will clean up my mistakes and then I will come home. You have nothing to worry about. I need to move now. I'll call when I can."

Mara hung up quickly before he could say anything else, then collapsed against the wall and slid to the floor. Her hands were fluttering like a leaf on the breeze. She had known that Master would be upset with her, but this was far worse. Something was terribly wrong.

Mara only allowed herself a few precious moments there on the floor, just a sip of panic, before forcing herself up off the floor.

It was not the time to panic, it was time to move, to think. She limped past the desk clerk in a daze. How long would it take for Master to find her and dispatch his goons? Could they hop on a plane and get here before morning?

"Sweetie? Sweetie?"

Mara, confused, stopped and swung around in a circle. The desk clerk was waving at her.

"Are you okay, sugar? You don't look so hot."

Mara smiled weakly at her. "I'm fine. Just having a run of bad luck right now. I'll be okay. I always am."

"You look like you're scared to death." The woman frowned through her heavy makeup. "Are you sure that there's nothing I can do for you?"

"Nah. I'll be fine," Mara lied. "I've got everything under control." She turned and tried to strut confidently out of the lobby. It was bullshit, of course. She had nothing under control. Leading them out of the woods and into the city was starting to look like a huge mistake. Things seemed to be unravelling in front of her eyes.

The game had changed. She wasn't sure exactly how, or to what extent, but Mara knew that the ground had shifted beneath her feet. Suddenly she had so much more than angry Mexican drug runners to worry about.

She had to think, and quickly. Master had a line on her now. He was going to kill her. It was time for Mara to break free. Case had been right all along. At least she had him, for whatever good it would do. He didn't seem to be much use in a fight.

Out on the sidewalk, Mara shielded her eyes from the midday sun and looked all around. She was looking for Case, or the gold Lincoln, or Master and his boys. She was looking for the noose that she could feel slipping around her neck. She was looking for Death, sharpening his blade, preparing to welcome her home.

Mara saw nothing. With a knot of fearing constantly tightening in her stomach, Mara hurried up to the room and locked the door. If only she were healthy, then she could just make a break. Master had taught her well and she was smart. She could disappear, but she wasn't healthy. She needed Case right now.

The fact that she needed anyone made Mara sick. She had long ago learned that relying on others was a surefire path to pain and disappointment. Case had stuck by her so far, but what would he do when the chips were really down? Would he be willing to risk it all when he was on the wrong side of a gun and there was no way out?

Mara thought over each intimate detail of their days together. She analyzed his every move. He'd faced off against the Mexicans three times now and the sheriff once and held his own, but he was shaky. He got rattled easy.

Case was also in love with her. Mara knew that she could use that, cultivate it. She could hold him close, at least for a while. Yet the truth was clear to her. At some point, Case was going to become a liability for her.

When that day came, she'd have to do what was necessary and put him down easy. The thought of having to kill Case didn't bother her. She was the Angel of Death.

That's what she did.

CHAPTER 12

Mara woke up to Case kicking at the door. She had fallen asleep face down on the bed, her feet where her head should be. She jerked up, a sudden movement that send tendrils of pain crawling through her from multiple sources.

"Mara, come on. Open the damn door," Case called from the hallway.

She rolled off the bed and limped to the door, trying to rub the sleep out of her eyes as she did. She took a second to look through the peep hole to make sure Case was alone before opening the door.

"About time," he growled as he stepped into the room. He was balancing two large pizza boxes on one hand, and several white plastic Walmart bags in the other.

"I fell asleep. Sorry," Mara retaliated, sounding somewhat pouty. She stuck her head out and looked up and down the walkway before closing the door and locking the deadbolt. As Case dropped his load on his side of the bed, Mara limped over and punched him hard in the left arm.

Case recoiled from the punch. "What the fuck was that for?"

Mara stood fuming inches from him, hands on her hips. "For

124

making so much goddamn noise. You want the whole fucking place to know we're here?"

Case looked confused for a second and stepped away from her. "They couldn't find us that quickly, Mara. Why are you suddenly so paranoid?"

"I'm not paranoid," she growled at him. "We are being chased, if you have forgotten."

"No, I haven't forgotten. Not by a long shot. But I also know that we had a huge head start. Those guys have no idea where we stashed the car or where we went from there. Yes, maybe they eventually pick up our trail, but it is impossible for them to do it this quickly. For all they know, we could be in Texas right now."

Despite her best attempts to stay emotionless, Mara gave something away. Case saw it immediately.

"What did you do?"

Mara dropped her eyes away from Case. "I didn't do anything," she said meekly. "Let's just eat and forget it. You're right. I'm being paranoid."

She started to reach for a pizza box, but Case yanked up her arm and pulled her into him. "Quit lying to me, Mara. I'm on the line here for you. I've lost my home and my car. I deserve the truth."

Mara wriggled and eventually pulled her arm free of his grip. "You will get exactly what I tell you and nothing more. The rest is for me to worry about. Now let's eat and get some rest. Tomorrow is going to be a busy day, and we need to be sharp."

Again she reached for the pizza. Case knocked the boxes onto the floor between the two beds. "Quit lying to me. You tell me what you did, or I'm walking out that door and you can fend for yourself." There was a fire in Case's eyes Mara had never seen before.

Mara stood and fumed. She could feel the pistol in the small of her back. She felt the fuel of righteous rage catch fire in her soul. It would have been so easy to end him there, but he was right and she knew it. Case did have a right to know. He had put himself in harm's way for her. She pushed the urges and the rage down and sat on the corner of his bed.

"I checked in while you were out. Master is very upset with me. He wants to bring me in. He'll send his muscle here to get me. They're probably already on a plane."

"Goddamn it, Mara, really? You called from the lobby, didn't you?"

"Yes," Mara said weakly. "I couldn't go far." She forced herself to look Case in the eye. "I told him that I was moving, and he knows that I know better than to stay where I called from."

"You're counting on him outguessing you?"

"Yes. I figure that they'll get here some time tonight, and they'll come here first off. As long as the same woman isn't working the desk when they get here, then no one will have seen me. But you've got to get moving first thing in the morning and find us a car. I'll feel much better once we're mobile again."

"Jesus." Case ran both hands through his hair and turned in a circle. "What? Did you think that we weren't in enough trouble already and just figured, 'Hey, let's make it more of a challenge'?"

"I knew that I needed to check in," Mara answered calmly. "I had been out of touch too long. Normally, I report within an hour of a successful completion. It's been days. I had to let him know that I hadn't run out on him. I had hoped to put him at ease, to let him know everything was fine. But he was different, odd."

Case's fuming anger began to subside and he eased down on the bed as well, though he stayed well back from Mara. "How so?"

Mara glanced at Case, and then quickly looked away. "I'm not sure. He asked me to tell him where I was, which he never

126

does. That's a rule; never broadcast your position, in case they're listening."

"Who are they?"

"Them," Mara said with a shrug. "Anybody. Cops. Feds. Other criminals. Master is very careful."

"Master sounds a little nutty," Case answered.

"The other thing," Mara said, ignoring Case's last comment, "Is that he insisted on sending his muscle for me, to bring me in. That's not how things work. When you go out on a job, you go alone. I don't work with his goons and we don't help each other out. Master is always very clear on that. If something goes wrong and we're on the hook, it's up to us to get out of it. He stresses that. We do nothing to lead authorities back to Master."

"You think he's written you off?"

"I think, maybe, but then I'm not so sure. He said that I needed…reprogramming." Mara couldn't hide the shiver that ran through her at the thought.

"I take it that's not a pleasant thing."

Mara looked at Case with a grave expression. "Death would probably be better than Master's programming. I did it once…I won't do it again. You see the way I am. He turned me into this. He breaks you down until you're nothing but an animal, then he brings you back. He burns the humanity out of you. You keep wanting me to love you, but I can't. That is what I just can't get you to understand. That part of me is dead. Master drove it out of me."

Case seemed shocked. "So why do you insist on going back to him?"

Mara stood sharply. "Because a gun is no good without someone to pull the trigger. I'm nothing without him." She edged along between the two beds and knelt to retrieve the pizza.

"That's not true," Case snapped. "You are a human being,

Mara. You always have it in your power to change your circumstances."

Mara tossed the two boxes back on the bed, opened the top one, and took out a long, thin slice of pepperoni pizza. "And do what? I have no history. I have no social security number, no driver's license, no job history. With Master I live in a good home, there is food and shelter and money. I have a purpose. I should trade all of that to work a drive thru window somewhere?"

"If that's what it takes, then yes."

"No thanks," Mara said around a mouthful of pizza. With her one free hand, she scooped up the Walmart bags and tossed them onto her bed. As she worked on the pizza she also began thumbing through the bag. She was aware that Case was coming toward her, but kept her focus on the bags. "What is this?"

Case was standing silently over her as Mara dumped one of the bags onto the bed. She held up a batch of sheer, silky bras. "Sexy underwear? I just needed something reasonable."

Case looked down at her and grinned. "Well, those are reasonably hot. Come on, I'm spending my money."

Mara stared at him silently, and then tossed the bras over her shoulder. "And the matching panties too. Not hard to see where you're going with this." Mara also tossed those aside. "Ah. Here we go." She held up a box. "Ankle brace. That's reasonable."

Case sat beside Mara on the bed. "I'll tape you up good tomorrow before we go out. With a night of ice on it, you should be able to get around okay."

"This I like," Mara said. She dumped the rest of the bags. Two pair of jeans, one blue and one black, several plain T-shirts, including one black one, socks, and a pair of cheap silver and pink sneakers. "A little flashy, don't you think?"

"It's Walmart," Case said defensively. "They have a limited selection. You should be fine. You're going to look like a young suburban housewife. Isn't that what you wanted?"

"I guess it'll do," Mara said. She finished her piece of pizza. "But let me tell you, if that underwear you got me is uncomfortable, you're going to wear it."

Case grinned at her. "Are you going to make me?"

Without smiling, Mara reached behind her, pulled out the pistol, and put it on the bed between them. "If I have to."

Case stood up, disgusted. "It was a joke, Mara. Jesus. There's no need for stuff like that."

Mara didn't back down. "Do I look like I'm in a joking mood?" Case didn't answer her. Instead he grabbed himself a slice of pizza and circled around to the far side of his bed. She watched him out of the corner of her eye, calculating. He was soft, weak, easily hurt. The time was coming.

Soon.

#

They ate in silence and then Case stared at the TV while Mara repacked the bags and laid out her clothes for the next day. "I still don't know what to do with the guns. They don't break down."

"Won't matter. Tomorrow I'll get us a truck and we'll just throw them behind the seat," Case said emotionlessly.

"How much will you be able to get tomorrow?" Mara asked. It was important. If it was enough, she could just kill Case and take off. If it wasn't, then she'd have to push him to his other stashes.

He finally peeled his eyes off the TV and looked across the room at her. He had never looked at Mara with such disgust before, and it made her wonder if he was seeing through her as well. "Enough to get a truck and to get on the road. I can get more later if I need it."

Mara tried to stay cool. "That's good," she said as she went back to packing their bags. "I'm trying to decide which way we should go from here."

"North," Case said, turning back to the TV. "You go any other direction and you're going into desert or prairie. Flat land, long stretches with nothing around. We head into the mountains, where we have cover."

"We just came from the mountains."

"It's a big range. Besides, I'm not talking here. I'm talking Colorado, Wyoming. Get up in the Rockies and dare them to find us there."

"We won't be able to stay any place for too long. We'll have to keep moving. Master has eyes and ears everywhere. He'll catch our scent."

Case went silent and after a while, Mara finished the bags and stacked them by the door. "Did you tell him about me?" Case finally asked.

Mara wheeled around on her good foot. "No, of course not. I'm trying to keep you out of this."

"But did you mention that someone was helping you? Tending to you?"

"No. I told him that I was hurt but recovering, and that I was moving. The less he knows the better for us both. But the Mexicans, they know all about you."

"I know," he said sullenly.

Mara stood by the door and let her eyes sweep over the room. She was making a list in her head, double checking herself, trying to make sure that she didn't leave anything behind. Confident that she had everything in order, she walked to the bed and turned the sheets down.

"Going to sleep?"

"Yes," she answered as she arranged two pillows at the foot of the bed.

"Let me go get you some more ice and a Baggie." Case

grunted as he pushed up off the bed. He grabbed the card key off the desk and stuck it in his back pocket. "Be right back." He grabbed the ice bucket, which was now filled with water, on his way out.

Mara watched him go. She had really hurt his feelings by pulling the gun on him. For a fleeting moment, Mara felt bad. She shook the thought out of her head. "Stay focused," she whispered to herself.

#

Case was pouting as he stepped out onto the cement walkway. Without thinking, he dumped the melted ice over the railing and started to circle around to the stairs that would take him to the ground level. He was still stinging from Mara's rebuke earlier in the day, but he was also embarrassed by his own actions. What exactly had compelled him to buy sexy underwear for her? Did he think that such a cheesy gift was going to change her mind?

He made his way quickly down the stairs and along the sidewalk toward the front of the building and the lobby. Leave it to him to find the one hotel in America that didn't have special rooms with ice machines.

He rounded the corner and started for the lobby. Case was paying no attention to his surroundings and it almost cost him. He was through the front door and into the foyer before he noticed the three goons in the lobby, crowded around the front desk.

"Shit," he muttered, skidding to sudden stop. Carefully he backed out of the foyer, keeping his eyes on the backs of the men. He backed up until he was certain that he was out of sight before hunkering down and scanning the parking lot. There was the gold Lincoln, parked facing the street by the turn in. It stuck out like a sore thumb, but he hadn't been paying attention. If he had something, anything, he might have made for the car and tried to sabotage it, but all he had was the ice bucket.

Instead he turned and ran, crouching low against the front wall. He reached the front corner quickly, then stood and finished his run around to the back of the building and up the stairs. The entire time, he was waiting for one of the goons to turn the corner and see him, to watch him go to the room. They'd be trapped up there.

Panicky, he fumbled the card key in the lock again before finally getting the door to open. Case paused and took a darting look around him. He saw no sign of the Mexicans. He ducked inside and slammed the door.

Mara leaned her head up as he entered. "That was fast."

He turned. "They're here. In the lobby. I almost walked right into them."

Mara pulled herself the rest of the way up. "That was faster than I thought. They must have guessed where we were going." She stared daggers at Case. "You go there a lot, don't you? To the casino? Enough that someone would recognize you or would rat you out?"

"I…." Case paused, thinking back. "Yeah, I went there sometimes. But not a lot, and never with anyone. Always alone. I didn't broadcast it."

"It doesn't matter," Mara said with disgust. She grabbed the ankle brace and slid it over her foot. Case saw the pain in her face, but she wouldn't show it. She dressed in the clothes she had laid out; blue jeans, soft pink T-shirt, socks, and shoes. When she was done, she picked up the Glock and tucked it into her waistband. "You said that they were at the front desk?"

"Yes," Case said.

"Where they talking to an older red-haired lady?"

"I don't know," Case stammered. "I didn't see who the desk clerk was. As soon as I saw them, I turned and ran. I don't think they saw me."

132

"You don't think," Mara scoffed. "So the second I pop that door I could eat a bullet. Great." She walked angrily to the door, then turned and wagged a finger at Case. "This is why you don't follow patterns. You don't go to places you know. People see you and remember you, even if you don't think they do. People like this, they have ways of finding things out about people, and they do it fast." She peered out of the peep hole, but could see nothing outside.

"You sure you should go out there?"

"It's either that or wait for them to come blow the door in. Sure do wish you'd gotten me those nine millimeters like I asked for. I've got two shots left."

"Take one of the other guns," Case shot back. "That's why I brought them."

"They're too big and bulky. I'll take my chances with mine." She put her hand on the door knob, checked the peephole again, and then took a deep breath. Finally, she turned back to Case. "Grab one of those guns for yourself. Make sure it's loaded and the safety is off. If I don't come back, or if they come up here for you, do yourself a favor and eat a bullet."

Case felt sick just thinking about it. Before he could think of anything to say, Mara turned the knob quickly and slid outside, pulling the door closed quietly behind her. Case looked out the peephole, but Mara had already moved out of range.

His eyes dropped to the floor and the bags stacked up. He got on his knees and rifled through them until he found one of the guns, the big revolver. As instructed, Case made sure the gun was loaded before standing and trudging over to the bed. With a heavy heart, he plopped on the end of the bed, held the revolver in both hands, and waited.

#

Mara reached the front edge of the building and peered

around. She spotted the Lincoln parked by the entrance to the parking lot. They were still here. She ducked back and looked behind her. Nothing there.

If she had more bullets, Mara might have made the ballsy play and just gone in, guns blazing. With only two, she had to be conservative. She peeked again, then darted from the corner into the parking lot and crouched between two sedans. She put her hand lightly on the fender of the car closest to the front door and prayed that it didn't have an alarm. It didn't. She duck walked back to the door, leaned up, and looked through the windows. Other cars blocked her view.

Mara cursed silently and made her way to the back of the car. Looking down the row of cars, she saw an old pickup just a few spots from the lobby. If she could make her way to the truck, she could hop in the bed and have a great view of the front doors.

Mara stayed low and moved fast. Once she reached the rear of the truck Mara grabbed the tailgate and lifted herself up. Just as she was ready to jump into the bed, a movement caught her eyes. The three goons were just stepping through the inner door. Quickly Mara dropped to the ground and scrambled around to the far side of the truck. A second later, the outer door opened. Estavio and Cairo were talking to each other loudly, but they were speaking Spanish and Mara had no idea what they were saying.

Crouched as low as she could go, Mara pulled the pistol and held it ready. The voices were trailing away from her. She risked a quick peek out from her position and saw the three of them heading for the car. Mara pulled back. With any luck, they'd drive on to the next hotel. She heard car doors open and decided to take another quick look. Rooney and Cairo were ducking in the left side while Estavio stood by the front passenger door, glaring over the roof. Mara gasped and pulled back.

She heard several sharp footsteps come back her way and Rooney called out, "What's up?" Mara scooted back further, flattened out, and rolled underneath the truck. Estavio was quiet for several seconds before he barked at Rooney to get in the car. Seconds later, it started and she could hear the car backing out of the parking space.

Mara decided to stay hidden. Soon enough, the Lincoln crept by and she realized that they were looking between the parked cars. Mara stayed very still and listened intently. Once she heard the car turn the corner, she rolled out from under the pickup, put the gun away, and scurried into the lobby.

Sure enough, the red-haired woman was still there and she looked scared to death. "What did those guys want?" Mara asked in a hushed but urgent tone.

"You," the woman answered with a shaky voice.

Mara's heart sank. "Did you tell them what room we're in?" The gun was right there in her waistband, calling to her again. She prayed that she wouldn't have to use it.

"Hell, no," Red answered back, some bravado bleeding back into her voice. She leaned forward on the counter. "I've seen that look. The one that you had earlier. I know a battered woman when I see one, sugar. Just tell me that it wasn't the big guy. You're too pretty to be taking up with a sorry wetback like that."

Mara couldn't help herself and laughed out loud. "We can't help who we love, can we?" She turned so that she could watch for the Lincoln when it came back around while trying to stay as far out of the way as she could. They both waited, and when the Lincoln finally did swing back around, they both held their breath. The car paused just in front of the door, and then Rooney turned. Only when he turned left out onto the street and moved on did they relax.

"Honey," the red-haired woman called out. Mara looked

back over her shoulder. "Is that a gun I see in your pants?"

Mara dropped her head. This woman had stuck her neck out to help and now this. Mara didn't want to kill her.

"Don't sweat it," Red said, clearly reading Mara's disappointment. She reached behind her own back and pulled out a gun of her own. "Beretta: a girl's best friend. I was a battered woman once too."

Mara smiled. "Nine millimeter?"

"Of course," Red said with a smile.

"You wouldn't happen to have any more ammo for that, would you?"

#

Red hooked Mara up with enough bullets to fill her clip, and gave her a fully loaded spare. They sat and talked, and Mara made up a detailed history of her troubled "marriage" to Estavio. When Red asked about the man she was travelling with, Mara claimed that Case was her brother, an artist who travelled the country painting landscapes.

When Red's shift was over and her replacement came on, she slipped Mara a piece of paper with her address and phone number on it, in case she ever found herself in another bind. Mara was honestly thankful for the woman's help, and wasn't even that bothered when Red hugged her goodbye.

Mara walked slowly back around to the room, enjoying the still warm night air and the feeling, no matter how brief, that she was safe. Still, the cartel men had found them fast, much faster than she'd expected. How they had found them couldn't be simple coincidence, Mara reasoned. She didn't believe in such things.

Mara got to the door and tried to go in before she remembered that she had left her card key in the room. She quietly knocked. "Case, open up. It's me. It's safe."

No answer.

Mara knocked more urgently. "Case, come on. Open up. It's clear." There was still no response. Fearing the worst, she stepped away from the door and pulled her gun, ready to charge into battle. "Case?" No answer. "Case!"

Finally, she heard the click of a lock and the door swung open. It was pitch black inside. Mara darted from in front of the open door to the side and peeked around the corner, gun held at the ready. She could see nothing.

Mara was about ready to edge into the room when she heard the click of a hammer being pulled back. She rolled her eyes upward, where the barrel of Case's big revolver was sticking out from behind the door and pointed directly at her face. Mara swallowed, trying to remain calm. "Case? Is that you behind that cannon?"

Still no response, but the barrel of the gun shook, just slightly. Mara let out a slow breath. "Case, I'm going to come into the room now and I'm going to turn on the light. I would really like it if you would not point the big gun at my face. Okay? Here I go."

She moved slowly, methodically. The gun tracked her every movement. Mara was terrified that he would flinch when she turned on the light and blow her face off. She kept her right hand on her gun, but felt the wall with her left until she found the light switch.

"I'm gonna turn on the light now," she said softly. "Please don't shoot me." She flicked the switch and quickly turned her head so that she wouldn't see the muzzle flash that would signal the end of her life. When heartbeats passed with no explosion, she gingerly turned her head back. Case was standing behind the door, still pointing the revolver at her face. He was white as a ghost, his hands shaking and his knuckles white from the death grip he held on the gun. He was sweating bullets.

Mara forced a smiled and slowly tucked her Glock back in her waistband. "Case, I would appreciate it if you would drop that gun." Case, breathing hard, didn't drop the gun. He was paralyzed with fear. Slowly, Mara lifted her right hand and grabbed the barrel. Case still didn't relax. Moving to the side, Mara gently pushed the barrel down toward the floor. Once she was out of the line of fire, she quickly wrenched the big gun from Case's sweaty hands.

"Jesus, Case, you almost killed me. What the hell?"

Case continued to inhale with jagged, broken breaths. Mara tossed the revolver on the bed, stepped in close, and wrapped her arms around him. "It's okay, Case," she said softly as she ran her hands up and down his back. "Just relax. They moved on. Nobody's coming for us. Just relax." Case stood there, frozen, for another minute before Mara's touch finally broke through, and then Case started to cry.

CHAPTER 13

Case woke up before dawn to find Mara's arms still wrapped around his waist and her head on his chest. He felt like a fool. The terror that had washed over him while Mara had been downstairs had completely short circuited his brain. Even in the depths of war, he had never felt as scared as he had, trapped in the little hotel room with three cold blooded killers just below him. He didn't dare move, didn't dare do anything that might attract attention.

Mara had been gone so long that he was certain that they had captured her. After that, it was only a matter of time before they came for him. He thought often of Mara's last instructions, to eat a bullet, but he couldn't bring himself to do it. Instead, he resolved that when they came, he would go out in a blaze of glory. Only the thought of a close quarters gunfight with professional killers had instead induced a paralyzing fear so deep that even when Mara did come back, he couldn't shake it. He'd almost killed her.

Then Mara surprised him. Instead of getting angry, or even putting Case out of his misery, she had come to him and calmed him. She had led him to bed and let him cry himself to sleep. That wasn't the action of a heartless assassin. That one moment of tenderness and compassion had convinced Case that somewhere deep inside, Mara felt something for him.

Only he was a coward. A despicable coward who had frozen up in the moment he most needed to be strong. Case resolved right then that he would be better for Mara. He would be stronger, tougher, and braver. He would prove to her that he deserved to stand by her side.

Slowly, carefully, he eased out of her arms and off the bed. He had a lot to do, and time was of the essence. He crept to the bathroom, cleaned up, and changed clothes. When he came out, Mara had curled up in a ball, fast asleep. He gave her a quick kiss on the temple. He saw the revolver lying on the foot of the bed and thought about taking it, but he was going into banks and would have no place to stash the gun. He'd have to take his chances unarmed.

Case snuck out of the room, all senses tuned in to what was going on around him. His every move was measured, careful. He walked to the end of the block and jaywalked to the other side of the street, which was still quiet in the last minutes before dawn. He made his way to a convenience store, where he called a cab and grabbed a cup of coffee while he waited. Case removed the list Mara had made for him and began studying it. She had identified her top choices for cars, and now as Case reviewed her list, he narrowed that list down in his mind. With any luck, he could buy something quick and be back at the hotel before Mara awoke.

He saw the purple and yellow cab pull into the parking lot and started to move. Case quickly finished his coffee and tucked the list of cars in his pocket. This he could do. He was used to moving among people without being seen. He could be invisible. Infused with fresh confidence, Case hopped in the waiting cab and set off.

#

Mara woke and stretched, really letting it go and loving the feeling as her muscles expanded as far she could make them. It had been a hell of a day, and when she'd finally fallen asleep she had slept like a baby. She finally sat up and yawned, rubbed her face, and looked around. Case was gone.

At first she wondered if he might have panicked and left. Then she remembered, it was Monday and the banks were opening. He had gone to get their money. His money, she corrected herself. It was his.

Mara couldn't shake the image of Case out of her mind. She had seen all kinds of fear in her life. She had felt all kinds. What she had seen in Case's face the night before was beyond anything she had ever witnessed. He was very weak, she thought. Then again, he was just a civilian. He was a healer, not a killer. Yet here he was, on the run with the reaper herself, and he was trying so hard to be what he thought she needed.

Mara shuffled to the bathroom and started the shower. She began stripping down, but stopped when she got to the ridiculous shiny green bra and panties he had bought her. She looked at her reflection in the mirror and turned this way and that, studying her reflection. "Crazy asshole," she muttered, astonished by what would persuade a man in his position to buy lingerie for a woman like her.

She started to take it off, then stopped again and stepped closer to the mirror. This time Mara studied her face, her eyes, her hair. She hadn't taken the time to really look at herself in a long time. She was always either putting on a face or taking one off, always focused on becoming someone else. "Crazy," she said again, though this time, it was directed at the girl in the mirror. The one who was starting to think about things that people like her should never entertain.

Like getting out.

#

Mara was fully dressed and sitting on the bed towel drying her hair when Case got back to the room. He came strutting in carrying a bank bag that looked stuffed to the gills, and twirling a set on keys on one finger.

Mara glanced up at him with cool indifference. "Cutting it close. Checkout is in five minutes."

Case grinned at her, a far cry from how he had been the night before. "We're out of here in three. Start grabbing bags and let's go." He stuffed the bank bag in his back pocket and gathered two bags.

Mara was up in a second. She grabbed the dirty clothes from the bathroom floor and threw them into the dirty clothes bag provided by the hotel, and tossed the revolver in after them. True to his word, they were out of the room in three minutes.

Case had bought a red Chevy pickup; an older, boxy one with chrome bumpers, white letter tires, and a roll bar in the bed. "Like it? I got a helluva a deal on it. This thing is cherry. Look," he said, pointing at the cab. "Extended cab."

"Don't get too attached to this," Mara said as she opened the passenger door and tossed the bags in the back seat. "We'll have to ditch this eventually."

"Not if we're careful," Case responded. "They don't even know what to look for." He pulled around front and ran the room keys inside. Two minutes later, he jogged back out with a receipt and they started out.

Once they were in the flow of traffic, Case took the bank bag out of his pocket and tossed it in Mara's lap. "That'll get us on up the road a ways," he said.

Mara unzipped it and found a wad of hundred dollar bills. She counted it out twice. "Nine thousand?"

Case grinned at her. "That was the biggest part of my stash, but I've got more. Got some up in Trinidad and in Colorado

142

Springs too. We'll grab that on the way up. I figure we make Cheyenne tonight, and tomorrow we head on up into Canada."

"What about the guns? They're not going to let us into Canada with those guns."

"We won't need them. Once we get to Canada, we hop a plane to England and we're gone. A fresh start for both of us. We'll find some little countryside village and just blend in. You'll see."

Mara turned away from Case and stared out the window. That girl she had seen in the mirror was all for the idea. She was getting excited about seeing new places and getting a fresh start. But Angel knew that she needed to get back to Master and make things right with him before things got worse. Angel didn't believe any place was safe from Master.

"We can't go straight through," she finally said. "We need to zig zag. Change course several times. Get off the main roads for a while. Make it hard to follow."

"You don't want to go to Canada," Case said. He glanced over at her. "You're not still thinking about going back to that Master guy are you? You said yourself that he was being weird."

"I never said that I was running away with you, Case. I said we needed to get out of the hills and get some space. I can't run from this. I won't spend the rest of my life jumping at shadows, waiting for someone to put a bullet in my back."

"No one is going to find us," Case argued.

"Besides," Mara continued. "We can't go to Canada. I don't have a passport or any kind of ID at all. I don't exist."

"Don't worry about that," Case said cavalierly. "This is something I can do. I know some people. I'll get you an ID. We'll go on up into Alaska, way up north in the wilderness. Let's see the fuckers find us up there."

Mara could see that there was no sense in arguing with Case.

He was quite proud of himself at the moment. "Fine. We'll figure something out. Let's just make it to Cheyenne tonight and we'll discuss it."

Case liked that answer and he let out a war whoop as they cleared the city limits and hit the highway, driving like a bat out of hell for the Colorado border. Mara looked out the back window at the city disappearing in the distance, and wondered how much time they had. She knew it wouldn't be enough.

#

Case drove casually and talked a mile a minute as they drove. He told her lighthearted stories about his time as an army field medic, and some of the funnier things he'd seen in his time as an ER doctor. He even told some stories about his childhood, but Mara noticed that he was always careful to never give any specific details about himself.

For the most part, Mara remained silent, only asking an occasional question or making some off-hand remark. She was watching the mirrors, constantly expecting the gold Lincoln to materialize out of nowhere.

By early afternoon they made the Raton Pass, and Mara couldn't help but look on in fascination at the natural beauty of the area. She had never taken the time to appreciate such things before. Staring out over the massive expanse, Mara was struck by just how little of the world she had experienced. The sight got the crazy thoughts started in her head again.

Minutes later, Case exited the highway in the town of Trinidad, just across the Colorado border. Mara sat in the truck and waited as Case went inside the local Wells Fargo to pull another stash of money. She continued looking around nervously, and at one point was convinced that she saw the Lincoln flash by on the interstate, but it was only a flash and she convinced herself that it couldn't be. They had no reason to be up here.

144

Case was inside for ten minutes and popped out with a bank envelope filled with money. "Another two thousand," he said proudly. "I got another nice stash in Colorado Springs, and that should set us up for a while. What do you think about grabbing some lunch before we hit the road?"

Mara took the envelope and quickly flipped through the cash, then nervously scanned their surroundings again. "Don't you think it would be better to just keep driving?"

"I'm tired of driving. Come on, this is a beautiful old town. There's a nice family diner on the other side of the highway with a beautiful view of the pass. Quit worrying, they have no idea where we are."

Mara reluctantly agreed, and as Case made his way to the diner he kept talking. "I love it up here. I wanted to live around here, but the land was too expensive and people were too close together. I settled for the land I did have." His voice trailed off and he was silent for a minute. "I'm going to miss that place."

Mara saw the sadness on his face and knew what she was supposed to say. "I'm sorry, Case. I made a real mess of your life."

Case looked at her quizzically. "You're sorry? Wow. Is that genuine regret you're feeling? I thought that you didn't feel."

Mara turned hard in an instant. "Don't make fun of me."

"I'm not," Case assured her. "I'm surprised. You really did sound like you felt bad about all of this. The entire time I've known you all you've talked about is how cold and detached you are. Could you be turning over a new leaf?"

Mara fixed Case with a flat stare. "I'm still the same person, but I recognize that you got wrapped up in all of this, that you helped me when you didn't have to, and because of that, your life has gotten fucked up. I do regret that."

"Hey, it's a start," Case said, showing more good humor than he had any right to.

He drove them to the restaurant, which did have a breathtaking view of the area. Situated on top of the mountain and looking back over the pass, Mara stood beside the truck in the parking lot and took it all in. Case nudged up next to her. "Sure beats the hell out of Bagdad or Detroit."

"I imagine it does," Mara responded.

They went inside and ordered. Case made small talk while they waited on their food. He told her lighthearted stories of his time in basic training, or of growing up in a small town outside of St. Louis. Mara kept an eye on the door.

After lunch was over Mara excused herself to the bathroom and discovered a pay phone just outside the door. She checked to make sure that Case wasn't watching before placing a quick call.

Master answered on the first ring. "Angel, what are you doing?"

This time she did a much better job of controlling her emotions. "I need to know if you can do something for me."

"Really? What would that be, Angel?"

"Do you think that you could get a message to the guys who are chasing me? Not directly, but a word on the street type of thing."

Master was silent for a moment before answering. "I'm sure that I could find a way. What do you need said?"

"Nothing yet," Mara said, keeping her voice low and constantly looking around to make sure no one was listening. "I've got to work out some details, but when I'm ready, I'm going to want to lure them someplace. I can't come back in until I get them off my back."

"You don't need to worry about them," Master said soothingly. "Once you're back with me, they won't find you. I'm not even sure that they are looking for you anymore."

Mara felt cold tendrils of fear crawling up her spine. "Why do you say that?"

"The girl's father. He met with a rather unfortunate end last night. Seems that someone discovered the real source of the problem and dealt with it. You should be safe now. Just come on in. Tell me where you are and I'll get Raven and Locke on a plane."

"I don't need those nitwits to help me," she snapped back. "Until I know for sure those guys aren't after me, I'm working off the assumption that they are." From her spot in the hallway, Mara saw Case finish paying their bill and turn to look for her. "I have to go. I'll be in touch."

She slammed the phone down. Master seemed entirely too eager to get her in the hands of Raven and Locke, who were Master's muscle. The only thing that they were good for were breaking bones and smashing skulls.

She hurried away from the phone and to Case's side. "Ready to go, love?" she asked Case with a flirty smile.

The older woman manning the cash register smiled. "Are y'all on your honeymoon?"

"Not yet," Mara said dreamily. "But who knows? By the end of this trip we might be heading in that direction. Isn't that right?"

Case was completely confused, but played along anyway. "Well," he stammered. "You never know what the future holds."

"For now, the future holds a week in Vegas, and we're burning daylight." Mara winked at the old lady. "You never know, might be a honeymoon after all." She took Case's arm in both of her hands and gently guided him to the door.

"What was that all about?" Case asked once they were back on the road.

"Just leaving a trail of breadcrumbs," Mara said as she watched the scenery fly past her window. "May not amount to

147

anything. If someone tracks us to that restaurant and asks around, it wouldn't hurt to point them in the wrong direction."

"Makes sense," Case agreed. "I can't say that I minded the show too much. I still think Canada is our best option."

"I'm thinking about it," Mara said, to appease him. She was leading the poor guy on and she felt guilty about it, which made her angry. She had never had to worry about such things before, and it had been easy to go about her business. Case was making her feel things, to look inside herself in ways no one ever had. No one had ever cared about her before. It was making things complicated. The old Angel would have already put a bullet in his head, taken the truck, and disappeared.

Then again, the old Angel never would have found herself in this situation. She didn't make amateur mistakes like missing an entire security detail. The fact that she had missed them was still gnawing at the back of her mind.

"Case, when we get to the next stop, do you think we could find someplace where I could get online for a few minutes? I want to check on a couple of things."

"Sure," Case said. "You're not trying to contact that guy, are you?"

"Why would you ask that?" Mara asked defensively.

"Just wondering," Case said, trying to sound casual. She could read the sudden worry on his face. "You haven't shown any interest in getting online before."

"If you must know," Mara started. "I want to read up on my…prior assignment. I missed something and it's bugging me. I'm not contacting Master. I don't dare do that until I've gotten this mess straightened out."

"Good," Case muttered. "Better yet, just don't contact him. After a while he should just assume that you're dead."

"Not without a body he won't," Mara answered.

148

"Tough business you're in," Case said. "After I get that last little bit of cash I can find a library. You can do your research while I try to find us a good hotel up in Cheyenne. We've got a little bit of money, so I want to splurge."

"You're not using credit cards, are you?"

"Of course not," Case answered. He sounded insulted. "You can't live off the grid and have credit cards. Everything is cash. I know what I'm doing here, Mara."

"I hope so."

They arrived in Colorado Springs two hours later and Case quickly cashed out his other deposit box. Mara counted all the money as Case found the library he had promised her. They had fifteen thousand all together…not a bad amount of money if you kept a low enough profile.

"How did you get all of this money?" Mara asked as Case negotiated five o'clock traffic on Colorado Spring's congested streets. "You didn't earn this writing for prepper magazines."

"Not all of it, no. Some of it came from the army, some from my job in Detroit. I live very simply."

Mara looked from Case to the bag full of cash and back. "Nope. Not buying it. You didn't manage to put back this much money on an army pension and a job as an ER doc. What are you hiding?"

Case sighed and looked away from Mara. "I may have had an additional source of income. I don't want to say. It's not something I'm proud of."

"What did you do?" Curiosity was brimming inside of Mara. She couldn't imagine what a goody two shoes like Case could be hiding.

Case shrugged. "Really. I don't want to say."

Mara wasn't about to let it go. "Case. I kill people for a living. I doubt that there's anything you can say to me that is going to be worse than that."

"No, it's not worse. But it was illegal."

"Really?" Mara was even more intrigued now. "Tell me. I really want to know what you could have done, because you seem like such a Boy Scout."

They got caught at a red light and Case finally gave up. "Fine. What I told you, about the baby and the mom and her boyfriend, that was all true. I really was disgusted by all the things I saw. But, the real reason I left was because...." He looked away from Mara as he struggled to admit what he'd done. "I was stealing and reselling medicine."

"You were a drug runner?"

"Not like that," Case said. "I wasn't selling them on the street. I was selling them to patients who really needed them and couldn't afford them. I thought I had it all figured out. I had a contact in the hospital pharmacy who would 'redirect' some of the stuff I needed. The rest, I would go to Canada every couple of weeks on shopping trips, and I'd buy some up there and smuggle it across. Then I'd sell stuff to patients for a markup, but a far lower markup than the big pharmaceutical companies get. It seemed like a win-win, and the only people who were getting hurt were the drug companies."

"They caught you?"

"They were about to. My contact in the pharmacy warned me. They caught him, but we were both vets and he promised to keep his mouth shut. He managed to give me enough notice that I was able to get out of Detroit. I had always known that it could come to that, so I was prepared to make a quick break. I grabbed my money and some clothes and took off. Been living in the mountains ever since." The light turned green and Case started driving again.

"Wow. I never would have figured. They'd put you away for

a long time if they caught you."

"I know," Case said, his face turning white. "That's why I've been so careful. I've tried not to fall into any patterns or stick my head up for too long at a time."

"Is that why you had the arsenal? In case you had to fight your way out?"

"God no," Case responded. "I do some hunting. The sniper rifle is a great gun for big game like elk. I'm not a bad guy, Mara."

Mara laughed. "I know you're not. I'm just surprised by all of this. You realize that, if the cops caught us, you'd probably get a harsher sentence than I would?"

"That's not funny," Case said.

"It is to me. I think it's hilarious."

Case finally located the library and found them a parking spot close to the door.

"Okay, listen," Mara said as Case killed the engine. "I don't want to be here long, so do what you've got to do quickly. Thirty minutes at most. Then we hit the road and we don't stop again until Cheyenne. Okay?"

"You got it." Mara started out the door, but Case caught her arm and held her up. "Does this change the way you feel about me?"

Mara looked back at him and smiled kindly. "Yes." Case's face dropped and it made Mara grin. "I think I like you a little better now."

CHAPTER 14

They took computers on opposite sides of a long table and began their work. Mara quickly found several newspaper stories related to the murder of Rafael Baca by "an unknown female assailant." The police weren't sharing much in the way of details, but they did have a composite sketch that looked nothing like her, especially with the rainbow hair and contacts. Good luck finding anyone who could connect her to that sketch.

A later report went on to name all five victims, including a twenty-one-year-old college student from Las Cruces. Mara winced at that one. They had blamed her for that death as well, though she hadn't been the one who fired the shot. She'd just used the poor girl as a human shield.

Mara moved on, searching for any news relating to the events in and around Springer. There was no mention of the fire at Case's place, but there was a story about the Fleming fire. According to the most recent reports, arson had not been ruled out and the fire was still under investigation. The entire family had been killed in the fire. There was no mention of the Mexicans or their gold Lincoln.

Finally, she found a story out of Minneapolis about the

gruesome death of a local business man named Joe Grasso. Grasso, his wife, and young son had been found brutally murdered in their suburban home the previous night. Details were sketchy at best, as the crime was still recent. There was no mention of the daughter.

Mara sat back in her chair and thought it all through. Grasso had somehow reached out to and found Master and hired the hit on Baca. She didn't understand how all of that worked and had never cared to know. Such things were often complicated. Master had, in turn, sent her to complete the mission, which should have been the end of it. She had been working similar hits for Master for years, and as far as she knew, no client had ever been tied back to the crime. So how had the cartel tracked Baca's murder back to Grasso and done it so fast?

If Master was right, she could be in the clear. Finding the person who took out the contract would be more valuable than killing the actual assassin, and should ease the family's need for vengeance. Still, Mara had made some sloppy mistakes recently; she wasn't about to make another one. She would contact Master and have him put the word out, in a situation where she could monitor her surroundings, and see if the Mexicans showed. If they did, she would clean up her mess.

She would still have a decision to make regarding Case, though. She looked over the top of the computers at him. She could just see his eyes and the top of his head as he worked on his side. Even though it went against everything she believed in and had been taught, she had become fond of him. Protocol dictated that she kill him as soon as possible in order to cut any remaining ties. Mara was no longer sure that she could do it. If she didn't, though, Case was likely to try and find her, which could cause huge problems for them both.

Or she could follow through with his plan and they could

run away together. Mara didn't think it would work. Master knew she was alive and out there, and he was desperate to get her back. Her job had always been simple: find her target, make the kill, and disappear. She was good at it, but had no clue how to work outside of those simple boundaries.

"You about ready?" Case called over his terminal. "I found us a place. We could stay for a couple of nights and really relax."

Mara leaned forward in her seat. "What about Canada?" she whispered.

"I don't think that there is a need to rush. New Mexico is way behind us now, and they have no idea what we're driving or where we went. I want to take our time and really think this through."

"I suppose we could do that," she answered. "Give me a second to shut all of this down." Mara started closing out the pages she had opened, but stopped when she came back to the most recent story of the Baca killing. Five deaths. She stopped and let her mind drift back to that night.

There was the killing of Baca, followed by the guard at the driver's side door. She pulled the girl in front of her as a shield, and then shot the guard at the back of the car. That was four. Then she ran. The last guard fired at her. She'd gotten a shot off and hit him, but the last she'd seen him, he was alive and still shooting. He could have died later, but Mara's impression was that the wound was far from fatal.

"Mar?" Case's hand on her shoulder woke Mara from her memories. "You okay?"

Mara shook her head to clear the cobwebs and quickly closed out her session. "Yeah, I'm fine. Ready to get back on the road. How long have we been here?"

"Almost an hour. I know you wanted to be out in thirty, but you were really intense over here and I didn't want to disturb you."

Mara looked back at the computer, which was now showing the library home screen. "Should be fine," she muttered. If only she had a few more details. There were things that were beginning to bother her, things she couldn't shake. "Let's hit the road."

#

It was dark by the time they hit Cheyenne. Exhausted from a full day on the road, Case drove straight to the hotel, a Radisson off I-25 that made for a quick getaway if need be. He registered them as a Mr. and Mrs. Bekker from Santa Fe. After that, Mara lugged their bags upstairs while Case ran down the street for some burgers.

Case had sprung for a king-sized bed, and after dinner they went to bed together. Mara feared that he would want another round of sex, but thankfully they were both too tired and they quickly fell asleep.

Throughout the night Mara routinely awoke, certain that some unknown assailant was right behind her. Mara's victims had never haunted her and they didn't now. What haunted her was the unknown. She knew that something wasn't right, and until she figured it out, she would find no rest. Beside her, Case slept like a baby.

Case woke her far too early the next morning, already dressed and ready to go. Mara struggled just to get her eyes open. "Hey, I figured that we could grab some breakfast and then go shopping."

"Shopping?" Mara rubbed the sleep out of her eyes and stretched.

"Yeah. There's a great sporting goods store not far from here. I figured we could buy some bathing suits and spend our day in the pool. I can't even remember the last time I went swimming. And I'd love to see you in a bikini."

Mara struggled to sit up and yawned some more. "You want

me in a bikini with this wound in my shoulder?"

"Sure. You're healing nicely. I stitched that thing good. If anybody says anything, we'll tell them that you had a hiking accident and got impaled by a tree limb. That's too crazy not to believe."

"I thought we were going to lay low."

"We are," Case countered. "Other than eating and going to the store, we'll spend all day here. No running around, no risk of exposure. I know Cheyenne isn't Chicago, but it's no small town either. It's highly unlikely that our friends would ever just stumble upon us here."

"Chicago?" Mara woke up quickly. "Why do you say Chicago?"

Case leaned back in surprise. "Alliteration. Chicago. Cheyenne."

"Oh." Mara relaxed slightly but remained on guard. She noticed Case watching her carefully. "Sounds like a good idea," she said, trying to put on a sunny disposition for him. "Give me a few minutes to get ready and we'll go."

Case didn't protest as Mara jumped out of bed and rushed to the bathroom. She locked the door behind her to discourage any romantic notions Case might be having. She took a scalding hot shower, the entire time debating if Chicago had really just rolled off the tongue like that or if Case knew something. She reached back through the days, wondering if she'd ever said or done anything to point him toward home. She couldn't think of anything.

After breakfast they made for the sporting goods store, which boldly proclaimed to be the largest in the Mountain West. They both bought bathing suits, and Mara added a box of nine millimeters and a double shoulder holster. Case gave her a funny look but didn't ask.

156

After that, they did as planned and swam the rest of the day and well into the night. Case got handsy on more than one occasion. Mara wondered if he might take a run at her in the pool, but they were never alone long enough for him to try anything.

As for Mara, she had never swam for fun before. Master had insisted on her taking lessons in case she ever needed it, and it was a good way for her to stay in shape and build muscle, but she had never just swam for swimming's sake.

The pool manager made them leave just before ten that night, otherwise they might have stayed there longer. They hustled upstairs and took turns showering. When Mara was done with hers she found Case waiting on her, dressed nicely in dark slacks, a white dress shirt with gray pinstripes, and loafers.

"Nice duds," Mara said. "We going somewhere?"

"Out to dinner," Case said. "I know this little place on the outskirts. It's a nice, quiet little place, dark, where we can be alone. It's not a fancy place…a lot of hunters hang out there, which is how I found it."

"You're taking me to a hunter hangout dressed like that?"

"It's not the location, it's the circumstance," Case answered. "Come on. It'll be fun. I got you something too." He pointed to a red and white box on the bed. "Go on, take a look." He was bouncing in his seat as he watched her.

Mara, still wrapped in a towel and dripping wet, smirked at him. This is what real boyfriends do for real girlfriends, she told herself. This is how normal couples act. Case was a normal man, used to doing normal things. She opened the box to find a short, rose colored dress and low top black suede boots inside. "It's… cute." She took out the dress and held it up in front of her. "It really is."

"Well, don't just stand there," he said giddily. "Get dressed and let's go. I've got something I want to discuss with you."

157

Mara dressed and took the time to look nice for him. She figured it was the least that she could do. On a very short list, this was one of the best days she could recall. She had long ago forgotten about Case's mentioning Chicago, willing to accept his explanation. She also hadn't thought about Master, or the cartel men, or the string of dead bodies she had left in her wake. She'd lived almost the entire day as a regular woman, and she liked it.

Case found the restaurant he was looking for far outside the city limits to the northwest of town. He pulled into a gravel parking lot just off the highway. There were two other vehicles, both large, late model American made pickups in the parking lot, which was dark except for the lights of passing cars on the highway and one single yellow bulb above the door that cast a tiny ring of light around it. Neon beer signs hung in the windows in front of dark curtains, and Mara could hear the thump of a jukebox from inside.

"I can't help but feel a little overdressed for this place," Mara said. She was nervous. Thankfully, she had discreetly tucked her pistol inside her right boot. It was uncomfortable as hell, but the piece gave her comfort, like a small, deadly security blanket.

Inside, some country song was blaring from the jukebox while three rednecks sat at a polished wood bar, throwing back beers and casually watching a baseball game on a small TV in the corner. There were a few tables in front, and a separate room off to the side with more tables. A middle-aged woman with a hawk nose and short black hair emerged from a behind a swinging metal door behind the bar, the kitchen, and invited them to seat themselves.

Case gently took her hand and led her into the side room. The room was a man's dream, with stuffed animal heads and signed sports memorabilia hanging on the walls. Case led Mara to a table set against the front wall under a shelf with a signed baseball bat.

As Mara sat, Case leaned up on his tip toes to read the signature on the bat. "Mike Lansing. No kidding." Case settled into the seat opposite Mara.

"Who is Mike Lansing?"

"Former major leaguer, played for the Rockies for a while. He's a Wyoming boy."

"Oh," Mara said, showing no interest whatsoever. "You said that you had something that you wanted to discuss?"

"Yeah," Case said as he unrolled the silverware on the table and put his napkin in his lap. "I was thinking, forget Canada. Let's go west, on into Montana, to Yellowstone and the Tetons. They'll never find us. And besides, if you were knocked out by Raton, wait until you see the sun come up over the Tetons."

Mara eyed him skeptically. "You're starting to treat this like a vacation. I don't think you quite understand what's going on here. Drug cartel goons are chasing us."

"Were chasing us," Case corrected. "As far as we know, they're still chasing their dicks back in Albuquerque. We're long gone, and headed for places drug lords can't track us."

"Or they could be pulling up in the parking lot outside as we speak."

Case frowned and parted the curtains beside them with one finger. "No cars." He looked at her smugly. "All clear."

A movement caught Mara's attention. One of the rednecks from the bar, a large man with a buzz cut and a ZZ Top beard, was standing in the doorway, sipping on a bottle of Miller and watching them intently. Mara instantly smelled trouble.

"I don't think this is the best place for us to be," Mara said with a subtle head nod toward the watcher. Case twisted around in his seat to see what she was looking at. The fat man slipped back out of the way.

"Ah, don't worry about it," Case said. "Men are drawn to

beautiful women. I've been the lonely guy staring at the dude with the pretty girl before. It's kind of nice to be on the other side for a change."

From where she was sitting, Mara could see the big guy talking to his two companions at the bar. They were both large, husky, but not as wantonly fat as the first man. The waitress/barkeeper was nowhere to be seen.

"I got a bad feeling about this," Mara said. "I really do think we should get out of here. We could find a nice place to eat somewhere in town."

"We're fine," Case assured her. "I've eaten here several times when I was up here hunting. Everybody's cool here."

Mara began drumming her fingers on the table nervously. "How many women have you ever seen in here?"

Case thought about it. "I don't know. Never thought about it. I'm sure some of the guys bring their wives."

"Okay, how many attractive, single women in the company of non-imposing men have you ever seen in here?" The three men were all peering at her now and whispering among themselves.

Case was offended. "You think I'm unimposing?"

"You don't exactly scream badass." She kept moving her eyes from the men to Case, until Case reached out and took her hands.

"Forget about them. We make our way across Montana and on over to Seattle. There's a guy I know through the prepper network who can get documents. I contacted him while we were at the library earlier. By the time we get there, he'll have our documents ready. We take a cruise ship up to Alaska, hop a plane, and we're gone. Poof. We can do this."

Mara was surprised. "You know how to get fake IDs? You're an ER doctor from Detroit."

"But I've been writing for right wing magazines, and I was in the army. I've got some contacts. It really isn't that hard, if you

160

know who to contact and how. Come with me on this."

Mara was about to protest when the three men walked into the room and headed straight for the table. "Shit, Case."

Case turned and a man in a sleeveless camo shirt, John Deere hat, and long blond hair reached out, grabbed him by the shoulder, and yanked him out of his seat. Case yelped as he was pulled back, and the fat man glided down into his seat. "Hey there, sweat pea," he said in a deep voice.

The third guy, who was the tallest and leanest of the three, with a circle of wispy gray hair around a bald head, slid in behind Mara and laid his hands gently on her shoulders. The blond guy drug Case by the hair to the side of the table and jammed his neck into the table as he knelt beside the now gasping Case.

"Now, what's a pretty thing like you doing with a lightweight like this? You look like the type of girl who needs a real man."

Mara tucked her hands in her lap and positioned her right foot so that the gun was as close as possible. Case was already starting to turn purple at her side.

"We just came here for a nice, quiet dinner. We don't want any trouble. Why don't you let him go and we'll go somewhere else?"

The fat man leaned across the table with a predatory smile. She could smell alcohol and nicotine on his breath. "I got a better idea. The boys and I, we got a cabin up in the woods a way that's just perfect for entertaining sweet young things. Why don't we lose the stiff and take us a ride?"

"I'll pass," Mara said frankly. She was flexing her fingers, preparing to go for the gun.

"I wasn't asking," he said.

The thin man behind her pressed in closer. In a moment, Mara realized that the gun wasn't an option. She decided to take another approach. She took her hands out of her lap and laid them on the table, the wooden handle of a steak knife beneath her fingers.

"Do you have kids, mister? A wife? Someone who cares if you come home?"

The fat man scowled at her. "It's none of your concern who I've got at home."

"If you do…," Mara continued unfazed. She carefully, slowly maneuvered the knife into a better position, trying to use her body to block the man behind her and keeping the fat man's attention. "You should get up and go home right now. This really isn't something you want to do."

All three of them chuckled. Case was trying hard to wriggle free of the blond man's grip, but having little success.

"Are you threatening me, little girl?" the fat man asked.

"I'm warning you," Mara responded. She felt the change sweep over her as it had done so many times before, the coming of the Angel. Mara could feel the air turn cold in the room as Angel began to take charge, maneuvering the knife into position. She felt the blood turn to ice in her veins and her heart go cold and hard. "Best decide quick."

The fat man chuckled and looked over at the blond guy at the side of the table. "This one's going to be fun," he laughed. Over her shoulder she felt the thin older man relax.

Angel closed her hand around the handle of the knife, spun it, and brought it straight back, hard and fast. The blade pierced the nice soft spot just below the rib cage and Angel heard the gray-haired man gasp. He stumbled backwards, letting go of her. Quickly, she put her hands on the edge of the table and shoved it forward, driving it into the fat man's gut and pushing him backwards. The blond guy was struggling to his feet as Angel jumped out of her seat. Case crumbled to the floor and began gasping for air, but he had the presence of mind to lunge for the blond man's leg. Case slowed him just enough that Angel got out of her seat, took it by the back, and swung it at the blond man's head. He saw it coming and covered his face, taking the brunt of the impact on his arms.

The fat man shoved back on the table and started up. Angel jumped up, grabbed the autographed baseball bat by the handle, twirled it, and swung. The fat man ducked down and her swing glanced off his shoulder. To her left, Case was struggling to his feet and trying to fight the blond guy, who punched him twice in the face, the second punch shattering Case's nose.

Angel lowered her next swing and caught the fat man right under the left arm, and felt the impact with his ribcage. He gasped and winced, dropped his arms, and she let loose a short, compact swing that hit the fat man in the side of the head and sent him falling back into the chair.

The blond guy had pulled a huge hunting knife from a sheath on the back of his belt and lunged at her. She danced out of the way. Case, holding one hand to his bleeding nose, picked a roll of silverware off a nearby table with his left hand and threw it at the blond guy's head. It distracted him enough for Angel to step up and nail him with the bat, hitting him just below the left eye. She heard the cheek bone crack as the blond man sprawled to the ground.

Beside her, the gray man was on his knees, staring wide eyed at the knife still sticking out of his chest and the blood that was coming out, trying to catch it in his hands. Angel took one long stride forward, grabbed the bat with both hands, and raised it over her head. The man sensed the movement, looked up, and his eyes got wide. "No, no, no," he muttered, but this was the Angel of Death standing in front of him, not the Angel of Mercy. She brought the bat down with a vicious swing that caught the man flush on the crown of the head. His skull cracked and he crumbled, his eyes going white and his face going slack.

Now Angel's cold indifference had been replaced with a burning rage. She turned and spied the fat man, with one hand pushed against his face, struggling up out of the chair. With one hand, Angel swung at the edge of the table, breaking the bat in two. The fat barrel flew off the side. Still holding the handle in her hands, Angel circled the table, pushed the fat man back down in the seat, and straddled him.

"No more trips to the cabin for you, fat boy," she growled. She put her left hand under his chin and pushed his head back and to the right before jamming the jagged end of the handle into the soft skin of his neck. She had to repeat the jabbing movement three times before she finally caught the artery and saw blood spurt out of the man's neck. She left the bat sticking in his neck and climbed down.

The blond guy was on his hands and knees, spitting blood onto the floor. Case was at his feet, cradling his broken nose in his hands. Mara grabbed him by the collar and helped him to his feet. "Go to the truck." He didn't immediately respond. His eyes got big when he saw the blood gushing from the fat man's neck. Angel took his face in her hands and made him look at her. "Go to the truck now," she repeated, more harshly this time, and Case nodded and scrambled for the door.

Angel bent over, took the Glock out of her boot, and jacked a round into the chamber. The blond must have sensed what was coming next as he began trying to crawl away. Mara put her boot in the small of his back and forced him down flat on the floor. She dropped, driving her right knee into his spine right between the shoulder blades. She pressed the barrel of the Glock to the base of the blond man's skull and pulled the trigger without hesitation.

Mara stood, straightened herself out, and turned to leave. The waitress was standing in the doorway between the two rooms, gaping at the scene. Angel started quickly towards her. "Did you call the cops yet?"

"No," the woman stammered.

"Good." Angel shot her in the face. As Mara stepped past her body the two cooks from the back rushed forward to see what was going on. They saw Angel coming, instantly knew they were in trouble, and turned to run. Mara shot the closest one in the back as he turned, and he fell in the kitchen doorway, but the other got away. Moments later she heard a backdoor slam open.

Angel tucked the gun back in her boot. Behind the bar the vast accumulation of liquor bottles caught her eye. She looked up, saw a hockey stick hanging on the wall, and took it down. Moving quickly, she stepped in behind the bar and smashed every bottle, sending the liquor pouring onto the floor. She picked up a tea light candle from one of the front tables and tossed it into the pool of liquor, and watched it ignite. She quickly threw anything she could on the fire and watched it grow to a satisfying size. With all the wood and old fabric in the place, the fire started to spread quickly to her satisfaction.

She hurried for the door, but took the time to smash the neon OPEN sign with the hockey stick before tossing the stick back toward the building fire and slamming the door shut behind her. Case was in the truck with the engine running, and torn up swaths of napkin shoved in each nostril.

"Move, now." Angel ordered. Case did as she instructed, peeling out of the gravel parking lot and onto the highway. "To the hotel, fast. We've got to get out of Cheyenne. Immediately."

CHAPTER 15

Case pulled up to the back entrance of the hotel and waited while Mara rushed inside and upstairs. She packed up their belongings quickly, and was ready to start lugging bags downstairs when she caught her reflection. She had blood all over her face and arms. There was some on the dress too, but the rose color helped disguise it to a casual glance.

Mara hurried to the bathroom, wetted a washcloth, and wiped off all the blood she could see. She then stuffed the wet washcloth in a bag, because she didn't want to leave it behind, and resumed her work. She struggled, but managed to get all their bags downstairs in one trip.

She tossed the bags in the bed of the truck, kicked Case over to the passenger seat, and gave him the washcloth. He cleaned himself up as Mara took the wheel and led them out of town.

Once they were safely out of town and on the highway, Mara relaxed. Case was sitting with his head reclined all the way back, staring at the ceiling. "For future reference," she said, trying to remain calm. "The next time the professional killer tells you that something is wrong and that you need to leave, you might want to listen to her. When you do what I do, you pick up a certain feel for things."

"I'm sorry," Case groaned. "I just wanted to have a nice night."

"Having fun yet?" Mara asked as a fresh wave of anger threatened to boil to the surface. She flexed her fingers around the steering wheel and tried to make herself relax. Beside her, Case partially rolled his head in her direction, caught one look at her face in the passing headlights, and rolled his head back to its original position.

"So where do we go from here?"

"I don't know," Mara answered tensely. They rode in silence for several minutes until Mara saw a green sign up ahead. "We have a town coming up in a few miles. What did you do with the license plate from the Blazer?"

"It's in one of the bags," Case muttered.

"Excellent," Mara said.

Case sat up straighter and looked forward. "What are you thinking?"

"I don't know yet, I'll have to check out the town. But if I find what I hope to find, I think I can get us some fresh wheels and some time. Just sit tight and let me see what's up."

They pulled into the sleepy Wyoming town of Pine Bluffs just a few minutes later, and Mara spotted what she wanted almost immediately. Along the right side of the road was a small used car lot with the cars angle-parked toward the highway and old metal key boxes attached to each driver's side window. "That's just perfect."

She turned right at the next corner and circled the block. She was looking for security, but there was nothing more than a dirt lot and a small portable building for an office. She saw no dogs or security cameras at all. "Gotta love small towns," she said with a grin. "Everyone is so trusting."

They rolled on through town and found a twenty-four-hour convenience store on the eastern edge. "Sit tight and try to stay down," Mara said to Case. "Keep your hand over your face. I don't want anybody getting a good look at you with that busted nose."

"You got it," he answered. He was still in clear discomfort.

Mara took some cash and hurried inside. The only person in the store was the young man working the counter, a slightly dopey looking kid with blond, comb over bangs and sleepy eyes. He was thumbing through an issue of Sports Illustrated when she came in. Mara saw him straighten up as she zipped inside, and she gave him a friendly, slightly flirty wave as she went by.

She walked up and down the aisles quickly and found exactly what she needed. She bought a plastic gas can, a quart of oil, a 32 ounce Styrofoam cup full of ice, some paper towels, glass cleaner, a plastic lighter, and a travel size portable screwdriver set in a plastic case. As the kid began to ring her up, she also asked for five dollars' worth of gas. She jerked her head toward the truck in the parking lot. "Boyfriend ran out of gas a few miles back. I'm always bailing him out."

"Yeah," the kid said with a chuckle that made him sound completely stupid. She paid out and gave him another smile on the way out. She threw the rest in the truck, handed Case the cup of ice for his nose, hurriedly pumped the gas into the gas can, and they were off.

Mara drove past the car lot and turned off the main street two blocks down, then doubled back and parked the truck at the curb of an empty lot directly behind the dealership. Mara turned off the lights, but kept the engine running and hopped out. "Drive down about three or four blocks, and go back to the highway and wait for me."

"Okay," Case acknowledged.

Mara slipped the screwdriver case out of the bag of items she had bought, found the two bits she needed, and put the rest back.

"If any cars start heading your way, just drive off and act casual. If you get pulled over, just say you're lost."

"I am lost," Case said.

Mara was concerned that the fight had caused more damage than just a busted nose, but she had no time to worry about it. "Go," she said softly but sternly as she closed the door. She waited for Case to move on down the street before she started walking the block back to the car lot.

The town was almost dead. They'd seen no other movement, no traffic on the highway, and she saw no lights on in any of the house windows. If it would stay that way for just a couple of more minutes, they would be home free.

Mara hurried alongside the car lot, looked both ways for cars on the highway, and noticed one west bound car coming up fast. She ducked back into the shadows and waited for the car to fly by, then looked again. With nothing else coming, she moved on. She picked out a white, late model Honda Accord and approached the driver's side. Looking once more for any sign of life and seeing nothing, Mara used the screwdriver bits on the key box, and in less than thirty seconds she had picked the lock. She took out the key, unlocked the car, threw the key box in the backseat, and started it up.

Mara sat and waited to see if anyone came running at the sound of the car starting up, but no one did and she backed out, keeping her headlights off until she was out of the parking lot and back on the highway. Case picked her up three blocks down, and together they cruised on through Pine Bluffs and out the other side without incident.

Mara and Case crossed into Nebraska a few minutes later. They travelled several miles further on before Mara started looking for a place to turn off the road. They found a dirt farm-to-market road that cut between two cornfields, turned off, and drove on for several miles, far enough that they couldn't be seen from the highway, and still had seen no signs of life. Mara stopped and waited for Case to pull up behind her, and then she turned around, pulled up beside the truck, and popped the trunk.

Case stepped out. "What're we doing?"

Mara started throwing bags into the trunk. "Find the license plate from the Blazer and put it on the back of this car. Tear off those paper dealer tags and throw them in the truck." Case nodded and started digging through the bags for the license plate while Mara took the glass cleaner and paper towels and cleaned the car's price off the Accord's windshield.

Once everything else was done, Mara poured the quart of oil in the plastic can on top of the gas, shook it up, and started dousing the pickup both inside and out with the mixture, then threw the gas can onto the floorboard and lit it up. The truck went up with a whoosh as Mara jumped in the Accord and drove away fast. She flew down between the rows of corn, watching the fire grow in the rearview mirror as she did. They got back to the main road, saw no sign of traffic, turned east, and Mara floored it for several miles to put as much space between them and the raging inferno as they could. Once they were safely away, Mara slowed down to just above the speed limit and set the cruise control.

"That was a sweet truck," Case said while holding a melting piece of ice to his nose. "Hated to do that."

"We couldn't take the chance that someone could identify it," Mara responded. "That fire will burn so hot and fast it will take them quite a while to identify it. By that time, this will all be over."

"This is pretty nice," Case said as he stretched his legs. "Kind of plain though."

"That's the point. This is one of the bestselling car brands in America. People see them every day and never notice them. There's no reason anyone should look at this car with that license plate and believe that this is stolen. Now, if some cop runs the plate or the VIN, we're toast, but I don't plan on giving them any reason to do that."

At the first major intersection they came to, Mara turned south and headed back toward Colorado. "That was pretty impressive," Case said after a long silence. "Taking out three guys like that. I mean, it was repulsive that you had to do that, but it was impressive."

"It's what I do," Mara said. "They were just some out of shape hicks. They weren't prepared for anyone who could defend themselves, and they certainly didn't know that they were fighting for their lives. I gave them a chance to walk away. That's more than I do for my marks."

"You weren't paid to kill those guys," Case pointed out.

"True." There was a pregnant pause before Mara spoke again. "I kind of like it, though. The killing. But not in a perverted way like a serial killer does."

"I don't follow. Killing is killing."

Mara debated internally and finally decided that she owed him something. "When Master took me in, I was one step away from hooking and I had been a victim my whole life. He fed me and clothed me and gave me a place to sleep, and then one day he asked if I wanted to learn how to take care of myself so no one could hurt me again. I said yes, so he enrolled me in a self-defense class, and I liked it. Then it was karate. After that, ballet and gymnastics for agility and balance. Boxing, wrestling, all kinds of martial arts. Whatever he introduced me to, I devoured it and begged for more. Then he started teaching me about guns and knives. By the time I was eighteen I was no longer a girl, I was a soldier."

"He was cultivating you."

"From the moment he laid eyes on me," Mara agreed. "I figured that out somewhere along the way, but I didn't mind because I loved it. I felt powerful. One day, he said he had a surprise for me. He took me to this old warehouse, and there was my dear old stepdad, tied to a chair and gagged. Master asked me if I wanted to watch while he took the guy apart, and I said no."

"Really?" Case said. "You turned it down."

Mara slid her eyes over to Case in the passenger seat. "I took the knife from Master's hand and climbed up in my stepdad's lap. It wasn't pretty, and I made sure to take my time. I made that bastard pay for every bad thing that ever happened to me, and he felt every last one. When it was over, Master asked me how I felt, and I told him that I didn't feel anything. That's how it started. Even now, when I kill, I feel that power. I'm reminded how I'm not a victim any more. Those guys were predators, but I took them down like prey."

Case shifted uncomfortably in the seat next to her. "I had no idea."

"I told you that I was a weapon. I'm a heat seeking missile, Case, and I'm at my best when the blood starts pouring."

"Would you still kill me?" Case asked, a slight tremor in his voice.

"Only if I absolutely had to," Mara answered.

CHAPTER 16

They pulled into Fort Morgan, Colorado and decided to call it a night. Mara found a cheap hotel just off the highway and pulled in. She paid for two nights in advance, and they quickly unloaded and crashed. Despite the adrenaline rush of the fight and the constant strain of being on the run, Mara found it difficult to sleep. She was haunted by a lingering thought that hung at the corner of her mind. She couldn't, or wouldn't, bring it into full focus, but it was there, eating at her.

By mid-morning she was up, pacing the room. The picture was trying to take shape in her mind, but she had to have more pieces in place to see it. Case was sleeping like a baby, with his head propped up against the headboard to help him breathe. Mara dressed quickly and ducked out of the hotel.

The highway was busy with morning traffic, and Mara waited patiently at the corner to cross. Once she was on the other side, she walked quickly to a convenience store up the road that could be seen from their hotel room. There was a pay phone mounted to the wall next to a large metal ice chest.

"Angel," Master said coolly. "Where the hell are you?" The angry edge in his voice was unmistakable. "I can't help but notice a string of dead bodies and unexplained fires all across the Rockies. Whatever kind of trouble you're in, you need to come in. Now. I'm not asking you anymore."

Mara fought to push down the sick feeling that was taking hold in her gut. She had complicated feelings about Master, but one thing she never wanted to do was make him angry, for more than one reason. "I'm doing what I have to do," she said with more confidence than she felt. "I'm making my way in. Now is when I need you to get that message out on the street."

"Angel," Master said with clear annoyance. "No one is chasing you. I've already told you that. I'm afraid that you're in need of some reprogramming."

Mara's knees almost buckled at the prospect. "If I'm not being chased, then I can come in, no problems. I have to know for sure. For my own sake. Can you please send the word out?"

Master let out a sigh that sounded like the long, slow hiss of a viper. "Angel, when I tell you that you're clear, you are clear. You know better than to doubt me."

"This isn't about you," Mara snapped back, driven more by fear than anger. She instantly realized that she had shouted it, and looked around bashfully as several people milling about outside turned to stare at her. She turned her back to the crowd and held the phone closer to her ear. "I need to know."

"Fine," Master hissed again. "I will put the word out, and when no one shows up, you come in. We're going to have a serious talk about your insubordination."

"I know," Mara said, her voice sounding tiny in her ears. "I'm headed to Safe Haven. If they're still behind me, I should beat them there easily. That'll give me time to set up an ambush." Master didn't immediately respond, and his silence made Mara uncomfortable. "Is that...sufficient? I could do it somewhere else."

"It's fine," Master said. "I can always find another safe house." There was another pregnant pause, and Mara was about to hang up when Master spoke again. "What about your travelling companion?"

Master's words sent a river of ice running through Mara's veins. "What?"

"Mr. Talley. Case Talley, formerly of Springer, New Mexico." She could see Master smiling as he spoke. He loved letting people know that he knew so much more than they did. "Seems Mr. Talley disappeared after his cabin caught fire a few days ago. Can't be an easy thing for an eighty-five-year old man with dementia to deal with."

Mara dropped the headset. Her entire body began to shake. She could hear Master calling her name. With trembling hands she managed to regain control of the handset.

"I'm assuming you didn't know that." Master was almost laughing. "Curious thing about Mr. Talley. He was a sickly old man with no family in Detroit, and suddenly, he's buying a large tract of land in New Mexico. This happened right about the same time that one David Dacus, a doctor at the same hospital Mr. Talley was being treated at, mysteriously vanished. Seems the good doctor was under investigation for drug smuggling and theft, and the Feds were about to drop the hammer."

Mara couldn't speak. She thought back on everything that had transpired and felt sick. Chalk up yet another sloppy mistake. How had everything gone so wrong, so fast for her?

"Mara? Are you still worried about those cartel men now? Very unlike you to take a complete stranger into your confidence. Very sloppy. Did you fuck him as well, Angel?"

Mara's head was swimming. Somehow she knew that something had flown past her. Something she should have known. At the moment all she could focus on was the fact that the man she had been travelling with was a liar.

"I take it that you did. I'm disappointed, Angel. You know that I don't like sharing my toys."

Mara struggled to bring herself back under control. She would deal with Case, whatever his real name was, in her own way. "Just get the word out," she said coldly. "I'll take care of the rest." Master started to respond but she slammed the receiver down. She felt the burning rage now, the kind that had swept over her in the restaurant.

She glared back at the hotel, and for the moment, all thoughts of cartel men and Master's promised reprogramming was forgotten. She had a bigger issue to deal with, and things were about to get nasty.

#

They were on a beach somewhere. Case was reclined in a pool chair, his bare chest golden from days upon days in the summer sun. He had a fruity drink with an umbrella in his hand as the water licked the shore softly. He turned and there was Mara, sauntering down the beach towards him. Her rainbow hair fluttered in the light island breeze behind her. She was wearing a hot pink bikini that barely covered her best parts, and her ever present Glock was strapped to her right hip. She was everything he loved in one package, sexy, beautiful, and dangerous.

As he watched her come towards him, Case felt the excitement sweeping over him. He couldn't wait to feel her soft skin under his hands, to lay her down in the sand and slowly, so very slowly, strip away that bikini. He could picture himself, taking his time, making it last. The water would roll over them, so warm and….

The water hit him with an icy slap that jerked Case awake and up with a start. He gasped for breath, confused, trying to separate his dream from whatever reality had just hit him hard. He rubbed his face and eyes, and then he saw her.

176

Mara was sitting on a backwards facing chair at the foot of the bed. The Glock was pointed directly at his forehead, and one look at Mara's face told Case everything he needed to know. Something fundamental had changed, and now he was in deep, deep trouble.

"Mara," he gasped, still recovering from his drenching. "What's going on?"

Mara calmly thumbed the hammer back. Case looked into her eyes and wondered if this was what her victims saw in those last moments of life. She looked back at him like an iceberg, no emotion, no soul, no humanity at all.

"You're going to explain some things to me, *Dr. Dacus*, and whether or not you ever see the light of day again will depend upon how you explain them. Right now, you should consider yourself lucky that I'm giving you the chance to defend yourself. Make no mistake, you're on trial, right now, and there are only two sentences available to you."

Case began trembling, and it wasn't all from the cold water. "Can I get dressed first? I'm cold and wet."

"No," Mara's answer was damning. "I have places to be. You'd best start talking."

Case struggled to gather his breath and his thoughts. He stalled, moving blankets and pillows around so that he could sit on something dry. Mara watched him frigidly, her gun hand never wavering. When he was finally set, Case forced himself to look into those killer eyes.

"How did you find out?"

"Doesn't matter. Talk."

"Okay." Case ran his shaking hands through his hair, slicking the wet hair back. "Most of what I told you was true, believe it or not. I was supplementing my income by selling prescription medicine. I was about to get caught. I knew it could happen and I had been preparing, but I knew that even if I ran, they'd find me. Then I ran into a guy I'd served with in Iraq. He was part of the whole militia thing, one of those guys with a spread in Montana, armed to the teeth and ready for the second civil war types. He told me that he could help me get some ID. Then Case Talley dropped out of the sky and into my lap."

If anything was getting through to Mara, it didn't show. She was as expressionless as a rock. Case continued.

"Case Talley was a sick old man. His mind was gone; he had no family or friends, no one to miss him when he was gone. Through his records and his insurance info, I could get all the information I needed. I gave it all to my friend and he got me an entirely new identity. I packed it away with the rest of my stuff. When Mr. Talley died and they came to get him, I had him listed as a John Doe. Nobody cared. The funeral home guys took him and they buried him in a potter's field. I buried Case Talley's records, certain that no one would ever look, or even notice that he was gone. Not long after that, my contact in the pharmacy got busted and I ran. David Dacus disappeared, and Case Talley bought himself some land in the Sandia Mountains. That's why I kept a low profile and stayed off the grid."

Mara continued to stare right through him. Case's eyes danced to the barrel of the gun. It was a black hole, out of which death was likely to reach out for him at any moment. He wondered what it would look like and if he would even have time to realize what was happening.

"I didn't tell you," he continued. "Because as far as I'm concerned, I am Case Talley. David Dacus is a dead man. If I could have attached my name to Case's body I would have. I thought about it, but I held on. I was hoping that I could wriggle out of the jam I was in. I should have known better. But I never lied to you, not really. Everything I told you was true. I just didn't tell you my real name. That's it. Everything else, everything I did and I said, it's all true. I've put myself on the line for you, Mara, even though I knew it could ruin me."

Mara continued to glare at him, but slowly, she lowered the pistol and eased the hammer back. "I'm not sure I should trust you."

"I haven't done anything you haven't," Case shot back, feeling a bit more aggressive now. "Mara. Angel. I still don't know who you really are. Not knowing your real name hasn't stopped me from helping you."

"I don't have a real name," Mara said softly.

"Neither do I," Case answered. "Not anymore. Not one I can use."

"So we stick together," Mara finally said. "At least for a little bit longer. I'm afraid that you're in much deeper than you realize."

Case's blood ran cold again. "What do you mean by that?"

This time it was Mara who looked away. "Master…knows. That's how I found out about you." She licked her lips and managed to look in his general direction, but not quite directly at him. "You're on his radar now."

"You called him?"

"Yes, I called him," she said defensively. "I had to report. He had to know that I was still out here. He's going to help me. We're going to set a trap for the cartel men. Then I can go home."

"Go home?" Case was disgusted. "Go home to some deranged psycho? Mara, I thought we were running away together."

"Mara," she said, almost like spitting out the name. "That's not who I am. Mara is some…concoction. Some dream girl that you've made up. She's a fantasy. I'm Angel, the reaper's right hand, the bringer of death. If I were smart, I'd just shoot you now and be done with it. I don't need you anymore. I've healed up enough to take care of myself. You're a liability."

"Why don't you then?" Case was sickened by Mara's sudden turn. After all he had done for her, how could she possible want to run back to a man who made her call him Master? It was beyond his comprehension. Case pushed himself off the bed, came around it, and knelt beside her.

"What are you…?" Mara started to ask, but Case reached across, took her gun hand, and forced the barrel up to his forehead. She tried to yank the pistol away, but he held it firm. This time, it was Case who stared daggers at Mara.

"If you really believe all of that, if you're really going back to him, then please shoot me, because I have nothing left but you. My alias, my home, it's all gone. I'm sure that they're looking for me now. I doubt that I can get to any more of my deposit boxes. I invested everything in you. If you're going to leave me, just put me out of my misery."

He didn't intend to, didn't want to, but he started to cry… just a few isolated tears that he couldn't hold back. They locked eyes and he saw something flicker in Mara that he'd never seen before, even after all their adventures. She blinked it away and pulled at the gun, but still Case held it in place. He saw the anger creep back in as Mara started breathing heavy, and with a snarl she thumbed back the hammer again.

"Is this really what you want?" Mara's face contorted with her anger. "Do you think I won't?"

"I want you to," Case whispered. "I can't live without you. I have nowhere to go if you leave me. I'd rather die."

"You stupid…." Her eyes flittered away from Case's again. She looked every way but at him. Case felt her hand trembling.

"Quit fighting and just do it," Case barked. "Finish it. But look at me when you do it."

Mara did as he asked and looked back down at him, but

again she uncocked the gun. "I won't." Case relaxed his grip just a tad and Mara yanked the gun away and tossed it on the bed.

Case wiped the stray tears from his cheeks, then rose and took Mara's face in his hands and kissed her. He kissed her over and over, on her lips, on her cheeks, on her neck. She responded the way she always did, with her animalistic intensity. As he kissed her she closed her finger tightly in his hair and bit his lip. Mara slowly worked her way up out of the chair and kicked it away. Case responded, standing and picking Mara up in his arms. She turned her head and kissed his neck, then bit his ear lobe. He hummed with pleasure and tossed Mara on the bed like a doll, then followed after her.

Only Mara turned him over and seized the high ground again. This time, though, Case didn't fight it. He let her control him, ravage him, and enjoyed each carnal moment of it all. When they were done, both caked in sweat, she started to get up, but Case grabbed her arm and yanked her back down. "Just lay here," he said. "Enjoy it. It's called basking in the afterglow."

"What is it about you men?" Mara asked. He could still feel her straining against his grip. "You get all worked up about something, and then you want to fuck."

"I don't want to fuck," he said. "*You* do that. I want to make love to you."

Mara pulled back out of his grasp. "Well, I don't want to do either. I can't stand it. The feel of it. To feel you all over me like this. I feel dirty."

Mara stood and headed for the shower, but Case called her name. She stopped and turned. "That's his doing," Case said calmly. "You feel dirty because he makes you feel that way. He's bad news, Mara. He'll be the death of you, sooner or later."

"You're probably right," she said before she turned away again, slamming the bathroom door behind her.

#

Case was still basking in the afterglow when Mara finished her shower. She padded quietly out of the bathroom and sat gingerly on the bed, careful to stay out of Case's reach. "I don't know what to do next," she said softly.

"About what?" Case didn't look at her or reach for her. He had learned that she needed space afterwards.

"Anything."

She left it at that. Slowly, Case opened his eyes and looked over at her. She was sitting on the edge of the bed, wrapped in a cheap hotel towel and staring at the floor. "Care to elaborate?" he asked her.

"I can't be responsible for you," she said without looking at him. "I don't want anything bad to happen to you, but I can't be with you. If you put me in that situation again…." Mara sighed heavily. "I want you to run, Case. I can get you some money when we get to St. Louis. You have to promise to leave. Find your friend, get another ID, and disappear. I can't have your life on my head."

Case reached for her, but she was too far and he didn't want to move…he was too comfortable. "I think I've made my position clear, Mara."

Her head snapped around and he saw the fire in her eyes. "I'm making my position clear. You can't put me in this position. I'm trying to get you free of all of this, so you can live your life. Don't be stupid. Even if I can't pull the trigger, Master won't think twice. He knows what we've been doing. He knows everything." The fire faded and she looked away again. "He knows," she whispered.

Case pushed himself up on his elbows. "Mara?" Reluctantly, she turned to face him. Case smiled at her. "Maybe instead of worrying about what you're going to do with me, you should worry about what you're going to do with him. Maybe it's time that this Master guy meets the Angel of Death."

Mara seemed shocked, as if she'd never even considered the possibility before. "You're suggesting that I kill my master?"

"He's not your master," Case said. "You're a free woman, Mara. He keeps you tied to him because he's afraid of you. He's afraid that if you ever decided to, you could take him down and he couldn't do anything about it. You're powerful...quit holding yourself back."

Mara went sullen and quiet. Case waited patiently, watching her face as Mara worked through it all. "He's helping me," she finally said. "He's going to get the cartel men off my back."

"And then what?" Case was trying to maintain a steady temper, but it was difficult. He had heard countless tales of abused women who couldn't break free of their tormentors, but he had never seen one up close before. It was maddening. "What will he do to you when he gets you back? You said he knows about us. What is the punishment for something like that? Ask yourself, Mara. What are you going back to?"

"Nothing you want to know about."

"Then don't go back," he pleaded. "You don't need him to fix your problems. You can do that. I can help you. Together we'll work this out." Case sat up fully and reached for Mara's arm. He rubbed her lightly. "Trust me, not him."

Mara continued to stare at the floor. "We should eat," she finally said. "We have to leave for St. Louis in the morning."

"What's in St. Louis?"

"Safe Haven," Mara said softly. She finally managed to tear her gaze off the floor. "And my master."

CHAPTER 17

Mara got dressed while Case cleaned up. Her mind was a jumbled mess, and it was driving Mara crazy. She couldn't get herself straight, couldn't think at all. She would try to replay her conversation with Master, because she knew that she had missed something, but then she would flash upon Case on the floor, crying, holding the gun to his head.

What was she going to do about him? They had come too far together for her to simply kill him and discard him. She had gotten him involved in this, and now put him squarely in Master's sights. She had to do something to get him clear, but he didn't want to go on without her. How could she make Case go away? She could just leave, but she was afraid he'd do something stupid and try to find her.

The internal debate raged non-stop while Case showered. Mara sat and chewed her nails, bouncing her legs up and down with nerves. Then she'd pace. She kept looking out the window, afraid that she'd see the gold Lincoln pull into town. Mara desperately wanted her brain to slow down, to give her a chance to regain some control, but it wouldn't. She felt like she was drowning in a churning sea of her own random thoughts, and nothing made sense to her anymore.

Mara was relieved when Case finally emerged from the shower. She was hoping that some fresh air and some food might put her racing mind at ease. She checked the window for the thousandth time, and still no gold Lincoln. "Hurry up, please," she said to Case as she surveyed the scene outside. The day was rapidly slipping away to darkness.

"What are you looking for?" Case asked, amused, as he toweled himself off.

"Cartel men," Mara answered. She felt panicked and she hated it. She could almost see Case losing respect for her for the way she was acting.

Case laughed. "Those guys are long gone. How would they track us down here?"

"Who's to say? How did they find me at your cabin? Or at the hotel? Why were they even at the hit?" Mara felt an anxiety attack coming and began pacing again. She ran her hands through her hair. "I've never seen these guys. Never had so much as a whiff that they were around, and then suddenly they showed up." She quit pacing long enough to look Case in the eye. "I should have picked them up before the hit. They weren't there. They couldn't have been. But they were." She stormed across the room to Case. "How did they do that?"

"I don't have the slightest clue," Case said. "You're the assassin, not me."

Mara went back to pacing and only stopped when she realized that Case wasn't getting dressed. "What are you doing?"

"Watching you. I've never seen you so frazzled before. It's kind of cute."

Mara snapped around. "Cute? We could have a team of hired killers on their way here right now, and you think this is cute? Do you really understand what's going on here? Do you get what's at stake?"

Case approached her slowly, treating her like a wounded animal. When he was close enough, he took her arms in his hands and pulled her into him. "Just relax. Let's just go eat and not think about this stuff for a little bit. Maybe, if you quit stressing about it, the answer will come to you. Okay?"

Mara let herself relax and lean on Case. She wrapped her arms around his waist and allowed him to hold her and rub her. It was a level of intimacy she'd never experienced before, and it felt good. "Okay," she said. "I'll try."

"Good," Case answered. He held her a while longer, then finally let go. "Let me get dressed real quick. What's around here?"

"I figured we'd just cross the highway. There's a diner right across the road from the hotel, just a little down from the convenience store. We should be able to get in and out quick."

"Are you going to tell me about St. Louis?"

Mara chewed on her lip as she thought it over. "I'll think about it. I'm not sure how I'm going to work all of this yet. There are too many angles. I hate this, being the prey. So much better to be the predator."

"I wouldn't know," Case answered as he finished dressing. "I've always been the prey."

They left the room and crossed the highway to a diner that advertised the best chicken fried steak in northeastern Colorado. "How much competition do you think they have?" Case asked as they walked in the restaurant.

"Damn little," Mara answered. "There's not much out this way."

"Well, I think I'll take their word for it anyway." Case said. They sat themselves and ordered water to drink. Mara kept staring out the window at the cars flying by on the highway.

186

"Quit worrying," Case said. "We're safe. What's the deal with St. Louis?"

Mara kept trying not to look out the window and kept failing. She began to mess with the silverware on the table. "There's a place in East St. Louis, we call it Safe Haven. When we come in from a job, we lie low there for a couple of days, make sure the coast is clear before we go on home. Master doesn't want us leading cops back to him."

"So we're going to lay low and wait for the cartel guys to come to you?"

"No. I'm going to set up a little sniper's nest and wait for them to come for me. When they do—"

"What about me?"

Mara shrugged and looked back out the window again. "You need to leave. Like I said, I can get you some money in St. Louis. I'll give it to you and you get lost. You don't need to be anywhere around when everything goes down. You'll only be in the way, and you'll likely get killed, and or get me killed."

Case still seemed amused by it all. "I can help. I did serve in the army, and I do know how to handle guns. I hunt all the time."

"Ever hunted a human?" Mara asked sharply. "Shooting a deer and shooting a man who's shooting back at you are totally different. No offense, but you seem to fall apart when things get crazy. You get all jittery."

"Kind of like you are now," Case shot back. She had struck a nerve.

"Yeah," Mara agreed. "Exactly how I am now. When the shooting starts, I'll be fine. I just need to know where they're coming from and who I'm shooting. If I count on you to help me and you choke, I'm dead. We're both dead."

Case looked dejectedly at his menu. "I have an idea."

"What?"

"What if I do what you ask and I take your money and run? Only, I tell you where I'm going. You take care of the cartel guys and then you come find me. Then we get ourselves good and lost. Best of both worlds."

Mara shook her head sadly and glanced outside again. "Never happen. Master will be there when it all goes down. He wants me back, and he won't risk losing me again. I'll never have a chance to run."

Case reached across the table for Mara's hands and forcibly pulled her attention back inside. "Shoot your way out. Three bullets versus four bullets. Who cares about one more? You kill the Mexicans with the rifle. You wait for this Master guy to show up. You shoot him with the pistol and you leave the guns behind. The cops will write it off as a gangland shooting and you just fade away. Like you told me the other day, you don't exist."

"You got it all worked out, huh?"

"Pretty much," Case said confidently.

"Who do you think taught me all of this stuff? Master knows me inside and out, and he already thinks that I'm compromised. He's not just going to walk up to me and let me blast him. Hell, for all I know, he's going to walk up to me and blast me. He's a very dangerous man, Case."

Case let go of her hands and collapsed back into his seat. "Didn't think about that," Case muttered. Their waitress came and took their order while Case thought. Suddenly, his face brightened. "I got it."

This time it was Mara who was amused. "Really? What did you work out this time, genius?"

"You set up your sniper nest and take out the Mexicans, just like you planned. Only I take one of the other guns, and I set up a second sniper's nest outside, where I can watch and see who's coming. When Master shows up to collect you, I plug him. He'll

188

never see it coming."

"That's not bad," Mara admitted. The swirling sea that was her mind began to clear, but only for a moment before the world spun out of control again. Out the window, Mara saw the shiny gold Lincoln suddenly appear out of the darkness, pulling off the highway and into the convenience store up the road. "Shit."

"What?" Case asked, craning his head to see what she was seeing.

"Cartel guys." Mara was up and moving, heading quickly for the door. Case mumbled and scrambled to catch up. From the front door, she watched the one named Cairo hop out of the back seat and go inside. Rooney was sitting in the passenger seat and looking casually in their direction, while Estavio sat in the driver's seat.

"That's the asshole who stole my shotgun," Case said, pointing at Rooney.

"We've got bigger things to worry about than that. We need to move, fast." Mara stepped back inside, clutched Case's hand, and led him quickly through the restaurant and into the kitchen. They pushed past their waitress, two cooks, and the manager, and pounded through the back door.

"How did you know that was here?"

"All restaurants have a back door," Mara said casually. They crept along the back edge of the building until they could see the Lincoln again. Cairo was coming back out and looked unhappy. "It's not going to take them long to find us," Mara said.

"What do we do?"

"Wait," Mara answered.

Cairo plopped back in the backdoor and slammed it shut. Rooney turned his head away from the window and Mara thought about making a break for it, but she knew that they had no time. After a moment, the Lincoln started moving again, back out of the parking lot and toward them. They ducked back behind the building and pushed themselves flat against the wall. The Lincoln turned into the hotel entrance and pulled up to the manager's office.

"Time to go," Mara said. She ran back across to the far end of the hotel and out the other side. With the car pulled in front of the hotel, they were clear for the moment.

"Good thing the office faces south, huh?" Case said, sounding too casual for the situation.

"Good thing," Mara repeated. They crouched low to the ground and hurried to the side of the road, both keeping a careful eye on the hotel. If one of them were to come to the corner now, there was nowhere for them to hide. Fortune smiled on them and no one came. At the first slight gap in traffic, the two raced across the highway, and didn't stop running until they got back to their room.

"Gotta move, gotta move," Mara said. She opened the hotel room with one key and pushed the door open. "Get the stuff," she ordered Case. While he darted inside, she pulled the car keys out of her jeans pocket and popped the front door and the trunk, then hurried inside. They gathered their bags quickly but left everything else, dirty clothes and the like, behind. Mara pulled the door shut quietly, but Case threw their stuff in the trunk and slammed the lid.

"Be quiet," Mara reprimanded, but they didn't have time to argue. Mara slid in behind the wheel while Case jumped in the passenger's side. "Get on the floor," she ordered as she started the car. Case started to argue, but when Mara pulled the Glock out of her waistband he decided to do as he was told.

"What's the plan?" he asked once he was tucked down as low as he could go.

Mara put the car in gear and started slowly out of the parking lot, edging toward the highway. "Shut up," she said. "Don't talk to me. Don't distract me." Her eyes kept flicking from the rearview mirror to in front as she waited for the Lincoln to present itself. She drove with her left hand at twelve o'clock and her right in her lap with the gun, the lights off until the last moment.

As Mara waited for a chance to go, she saw red lights coming from the other side of the hotel. They were coming, backing out. Unable to wait any longer, she flipped on her lights and charged into a hard left turn, pulling right out in front of a speeding SUV and gunning the engine to get up to speed. The Lincoln appeared in her rear view a second later, and Mara watched as the car paused, then continued around the corner and towards the room. "Did you close the door?" she asked Case.

Case uncurled himself and took a seat beside Mara. "I don't remember. Why?"

"Because," she started to say, but when she glanced back in her mirror she saw the Lincoln tearing out of the parking lot. Mara floored it. "Because if you left it open they'll know we're gone. Dammit."

They were headed north toward the river, the Lincoln stuck behind slower traffic. Mara took a hard right and headed off into a residential neighborhood. She hoped to get herself lost in a dark tangle of side streets, and eventually make her way back to the main road. Instead, the Lincoln saw her move and turned right as well, moving to cut her off. Mara rolled down her window and switched the gun from her right to her left hand.

As the Mexicans raced to cut them off, Mara wrenched the wheel hard right, skidding into a turn just as the Lincoln reached the intersection. She had a moment to register the shocked faces of their pursuers' faces before she opened fire with the Glock. The muzzle flash lit up the night and the gunshots sounded like thunder as she let loose three fast shots. The Lincoln bucked, skidded right, hopped the curb, and bounced down onto the perpendicular street, while the sound of shattering glass filled the air.

With no time to waste, Mara gunned it again and made a dangerous, no look, left hand turn back onto Highway 52, headed south now. Interstate 76 was just ahead, and if she could get there before the boys in the Lincoln caught up, they might make it.

She barely held the turn, the car teetering dangerously on the verge of going off into a ditch before she straightened back out. She had seconds to get out of sight, and decided that a full speed run to the interstate was a bad idea, especially after the gun shots. Instead Mara took the next right, and again decided to disappear into a residential neighborhood.

She wound her way further and further away from the main road, snaking her way deep into a tangle of houses, and finally, ducked the car into an alley between two houses that both had tall security fences and parked. They both ducked down in their seats and waited.

"You think we lost them?"

"No clue," Mara whispered. "But I do know one thing now."

"What's that?" Case asked.

"Master was wrong. He told me that they weren't chasing me anymore. Not only were they still chasing me, but they were a hell of a lot closer than I thought."

CHAPTER 18

They waited in the alley for over an hour, afraid to speak or even move. Mara constantly monitored the mirrors, but there was never a hint that the cartel men were in their area. She finally decided to take a chance and started the car again, carefully making her way back to the highway.

They saw no sign of the gold Lincoln, and soon Mara merged onto I-76 and sped out of town. Once they were safely out of harm's way, Case cleared his throat.

"Something on your mind?" Mara asked.

Case fidgeting in his seat. "Have you given any more thought to my plan about setting up a second sniper's nest outside?"

Mara sighed and flexed her hands around the steering wheel. She was keeping an active watch all around her. "First chance I get," she said, ignoring Case's question. "I'm going to cut south and catch I-70. From there it's a race to see who gets to St. Louis first. If they beat me, I'm screwed."

"Stop avoiding the question."

Mara glared at him out of the corner of her eye. "I've been very clear with you, Case. I want you gone. All you're going to do is confuse things. I can handle three guys walking into an ambush. Besides, I suspect Master will have something planned."

Case looked away, staring out the window at the passing darkness outside. "You're still going back with him. No matter what I do, no matter what ideas I come up with, you were always going back with him. Weren't you?"

"I don't have a choice," Mara said with exasperation.

"You always have a choice," Case pouted.

Mara didn't respond immediately, and several miles disappeared beneath their wheels before she finally spoke again. "Listen. I can research, plan, and execute a hit with no problem. But I don't know how to live. I was a kid when Master took me in. I don't have a clue about paying bills, balancing checkbooks, writing resumes, and things like that. I have a certain, very specific skillset that doesn't really translate to normal life. I *am* my job. Without it, I'm…nothing."

"You're not nothing," Case argued, finally looking back at her. "If you can learn how to kill someone, then you can learn all of those things too. Leading a normal life isn't that difficult."

Mara glanced at him, then looked away. "There's something else."

"What's that?"

Mara paused. "What if I don't like it? What if I can't handle being a normal person? I'm afraid that I'll miss the thrill of it all. I know that this sounds bad, but I love what I do. Even though I'm scared because I don't know where those cartel men are, I'm loving this because it's exciting. The thought that they could be right around the corner or just down the road, the feel of a gun in my hand and the thrill of pulling the trigger, those are the things that make me feel alive."

Case let that sink in for a moment and slowly turned to look back out the window. "I can't help you with that. I know some guys who served that had the same problems. They never could adjust to a civilian life. A lot of them wind up going back in. Some of them snap when they're out for good." He went silent again as Mara made her cut to the south toward I-70. After a long silence, Case finally spoke again. "I don't suppose that you could go into business for yourself. You could be an independent contractor."

Mara chuckled at the thought. "I don't know anything about the business side of murder. I don't know how to find the clients and arrange the money and all of that. It is an interesting thought, though."

Case went silent, and there was nothing but road noise between them. Mara slipped into automatic pilot when Case suddenly snapped, and it startled her. She jerked the wheel and had to make a quick correction to avoid being steamrolled by a semi. "Case, what the hell?"

"I've got it," Case said, completely oblivious to their close call. "You could go into security. You could be a bodyguard or something like that. Then you could still use some of your skills in a legal way."

Mara shook her head and smiled out into the darkness beyond the headlights. "You never stop trying, do you?"

"Not when it comes to you," Case answered in all seriousness. "I'll never quit on you."

#

As the sun began to rise, Mara decided to pull over for breakfast. She found a roadside diner and pulled in. As they waited for their food, Case asked a question that had been gnawing at Mara for some time already. "So where do you think those guys are now? You think we're ahead of them or behind them?"

Mara chewed on her thumbnail as she thought about it. "Hard to say," she finally admitted. "I want to say that we're ahead of them, because I need to be ahead. If they started for

195

St. Louis as soon as they realized that they lost us, then we're probably behind them. There are just so many variables. When we get there, I'll have to be very careful and scout everything out."

"But for all you know they could still be in Colorado. You don't know for sure that they've even gotten the message about St. Louis yet."

Mara shrugged at him. "Hell, they could be in California for all I know. Or they could pull up in the parking lot at any minute. They seem to have a nasty habit for doing that." She turned to look out the window, her eyes scanning the parking lot, almost certain that the Lincoln would suddenly appear. "That was very bad luck, them showing up when they did."

Case nodded in agreement. "That was crazy. I was so sure that we had seen the last of them. I sure would like to know how they tracked us down."

"Yeah," Mara said absentmindedly as she continued to study the parking lot One second later, everything that had been eating at her, all of the angles that she couldn't figure, snapped into place. She knew beyond a shadow of a doubt how they had tracked her down. She knew that the cartel men would be in St. Louis well in front of her, and that her entire plan would need to be altered.

Case saw the realization dawn across her face. "What is it?"

"Nothing," Mara said. Her mind was racing, already calculating. Things would be more difficult now, but in a way, she felt better than she had since she had first approached Rafael Baca that night. Now she knew exactly where she stood and who her enemies were.

"I don't think that it's nothing," Case prodded her. "Don't try to give me that crap. What's going on? What are you thinking?""

"Nothing that you need to be concerned about," Mara

snapped. "I'll take care of everything when we get to St. Louis. One or two more days and this is all over."

Case looked nervously across the table at her. "And what about us? Where will we be after all of this?"

Mara pulled her attention away from the window and back into the restaurant, and glared hard across the table at Case. "Out. We'll be out. One way or another."

#

They finished their breakfast and paid out. Mara was chomping at the bit to get back out on the open road. She knew this feeling well, the anticipation of a job coming to an end. She felt powerful again, in control.

That feeling evaporated the instant she stepped outside into the cool morning air, when she noticed that a Missouri state trooper had pulled up to their car and was getting out of his cruiser. "Shit," Mara muttered. She reached behind her and felt the Glock riding in the small of her back.

Case put a resisting hand on her arm. "Relax, let me talk to him. You overreact and you'll have the entire state on our ass." He strolled away from Mara and approached the cop casually. "Morning, Officer," he said with a wave. "Something I can help you with?"

The officer, a young man with the build of a small refrigerator, pointed at their car. Luckily, Mara had backed into their parking space specifically to avoid curious cops from running the plates. "How long have you had this car?" the officer asked.

"Just a few days," Case said jovially. He could hear Mara's slow footsteps on the gravel behind him. "My wife and I are taking her on her maiden voyage. Why?"

The trooper eyed Case for a minute and then walked around the front of the vehicle and down the passenger side, peering into the windows. "A white Accord matching this description was reported stolen from a car lot in Wyoming a couple of nights ago."

"Oh," Case said, sounding confused. Mara was moving to Case's right and making a wide circle around the car, keeping her eyes on the cop and her right hand tucked discreetly behind her back. He stole one quick, sideways glance at her and then back to the cop. "There's got to be thousands of these things running around. The Accord is one of America's best-selling cars, and I figure white is the most popular color. I mean, look at how many white cars are in this parking lot alone."

The trooper grunted as he quit peering into the windows. He turned to Case, then quickly scanned the parking lot. There were at least a dozen white cars around them. "You got the papers?"

Case sidled up next to the trooper as Mara crossed the front of the car and headed for the driver's side door. Case shot her a quick warning look. "Haven't had a chance yet," Case said.

"Uh huh," the trooper grunted again, and he started for the back of the car. Over the roof Case saw Mara tense, and he knew she was reaching for the gun.

"Wait," Case called out. The trooper stopped and looked at Case expectantly. Case looked quickly from Mara to the cop and pulled out his wallet. "I do have the receipt. That'll show you when we bought it." When Case had bought the truck in New Mexico he had insisted on the seller writing him out a receipt. The annoyed man had quickly scribbled out a receipt that was thankfully sparse on details. Case took it out of his wallet and unfolded the paper. "Here."

The trooper took the paper and read it over while Case and Mara eyed each other over the roof of the car. Mara was prepared to act at the first sign of resistance from the cop, an eerie calm settling over her. She envisioned it all, the trooper's continued suspicion, the gun there in her hands. At this range, it would be almost impossible to miss him.

The trooper looked up from the paper and gave them each a quick once over, then handed the paper back to Case. "Works for me," the cop said cheerfully as he started back towards his cruiser. He stopped, turned, and looked at the car again. "You know how many of these things I've looked at in the last two days?" he asked with a shake of his head. "It's like trying to find one particular needle in a box full of needles. You all have a nice trip."

The trooper waved and went on his way. Once his car disappeared, Mara let out a long, slow breath. "That was close."

"Yes it was, but you see now that you don't have to use a gun to get yourself out of a tight spot. You might want to remember that." He looked at her smugly from over the top of the car. "Looks like I can be of more help to you than you give me credit for."

Mara rolled her eyes and unlocked the door. "Don't start getting cocky on me. We've got work to do."

#

They pulled into the western outskirts of St. Louis just after ten that morning. Mara pulled into a convenience store, and while Case went to the restroom, Mara found a pay phone.

"Angel," Master said cheerily. "I've been waiting to hear from you."

"First thing," Mara scowled on the other end. "Is that you were wrong. The cartel men rolled right up on us last night."

"Really? That's fascinating. It's not like someone of Baca's... stature to waste resources on something as petty as a simple killer. I would have thought that eviscerating the man who contracted the killing, along with the rest of his family, would have been enough to satisfy the blood lust."

"Well, you thought wrong, so I guess you don't know

everything," Mara snapped. "And you tried to convince me to come in, that everything was fine."

"Now, Angel," Master said with a hint of warning in his voice. "I don't like your attitude. You'd best remember who it is that you are speaking to."

Mara tightened her grip on the handset and bit her tongue to keep from firing back. Instead she waited for her momentary surge of anger to pass. "I'm sorry, Master. I'm just upset because we barely got away from them."

"We? Are you still traveling with that phony?"

"He still serves a purpose," Mara responded. "I'll get rid of him before I come in. He's not a problem at all. I can deal with him whenever I'm ready. The cartel men are the problem. I'm afraid that they beat me here." Master remained silent on the other end of the line. "I'll have to be very careful and scout Safe Haven thoroughly."

"So?"

"So, I'll scout it today and make sure that they're not watching it yet. If I like what I see, I'll slip inside a little before dawn and set my trap. They can come in any time after that. I was hoping that you'd put the word out on the street that I'm not coming in until tomorrow. That should buy me some time."

"Sure," Master said, his voice smooth as silk. "I'll put the word out, for what it's worth. And I'll send Raven and Locke to help you. Even the odds a bit."

"I don't need those two goons," Mara said sharply. "I can take care of this myself. I'm going to have a nice, cozy little sniper's nest set up, and I'll pick them off clean."

"I'm sending Raven and Locke," Master repeated more strongly. "They can wait in the wings if you want, but if things don't go as planned, like everything else on this job, you might need the extra muscle."

200

"Sure. Or if things go really wrong, they make sure that the cartel men don't take me alive. Is that right?"

"Or course," Master said flatly. "You know that you can't allow yourself to be taken alive. Anything that risks exposing the family is forbidden. Frankly, my confidence in you is flagging. You've gotten sloppy, Angel."

"We'll see how sloppy I am. Tell the goons to stay in the shadows and out of the way. I'm assuming they're smart enough to know if they should interfere or not."

"You don't give your brothers enough credit," Master chided her. "They are very good at what they do. They are very well trained, the way you were. They'll know what to do."

"Good," Mara said. "Tell them to stay out of things unless absolutely necessary. These guys have been hounding me for days. They've shot me, driven me off the road, and almost killed me. I owe these guys, and I don't want anybody getting in my way. I might not take them out immediately. I might neutralize them first."

"Ahh," Master said. "There's my Angel. I do love that nasty streak of yours. I'll get the word to them. Just remember, they're not taking any chances, so you'd better be as good as you think you are." Master hung up and Mara stood there listening to the dial tone until she saw the men's room door push open. She quickly hung up and scampered back to the car. She was already sitting in the driver's seat waiting when Case got back to the car.

"What now?"

"Several things," she said as she started the engine. "We need to dump this car and find a place to lay low for today. Then I'll get you your walking away money."

"Mara—"

"Don't argue with me on this, Case. I've been thinking about it this entire drive. We'll talk about it later and you can try to

201

talk me out of it. Now I need to focus. The last thing I need is to stumble upon those cartel guys now. So just shut up and go along for the ride."

Case made it clear that he didn't like it, but he did shut up and watched as Mara drove, winding her way through a nest of main roadways, skimming southeast of the city proper. The drive took over an hour, with Mara making certain that no one was following her before she finally pulled up in front of a generic looking, single story brick home at the end of a cul-de-sac in a solidly upper middle-class neighborhood. Mara parked on the street and killed the engine.

Mara pointed a finger at Case. "You stay here. I won't be in there long. You just sit here and try to look casual. Listen to the radio or something."

"Whatever you say."

"Don't be flippant," Mara scolded. "If you walk into the house, you won't walk out. That's not my call and I can't save you. Do you understand?"

"I've got it," Case answered defensively.

Mara hopped out of the car and strolled up to the front door. She rang the doorbell three times in a rapid, short progression, and then stepped back. Moments later the curtains in the room to the right of the door fluttered. Mara heard locks turning and then the door cracked open. Mara took a cautious glance around before stepping inside.

"Lady Gray!"

As soon as Mara pushed the door closed she was enveloped in a big hug. The woman on the other side of the door was a short, somewhat pudgy black lady at the tail end of middle age. The woman had aged considerably since the last time Mara had laid eyes on her, yet her hugs were as strong as ever.

"Ms. Crawford," Mara said softly.

The woman slapped Mara on the shoulder. "Nancy. You know better than that Ms. Crawford stuff. You're a grown woman now."

"Nancy," Mara repeated, suddenly feeling very much like a child. "I can't tell you how glad I am to see you again."

"Oh, I'm glad to see you too," Nancy said. She held Mara at arm's length and looked her over. "You look terrible. Are you okay? Is that man of yours treating you right?"

Mara looked to the floor and shrugged. "It's been a tough couple of weeks," she said. "Things aren't going so well for me right now."

Nancy let go of her and huffed. "I told you that man was no good. You need to break away."

Mara peered back up into Nancy's eyes. "That's why I'm here, Ms. Crawford...I mean Nancy. I need my bag."

The older woman smiled at Mara. "My, my, Lady Gray. Are you finally going to do it?"

"Yes I am," Mara said softly. "I'm leaving tonight. I'm going far away and never looking back, just like you've always wanted me to do. He doesn't know that I've left yet, and with any luck I'll be on a plane before he does."

"Good for you," Nancy crowed. "I pray every night for you. I lost so many of you girls over the years. Come on." Nancy turned and led Mara through the house, out the back door, and into a well-organized storage shed in the back. They stepped past lawn tools of all sorts to a locking metal cabinet set against the back wall. Nancy took a butterfly keyring off a hook and opened the cabinet. Inside there was an assortment of small gardening tools and chemicals, and on the bottom shelf, an olive green duffle bag. Mara bent over and pulled the bag out.

"You think that you have enough?" Nancy asked as she locked the cabinet back up. "I could float you some more if you need it."

"No, Ms. Crawford," Mara said with a blush. "I'm perfect."

"Well then," Nancy said with satisfaction. "Come back inside for one minute. I have a going away present for you. It's something that I've been saving for a while, hoping that this day would come." Mara slung the bag over one shoulder and followed Nancy back into the house. "You go to the kitchen," the older woman ordered. "I'll be right there."

Nancy disappeared into the back of the house while Mara strolled into the kitchen. She tossed the bag up on the kitchen counter, unzipped it, and confirmed that there were still several stacks of hundred dollar bills inside. Checking over her shoulder to make sure Nancy wasn't coming back yet, Mara pulled out a Beretta nine millimeter with the serial number filed off. She checked the clip to make sure it was still loaded before stuffing it back inside and zipping the bag up.

Nancy came back a minute later with a manila envelope in her hands. "This is for you."

Mara took the envelope, carefully opened it, and dumped the contents out on the counter. A black leather passport wallet fell out. Mara looked up at her in shock. "You got me a passport?"

Nancy shrugged. "When you do what I do, you meet people and sometimes you do things that are a little...unorthodox." Mara opened the wallet and looked it over. The name was wrong and the picture was a couple of years old, but it should pass. It looked highly official.

Nancy chuckled. "You're not the first one of my kids that I've needed to help disappear. I've managed to save a few of you over the years," she said softly. "When I have the chance, I'll do whatever I have to do."

Mara unzipped the bag and tucked the wallet inside. "Thank you, ma'am. I really do appreciate everything that you've done for me. God knows that you didn't have to."

"Yes I did," Nancy said. She took Mara's face in her hand. "You've always been a special one to me. I saw it the first time they brought you in. I looked in your eyes and I saw something that I didn't see in a lot of kids. You've got a fire, a determination inside you. I knew that you'd make it. You're a survivor, Lady Gray."

Mara closed her eyes and put her hand over Nancy's, allowing herself to enjoy the lingering feel of her touch. The moment lasted for but a few precious seconds before Nancy pulled her hand away. "Now you get out of here," Nancy said as her eyes began to cloud with tears. "And don't you look back. You go somewhere that man of yours will never even think to look for you."

Mara fought back her own tears as she gathered up the duffle bag and threw it up over her shoulder. "I will." There was a pause, a tense silence between them. "You know," Mara started. "In case I never see you again—"

"Don't," Nancy said. "There's nothing you need to say to me. I don't *want* to see you again. I want you to disappear. Just do me one thing."

"What's that?"

"Whatever you do next and wherever you go, just be happy. You've suffered enough."

"I'll do my best," Mara said. "I promise."

#

Mara and Nancy shared one last hug at the door before she left. Mara struggled to regain her composure as she walked back to the car. She knew that Case would be watching and that he would pick up any emotion that she was trying to hide. Mara opened the back door and tossed the bag on the seat before getting back behind the wheel.

205

"Are you okay?" Case asked.

"I'm fine," Mara answered sharply as she started the car and drove quickly away. She jerked her head towards the backseat. "There's your retirement money."

Case shook his head. "You said that we were going to talk more."

"Not yet. I have another stop to make first. I haven't forgotten."

That appeased Case and he sat quietly as Mara again worked her way back across the metro area and out to the north. Their next stop was a greasy, run-down garage attached to the side of a low quality used car lot. Mara pulled up to the curb.

"Let me guess," Case said. "Stay in the car and be inconspicuous. If I follow you, I die."

Mara laughed at him. "You won't die. You might get the shit beat out of you though. Just sit tight. This won't take long." She reached over the back, unzipped the bag, and took out a single stack of hundreds. Case's eyes got wide as she zipped the bag back up. Just as she was getting out of the car, she read Case's mind. "Significantly more than nine thousand." Then she was out.

The garage had two bays, and both were open. In the far bay, an old Ford pickup was getting an oil change, while the first bay was empty. Mara strolled confidently into the bay and spotted the man she was looking for at a work bench wiping down his tools.

"Inky," she called out. "Hey Inky."

Inky was a short, skinny man with a shaved head who was nicknamed Inky because he was tattooed from head to toe, except, he told people proudly, for his genitals. "A man has to be a special sort of dipshit to tattoo his dick," Inky would often tell anyone who asked about his tats.

Inky turned, saw Mara, and smiled widely. "Lady Gray. Long time no see, chica. Get over here." Mara walked over and accepted a warm hug from Inky. "Man," he said as he pulled away from her. "You're looking rough, girl."

"Been a rough week," she answered cryptically. "I was hoping that you could help me out. I need some fresh wheels and I need them to be discreet. Very low profile."

"Uh huh," Inky said.

Mara showed him the stack of bills. "I've got this and a white Accord out front. What can I get right now?"

Inky took the bills, thumbed through them, and broke out in a gap-toothed grin. "I can hook you up. Let me see the car."

Mara led him to the bay door and pointed at the Accord.

"Who's the stiff?" Inky asked.

"He's part of an assignment I'm working on. He's just a beard."

"And you brought him here?" Inky said, anger seeping into his words. "What are you thinking?"

"I told him that the Accord was a loaner while you were fixing my car," Mara said quickly. "That's all he knows. Besides, I'll be done with this assignment in a couple of days. You know what happens to a beard after they're no longer useful."

"Yeah," Inky grinned. "They get shaved off." They shared a quick laugh and then Inky started for the office. "Let me get you your car, my lady," Inky said sarcastically. Mara fell in stride with him. "You seen Ms. C lately?" he asked.

Mara tried to be non-committal. "It's been a while. She was looking pretty good the last time I saw her though."

"She sure is," Inky said. Mara had the impression since they were both young that Inky had a serious crush on Nancy Crawford. "You know that she's still working? Still trying to save the world one street kid at a time."

"I doubt that she'll ever stop," Mara answered.

"She probably wouldn't be too happy if she knew what we've done with our lives, huh? We're not exactly the success stories that she thinks we are."

They reached the office door and stopped. "I don't know," Mara said. "We've turned out better than some. We're surviving. That's more than a lot of kids can say."

"That we are," Inky agreed. "I'll get your new keys and pull around to the car."

"Gotcha." Inky started into the office when Mara grabbed his arm. "That Accord out there should probably wind up in a junkyard."

Inky shrugged her off. "Nah. A fresh coat of paint, a new VIN plate, and a month from now some underpaid secretary in Toronto will be driving it and nobody will know nothin'. No sense in wasting a perfectly good car."

"Just move it quick," Mara warned.

"It was never here, sweetheart," Inky said with a smile as he ducked inside the office.

Mara returned to the Accord, and soon Inky pulled around in a red Grand Am. He jumped out and patted the roof. "There's a million of these things running around St. Louis. Nobody even sees 'em."

"Perfect," Mara said. She turned to Case, who was still sitting in the passenger seat. "Start loading up. Time to go." Then she tossed Inky the keys to the Accord, which he caught with one hand. "Pleasure doing business with you, Ink."

"Hey, no problem," Inky said as he stepped away from the Grand Am. "And next time you see Ms. C, let her know that I'm thinking about her. Okay?"

"Sure," Mara said. She waved goodbye to Inky and helped Case move their stuff to the Grand Am. They soon started off again with Mara repeating her meandering ways. She eventually found a Hilton not far from Busch Stadium and rented a room. Once they were checked in and the car was unloaded, she pulled a chair over by the bed and sat down. "Sit," she ordered Case.

Case plopped down on the king-sized bed. "You really went for luxury with this room," he said, impressed.

"I figure we both deserve it."

"So what next?" Case asked.

"Now we talk."

Chapter 19

"What are we talking about?" Case asked.

Mara looked hard across the room at the man who had become so ingrained in her life. Case had a strange effect on her that she couldn't explain. She knew that she never should have brought him this far, and that once she was healthy enough to travel she should have abandoned him or killed him. She certainly didn't need to risk her neck for him, and she never had to have sex with him. She had done those things because she wanted to.

Mara looked away from him while she composed her thoughts. It took a great effort to force herself to look him in the eye when she was set to speak. "First off, thank you. I would have died in those woods if you hadn't taken me in. I know that you've stuck your neck out for me, and I want you to know that it is appreciated."

"Of course," Case answered.

"That being said, I have to finish this on my own. I can't take you with me. You've done your part." She pointed at the bag full of money. "Master doesn't know about my stash. He doesn't allow us to keep much money on us. When we go on a job he gives us some, and we can get more as needed, but it all comes from him. That's how he keeps us dependent on him. I've been saving that for years. That's our retirement money."

"Ours?" Case asked.

"Yes, ours. I made a friend of mine a promise, and I intend to keep it. What I want you to do is to take that money and get far away from here. I'll catch up to you. You said that you had a friend in Seattle that could hook you up with papers?"

A huge grin spread across Case's face. "Yeah. He was expecting us days ago."

"Call him, but not from here. Tell him that you're coming, but it's going to be a few more days. In the morning, you catch a bus. Don't go direct. Switch buses a couple of times along the way. Keep a low profile. Got it?"

"Yeah I do." Case was almost giddy. "I'm glad you changed your mind." He stood up and started toward Mara. She knew what he was coming for. She quickly shot up off the chair and put both hands flat against his chest.

"I have work to do. I'm going out. Take a walk, a long walk, and call your friend from a payphone while you're out. Make sure you're far from here before you do. I'll be back tonight."

"I could wait for you," he said. "We could leave together."

"No," Mara said definitely as she backed away from Case. "This is the way it has to be." She opened the door. "Remember, be far from here before you call. Don't do anything to lead anyone back here." She ducked out the door and was gone.

#

Case watched the door, trying to will Mara back through it, but she never came. He waited a few minutes more as he processed what she had told him. Case had hoped that he would change Mara's mind, but he never believed he would. Now it was happening and he was ecstatic.

Case knew then what he had to do. He took some money and

211

called down to the front desk for a cab. He had spotted a grocery store on their way in that should have everything he needed. He would prove to Mara that she was making the right choice.

The desk clerk called up to the room a few minutes later and Case started to rush out of the room, then remembered that he still needed to call his friend in Seattle. He picked up the phone and made a quick call, knowing that it would go directly to voicemail. When the message came on, Case simple said, "This is David. I got delayed but we're coming. Heading out tomorrow. See you in three days."

Case hung up and hustled down stairs. He didn't know how long Mara would be out, and he wanted to be sure that everything was perfect before she got back.

#

Mara couldn't see them from the street. She had bought a Cards hat and some cheap sunglasses and thrown her hair into a ponytail before heading to Safe Haven, hoping that it would be disguise enough should the cartel men spot her.

She drove block after block in a widening circle, checking every street and alley for signs of the gold Lincoln or the men themselves, without luck. Mara was certain that they were out there though. They had to be. It was possible that she was wrong, that they had beaten the cartel men there. Maybe they hadn't gotten the message at all and were still running around Colorado looking for them. She decided that she needed a new vantage point.

Safe Haven was a former department store located in a long since abandoned commercial area of St. Louis. It had gone through several incarnations over the decades. It had gained the name Safe Haven when the Methodists had purchased the building at auction and converted it into a shelter for abused women and runaway teens. This was where Mara had met Nancy Crawford, and where she had been living when Master had found her and offered her a permanent way off the streets.

When the Methodists had given up hope and closed the shelter, Mara had talked Master into purchasing the building for a bug out location, and he had agreed. Since then, Mara had always stopped and stayed in Safe Haven for at least two days before going back to Master, who had since relocated to Chicago. It gave her a chance to decompress and to make sure that her back was clear.

It also gave her a chance to slowly lay the groundwork for breaking free. She'd been working odd jobs and even performing the occasional burglary for years to build up her nest egg. She hadn't planned on leaving yet, but recent events were forcing her hand early.

Mara pulled the car into a parking garage four blocks away from Safe Haven and drove all the way to the top. From the fifth level, she spotted two men on the rooftops. From where they were, they could each easily keep an eye on two sides of the building.

With her suspicions confirmed, Mara crouched down along one wall where she could keep an eye on the nearest rooftop and waited. It was late afternoon before the men finally started to move. Once Mara saw the closest man start down off the roof, she started moving fast. Mara ran for the car, and raced down the ramp and back out onto the street.

Mara started toward Safe Haven, driving as fast as she could on the narrow streets. She had to do this exactly right. If she got too close, they would see her. Worse yet, she could lose them altogether.

She got lucky. Mara saw the gold Lincoln cross her path two blocks away, headed west. She quickly turned right and travelled a parallel path. She watched at each intersection to make sure she could still see the tail end of the Lincoln clearing the same intersection two streets down.

The cartel men cut across her path and she fell into traffic behind them. Mara slowed and let a couple of cars get between them. Her heart was pounding with the thrill of it all. She followed them back to a motel that looked from the outside like it had remained unchanged and uncleaned since the glory days of Route 66. They turned right into the parking lot while Mara went left and pulled into the parking lot of a payday loan building across the street. Watching the rearview mirror, Mara smiled as she watched the three men pile out of the Lincoln and head into their room.

"I got you," she said out loud. "Now you're mine."

#

Mara had certain places she liked to shop in St. Louis, and she made her rounds quickly, gathering everything she needed for the night. Weighted down with bags and distracted by purpose, Mara burst into the hotel room and straight into Case's surprise.

Case was lying on the bed wearing nothing but a smile. The room was dark except for small scented candles that he had placed all around the room. Mara dropped her bags in shock. He had left rose petals all over the floor and the bed, and had a bottle of wine in a bucket full of ice on the nightstand.

"Case, what the hell?"

Case got up slowly and crossed the room. He was wet, his hair was slicked back, and tiny drops of water still beaded up on his chest. Mara put her hands on her lips and cocked her head to the side.

"Case, this is not…"

He reached past her and pushed the door closed, then pulled her to him and kissed her hard and passionately. He pressed against her, turned her, and drove her back until they hit the bed, and Mara fell with Case falling on top of her.

"Case," Mara said, trying to catch her breath. "I've got things to do. I—"

He kissed her again as he ran his hands all over her body, up under her shirt. His touch did strange things to Mara, made her forget who and what she was. She felt herself slipping away, as she always did. She felt the passion climbing into the driver's seat. She dug her fingernails into his back.

Case pulled back sharply. "No."

Mara was stunned. "What? What do you mean no?"

Case sat up, took her wrists in his hands, and pushed them gently to the bed. "We're not doing that this time. This time I'm going to make love to you, slowly, the way it's supposed to be. And don't tell me that you don't want to, because I know you do. I see it in your eyes."

Mara looked up into his face and swallowed hard. He was right; she did want to, and had since their first time together. All she knew of sex was what Master had taught her, hard and fast and violent, and she hated it. With Case, it had always been different, even if she had tried so hard not to let it show.

Case moved in for another kiss, but Mara turned her head away. "Don't be afraid," he whispered. "I'm not going to hurt you. I love you, Mara."

She looked back up at him, still struggling to gain her breath. She knew in that moment that this would happen. She had to tell him something first. "Jamie," she whispered.

Case stopped, lifted up slightly, and looked down on her, confused. "What?"

She took a deep breath and spoke softly. "My real name is Jamie," she whispered. "If we're going to do this, I want you to know."

Case smiled and kissed her softly on the lips. "You're still

215

Mara to me, if that's okay."

"I still call you Case," she answered.

He smiled again. "Just relax. Let me take control." Mara closed her eyes and nodded her head, and let Case do what he wanted. It was a strange sensation, letting Case have his way with her. At times she wanted to resist, to push back against him. At other times the passion wanted to sweep over her and turn their love making into something more animalistic. Yet Mara held off, and eventually, he swept her away.

#

Angel had trained herself well over the years, and her eyes snapped open at exactly nine o'clock. She'd only been asleep for a little while, but she felt like it had been days. Chase lay beside her, one arm thrown protectively across her chest. Angel turned her head to look at his face, studying his features in the dancing candlelight. The sight of him put a warm feeling somewhere deep inside her, and it made Angel sick.

She'd honestly thought that Jamie was dead and gone. Sure, she could put on a show when she needed to, like when she visited Ms. Crawford, but in reality Jamie had died a long time ago. Or so Angel had thought. Now, as Angel peered into the face of this man, she found herself hating him. All this time, Angel had viewed him as a weak link, an anchor holding her down. Only now, with the last lingering feelings of afterglow fading away, did Angel realize just how dangerous he was. Case had awakened a part of her that Angel *needed* to be dead.

Angel slid out from under his arm and to her feet. Case stirred and mumbled, but did not wake. Silently, Angel made her way to the door and the bags she'd dropped when Case had assaulted her. She gathered them up, fearful that the rustling plastic might wake him, but he seemed to be too deeply under to be bothered. As she started toward the bathroom, she spied her shoulder

216

holster on the floor, the two pistols still tucked neatly inside.

Angel gently put the bags down, padded over to her clothes, and pulled the Glock. This was the gun she'd pointed directly at Case's face and pulled the trigger on back in the mountains. Then it hadn't been loaded; now it very much was. Feeling the comforting hardness that made her what she was, Angel tiptoed to the side of the bed and pointed the muzzle of the Glock directly at Case's head. One little pull of the trigger was all it would take.

Angel leaned over and put the barrel close to his temple, centimeters from touching. Her hand was steady, her finger deliciously close. She stared down at him, watching Case breathe slowly, and found to her horror that she couldn't do it. She just couldn't tap into that vital spark that enabled her to act without thought. Jamie was blocking her.

Disappointed and relieved at the same time, Angel lowered the gun, turned, and went back to her bags. That spark was still there, still burning, but there were other names on her list that needed killing far worse than Case did. She would still have her reckoning and her bloodlust would still be satisfied. As for Case, he would never know just how close he came.

Angel put the gun back in the holster, tossed the holster over one shoulder, then gathered her bags and locked herself in the bathroom. The bright light hurt her eyes, and she had to wait for what seemed like an eternity for them to adjust. She could still feel Case all over her and inside her, and it made her sick. She wanted to jump in the shower and wash him away, but she had to wait. Preparing herself for battle was a process, and it had to be done in the right order. The shower would have to wait.

If Angel felt happiness, this part was what happiness was. The putting on of the "war paint." The physical transformation of herself from the mousy Jamie to lethal Angel. The ritual was the main reason she insisted on the outlandish disguises. It made her feel invincible.

Once the hair dye had set and she'd showered, Angel went to work on the make-up. She was careful, crafting the exact look she wanted. As she worked, the thought occurred to her that this was probably the last time she would ever do this, and it made Angel stop midstream. She pulled back and looked at herself, damp hair still drying, makeup half applied, looking pale and gaunt from too little food and rest. Amazingly, Angel felt sadness creeping over her. She allowed it to linger for a few seconds, then she turned that sadness to anger and went back to work.

When she was done, Angel dressed, taking just as much care with that as she had with the make-up. Tonight she dressed all in black...tight black pants and low topped black boots, with a body hugging top. She slipped the shoulder rig on and checked the action on both guns before sliding the fully loaded clips back into the butt and jacking a round into the chamber for both. She had a second clip for each gun, and she tucked them into her belt. Then she clipped a switchblade to the waistband of her pants at the small of her back. She had a razor blade discreetly hidden in the belt in case she wound up tied up for any reason, and she checked to make sure that she could get her fingernails under it. Finally, Angel slid into a black bomber jacket to complete the look.

With it all done, Angel checked herself in the mirror one last time. She was a vision, pale skin and silver hair contrasting against the black clothes. Her lips were silver, outlined in black, and she had glittery silver eyeliner that made her light blue eyes look almost clear. She looked like a vampire; alluring, deadly, locked and loaded, and ready for blood. She *was* the Angel of Death.

Satisfied, Angel slipped on a pair of skin tight, fingerless black gloves and headed out, careful to turn off the bathroom light before opening the door. Case stirred and she paused. As she looked back over at him, she felt the pangs of regret and longing stirring within her. Jamie wanted to climb back into bed or wake him so they could run. Angel knew that there was no running—that had never been an option—and that she'd been doomed from the moment the gold Lincoln had screamed toward her. All roads had been leading her to this moment. Jamie would just have to be satisfied that when all was said and done, Case would be safe. If not, it was all for nothing.

She started for the door, but as soon as she turned the handle, Case stirred again and called her name. Angel froze as she heard the sheets rustling behind her. "Mara? Where are you going?"

Angel didn't turn around. "I'm going to work," she hissed.

"Don't," Case called. She heard more rustling and glanced over her shoulder to see Case getting up out of bed. "Don't do this, Mara. There is another way."

With a heavy sigh, Angel turned around and stepped into the circle of light the candles created. Case's eyes got wide as he got a good look at her. "There is no other way," Angel said coldly. "I have to be Angel tonight. I won't spend my life looking over my shoulder. This ends now."

Their eyes locked, and deep inside Jamie screamed out in pain, but Angel silenced her thoughts. This wasn't Jamie's fight. She'd lost long ago. Angel was in charge. She broke the contact and started for the door.

"You're not coming back, are you?"

Angel pulled the door open the rest of the way before glancing back at him. "No."

He took two steps forward. "I love you, Mara."

"Then do me a favor," she interrupted. She dared not look back at him again. "Take that love you feel, and find someone who deserves it. Someone who can love you back and give you a decent life. What I do tonight, I do for you. This is your second chance, don't waste it."

"Mara," he called out desperately, but Angel was out the door quickly, pulling it to behind her. She hurried down the hall to the stairs and then down into the humid night air. She didn't stop rushing until she was in the car and moving out of sight of the hotel. Only then did Angel allow Jamie to say one last, whispered goodbye. Then Case and Jamie both were gone and only Angel remained, death riding at her side.

CHAPTER 20

Angel cruised past the Explorer Motor Inn and found the gold Lincoln still parked there. Perfect. She'd been afraid that she'd taken too long at the hotel, that the tryst with Case had delayed her too much. She need to get this out of the way *before* she moved to Safe Haven. She needed to even the odds.

Confident she had caught the cartel men just in time, Angel circled the block. Just beyond the hotel was an empty lot full of junk, and beyond that a lightly travelled road and a decaying residential neighborhood. The lights of the hotel parking lot shone bright, but they were not powerful enough to lighten the shadows this far away.

Angel parked the car on the far edge of the vacant lot, and left the keys in the ignition and the door unlocked. This wouldn't take long. She moved quickly, taking a furtive look around, but there appeared to be no movement on the street and thankfully, no one loitering around the outside of the hotel. As she moved quickly across the field, she scooped up a chunk of concrete roughly the size of a brick and bounced it in her right hand. Her eyes were locked on the Lincoln and the hotel room door just beyond. For the first time since she'd approached Rafael Baca,

221

she felt like herself again.

She stepped out of the field and into the parking lot. Traffic whizzed by to Angel's left, the drivers completely unaware of what was about to happen. She began to pick up the sounds of the hotel…TVs blaring, voices filtering through the doors. From the courtyard she heard laughing and a splash from a pool.

Once Angel was within a few feet of the rear of the Lincoln, she stopped, readied the chunk of concrete, and threw it through the back window. It shattered loudly, but Angel was already on the move, pulling the two guns from their holsters, eyes pinned to the hotel room door. She heard the cry from inside. As the door first moved, she'd reached the sidewalk. She levelled the barrels of the two guns in front of her and peered through the sights as the door opened.

The man known as Cairo flew out of the door, gun in hand but held low. He was wearing black slacks and a white undershirt and was barefoot, completely unprepared to fight. He stormed out, already cussing a blue streak, but he went suddenly silent as he saw Angel coming at him from the darkness. He never had a chance. Angel fired both guns simultaneously, and Cairo took both shots to the face, blood spattering on the wall behind him, his gun clattering to the sidewalk as his body fell to the ground.

Angel stepped over him quickly and easily, letting the pistols lead her into the hotel room. From behind a closed door she heard a voice calling out. "What was that? C? Man, what's going on?" The voice sounded vaguely panicked. She recognized Rooney's voice instantly. The big guy, Estavio, was nowhere to be seen.

Rooney kept calling from behind the bathroom door. Angel was ready to bust in when she spied Case's shotgun laying on one corner of a bed among the rumpled sheets. She tucked the pistols away, scoped up the shotgun, and checked it. Loaded. With a vicious smile, she pumped the shotgun and kicked the door open.

Rooney was sitting on the pot, pants around his ankles and completely unarmed. As she burst in the door, the color drained from his face. "Oh Jesus," he whimpered as Angel stepped into the room with the shotgun held out in front of her. "Ah, come on, lady," Rooney whimpered. "I'm on the john here."

Angel ignored his pleas. "This is a nice gun," she said coldly as she sighted him over the barrels. She was close enough to be deadly, but far enough away that he couldn't grab the gun. "Do you mind if I keep it?"

"No," Rooney yelled. "No, no—"

She let him have it with both barrels, the sound deafening in the enclosed space, and Rooney's body jumped backwards and then slid off the toilet and onto the floor. Angel watched him fall and pumped the shotgun again. She turned, ready to go find Estavio, when he suddenly appeared on the sidewalk outside the doorway, chrome plated .45 in his hand. She dove out of the line of fire, losing the shotgun, as Estavio opened up with his pistol. She hit the ground, rolling towards the partially open door. Angel stopped her roll in a crouch and kicked the door. Estavio was coming in, leading with his gun, and the door caught him on the wrist.

He yelled out in surprise and shoved the door back open, but the brief delay had given Angel time to move. She squirmed back between two beds and fired a quick shot at the overhead light, throwing most of the room into darkness, except for a tiny sliver of light coming from the bathroom. Then she flattened herself against the floor and waited, watching for Estavio to show himself.

"Ah, you little bitch," Estavio growled from the doorway. She heard the door hinges squeak, and a second later he fired a quick shot into the room. The bullet slammed into the wall on the other side of the room. Not even close. Angel held her breath and waited.

He didn't speak again but she heard the floorboard creak, and a moment later another shot hit the floor just off to her right, too close for comfort. As quietly as she could, Angel shifted to her left until she was right up against the cheap wood frame of one of the beds. Off in the distance, sirens started up.

The following silence seemed to stretch on for minutes, though Angel knew it was mere seconds. She heard him move again and another shot hit the floor; this time Angel grunted as if she'd been hit.

Almost instantly she heard the door swing open. Angel popped up onto her knees as Estavio lunged into the room, but he was firing in the wrong direction as Angel was further to the right than he'd fired. His shots impacted the floor and the cheap nightstand between the beds, and then Angel fired two shots at the chest of the big man silhouetted in the doorway. His body jerked, and he dropped the pistol and fell over.

Angel sprung up off the floor, hurdled the corner of the bed, and kicked the door closed, only Estavio's leg was still in the way, keeping it from closing all the way. Estavio was on his back, grunting and wheezing, trying to work his right hand up under his jacket. A hissing noise from outside caught her attention and Angel chanced a quick glance to her left. On the sidewalk outside, a bottle of Coke was spewing and foaming next to a small bag of potato chips. He'd been on a snack run when she'd attacked.

She looked back down at Estavio, his face contorted in pain as he tried to work his hand up to what she assumed was a second gun. The orange lights from the parking lot cast a strange pall over his face. The thought occurred to her that she should say something witty, but then what was the point? Instead, Angel let the gun hang there as Estavio slowly inched his hand up under his jacket, then she ended his life.

With the battle over, she holstered her pistols and moved quickly to retrieve Case's shotgun. She stepped over the fallen bodies and the pooling Coke, and back out into the night. The sirens were closing, but still too far off to be any threat. As she made her way back into the parking lot, she was aware of voices muttering. She turned to see several people outside their rooms, watching the goings on, and all of them were black. She twisted around but kept walking, the shotgun casually propped up on one shoulder, and shrugged. "White people problems." With a smirk, Angel turned back around and disappeared into the shadows.

#

Case stood naked in the flickering candlelight, staring at the door. The sight of Mara made up as some sort of malevolent spirit had stopped him dead in his tracks. Only a couple of hours earlier, he'd looked deep into the eyes of a beautiful girl named Mara, and he'd seen a future for himself. When Case had looked in her eyes now, that girl was nowhere to be found. Instead, he saw that same detachment that he'd seen far too often in the eyes of soldiers. The ones who'd lost a piece of their soul out there on the battlefields. The ones that were too far gone to ever be themselves again.

Case stood for the longest time, feeling hopeless, useless, and impotent. He had no car, no idea of where she might be headed, and no knowledge of the city. Mara was gone, long gone, and he had no way to bring her back. Dejected, he shuffled back to the bed and collapsed onto it. No matter how hard he tried, he couldn't drive the chilling image of Mara's made-up face out of his mind: the black lips, the silver hair, and the cold, emotionless eyes of a killer.

Or of a person resigned to death.

225

He fell asleep, but only realized it when someone started pounding on the door outside. He awoke with a start, his heart going a thousand beats per minute. The knocking on the door was fierce and relentless. Someone was calling out on the other side of the door, but all Case could make out was an undistinguishable sound.

Case stormed over to the door, slipped the security bar on, and opened the door just as far as the bar would let it open. He peeked out into the dimly light hall to see a slight man in a powder blue dress shirt, red and yellow striped tie, and belted khaki slacks on the other side. He had mousy brown hair that formed a widow's peak on the top of his head, and wore wire-rimmed glasses. Over his shoulder, a large man in green scrubs stood scowling.

"Whaddya want?" Case snarled at the man.

The man stopped suddenly, his hand already coming down to beat on the door again. He peered up at Case with watery blue eyes. "Jamie," he said. "Jamie Grayson. I need to see her."

"You're barking up the wrong tree, pal," Case snapped back. He was in no mood to fool around. He could feel his heartbreak turning to anger with each breath. "There's no Jamie here. Now get lost." He started to slam the door, but the man stuck the toe of his discount loafers in the doorway.

"I know she's here, sir," the man answered, his voice wavering. "She checked out this room earlier today. I need to speak to her, urgently. Please let me in."

Case rolled his eyes and glowered down at the smaller man. "I told you, there's no Jamie here. Now get lost." He kicked the man's loafer out of the doorway with his bare foot, and again went to slam the door when from someone out of his field of vision, a meaty hand, hit the door with a flat palm hard enough to send Case stumbling backwards.

226

"No," the man barked at whoever was standing out of view. Case rebounded quickly, only to find the man had again thrust his foot in the door.

"Jamie," the man called, trying to work his face through the crack in the door. "I need to speak with you. It's Doctor Byrd. Please, Jamie, let me in."

"There's no Jamie," Case snarled. "It's just me in here."

"But she's been here," Doctor Byrd persisted. He glanced down and saw Case was naked on the other side of the door. "Oh God," he muttered. "You had sex with her? Oh my God, you have to let me in, sir. You have no idea what is going on here."

"I know that there's nobody here but me, and I'm trying to sleep. Go fuck yourself, pal."

The meaty hand slammed into the door again and it buckled, the wood splintering around the strained security bar. "Enough," Doctor Byrd barked at the still unseen man. He turned his attention back to Case. "Sir, please listen to me." He pulled a faded Polaroid out of his breast pocket and shoved it in Case's face. "This is Jamie Grayson. Look at her. Look close."

Case only needed to glance to know that it was his Mara. She appeared much younger in the picture. She looked up at the camera with hangdog eyes and a bruised face. Her hair was a stringy mop that fell in dirty strands in front of her. She was far from the sinister vision that Case had seen minutes earlier, but it was the same girl.

Byrd pulled the picture back. "You have seen her," he stated calmly. "I take it she's gone now?"

Case let the air slowly hiss out of his lungs. "What do you want with her?"

Doctor Byrd seemed to relax. "My name is Thomas Byrd," he started. Byrd reached back into his pocket, produced a business card, and held it through the crack. Case took it and leaned

227

back, trying to read the card in the poor light. It said Dr. T Byrd, Psychologist, Midwestern Centers for Mental Health.

"What is this?" Case asked, holding the card in his fingers.

"That's what I'm trying to tell you. Ms. Grayson is a very sick young woman. I am her doctor, and I am desperately trying to locate her. Can we please come in? I can explain everything."

Feeling defeated yet again, Case dropped his head and muttered, "Fine." He pushed the door to, slipped off the security bar, and opened it fully. Immediately a barrel chested man in scrubs, the one who had been out of view, pushed in, moving urgently. Byrd came in next, followed by the other large man in scrubs who could have been the first guy's brother.

Byrd took Case's arm in one hand and directed him toward the bed. He scanned the room disapprovingly as the men in scrubs turned on all the lights and began rifling through their bags. "Have a seat, Mister...."

"Talley," Case said as he settled down onto the bed.

"Mr. Talley," Byrd responded. He sat gingerly next to Case. "I can see that you and Ms. Grayson have gotten close. There are some things about her I need to let you know. She's in very great danger, Mr. Talley. She's a danger to herself and to everyone around her. This is not the first time she has escaped."

Case's eyes shot up to meet Byrd's. "Escaped?"

"From the home," Byrd continued. He looked around nervously, like someone might be listening in. "I shouldn't tell you this," he said softly, leaning in close to Case. "But given the circumstances, I believe you have a right to know. Ms. Grayson is psychotic, extremely delusional, especially when she's off her meds. She has a fantasy that she is some sort of killer for hire."

Case's blood ran cold as Byrd laid out the story. As he spoke, pieces began snapping into place for Case. He thought back over their time together, and it all suddenly began to make sense.

"The problem is," Byrd continued. "That she believes this to be true, and she acts on the fantasy. I believe that she may be responsible for a series of grisly murders out west. I fear that she's gone too far now. The police are hunting for her, and they will kill her if they catch her. I have to find her and bring her back to the home before more people get hurt."

Case ran one hand over his face as he processed the information. "This is...crazy," he muttered. "I knew she was in trouble, but...." He couldn't believe what he was hearing. "All that stuff about Master—"

"Master?"

"Yeah," Case said with a sad chuckle. "She said she belonged to some guy named Master."

"Yes, she references him often." Case looked up at him and Byrd shrugged. "Master is the voice in her head that drives her to do these things. She related to him like a real person. She will call random strangers and have conversations with him. I have my theories about this, but that's really neither here nor there at the moment. What I need from you is information. Where did she go?"

"I have no idea," Case said. "I really wish I did. I would like to help, but I just don't know."

"Boss," one of the large men called out. They both turned to see him standing in the bathroom door, holding a box of hair dye and a bottle of makeup high in his beefy hands. "She put on her war paint."

"Oh dear God," Byrd said. "She's on the hunt." He grabbed Case by both shoulders and shook him violently. "I need you to think, sir. She must have said something. Anything you can give me. People are going to die tonight, innocent people, if we can't find her. Think sir. Think."

Case wracked his brain and finally remembered the one

tidbit she'd given him. "She said something about Safe Haven."

"Safe Haven," Byrd muttered. "Safe Haven, Safe Haven...." Then he snapped his fingers. "I know what she's referring to. Excellent." He looked back up at Case. "Thank you. We might still have a chance. Thank you." He stood quickly and headed for the door. "Mr. Raven, Mr. Locke, we must go. She's on her way to Safe Haven."

The large men promptly followed and soon disappeared into the hallway. Case buried his face in his hands, wondering just how much worse this all could go. He was disturbed by a subtle throat clearing. He looked up to see Doctor Byrd standing in the doorway.

"Mr. Talley," he said softly, and pushed his glasses back up onto his nose. "She's armed, is she not?'

"Yeah," Case muttered.

"And she's very dangerous. Given that you two have clearly become...intimate, it strikes me that you could still be of some help to us. If she's agitated, you might be able to reach her, to talk her down. I'm afraid that once she sees us, she'll lash out. I wonder if you would mind getting dressed and coming with us. If not, I understand. In fact, I'm hesitant to even ask given the situation. It's just that—"

"Say no more, Doc," Case said as he struggled to his feet. "If there's anything I can do to help, I'll do it."

"Very good," Byrd answered with a thin smile. "Please hurry. Time is of the essence, and I fear that we might already be too late."

#

The problem with a sniper's nest, Angel reasoned, was that it was impersonal. That, and given the circumstances, impractical. There were two entrances to Safe Haven, the main door that faced the street and a side door by the alley. She checked each of the two perches that the cartel men had scoped out, and discovered that she could only see one door from each. Guess wrong, and her target would slip right past her. Besides, it would be no fun to pick him off at a distance. She wanted to do it up close and personal. She wanted to see the terror in his eyes when he realized she had figured it all out.

Angel decided to spring her trap inside. She popped the side door open using her key and quickly ducked inside. Just inside the door, she found a light switch and was satisfied when the florescent lights flickered to life. It wasn't great light—the bulbs were old, some completely burned out, while others continued to flicker, creating deep pools of shadow in the deserted old department store—but it would work.

When the Methodists had finally given up their dream of saving the homeless of St. Louis, they'd left a mess in their wake... broken cots and dingy mattresses, wobbly chairs and folding tables, clunky old phone systems and computers and faxes, piles of dirty clothes, used sleeping bags, and empty food cans.

Aware that time was working against her, Angel worked quickly. She drug the cots and mattresses over and piled them up against the front door. Anyone trying to come in through the front door was going to make a hell of a racket doing so. She scattered empty food cans along the way as well, particularly in the shadowy places where the lights didn't work so well, and she used the office furniture to create a perimeter. By this time she was hot and dusty, but Angel felt relieved. She pulled another desk against the wall next to the light switch, took a seat, and killed the lights.

In the darkness, she waited patiently, Case's shotgun in her hand, two more shells loaded and ready. The twin pistols comforted her with their weight in the shoulder harness. She tried to envision the moment, to imagine how it would all play out. As the minutes slowly ticked by, her mind began to wonder back to the hotel and Case, and the sensual night they'd spent together.

Angel had lapsed into a trancelike state, but the creaking of the heavy metal door snapped her out of it. She tried to shake the cobwebs out of her head as she picked up the shotgun with the left hand and found the light switch with her right.

A shadow appeared in the doorway, and a moment later a soft voice called out. "Hello? Jamie? Are you there?"

She stayed silent and still. The figure drew back. There was some muttering, and then the figure reappeared in the doorway, this time waving a flashlight around, the bright blue beam dancing through the dark and lighting up the swirling dust particles in the air.

"Jamie," the voice called out again, stronger now. Somebody out of sight whispered and the figure said okay, then started again. "Angel? Are you there Angel?" The figure stepped fully into the room, still playing the flashlight about but never coming anywhere near Angel's location. Someone was holding the door open on the outside.

"Angel, it's me. It's Case."

Before she could think to stop herself, Angel called out, "Case?"

Everything happened in a blur. Case wheeled, the blue beam of the flashlight reaching out for her, but Angel was already moving as someone slammed the door open. She flashed through the beam and Case yelled out for her. Another voice from the doorway shouted, "There!"

Someone slammed into the desk she'd been sitting on, but Angel jumped off. Now she turned, brought the shotgun to bear, and let fire with one barrel. The room lit up, Case dropped the flashlight with a yelp, and Angel saw very clearly for one brief moment Locke's face in the fire of the shotgun. He gurgled and fell and Raven appeared in the doorway, his silhouette clear against the streetlight outside. He fired a gun in her general direction, and Angel answered with a second blast from the shotgun before scrambling out of the way. The silhouette fell backwards and the door slammed shut.

"Jesus," Case called out. "Jesus Jamie…Angel…Mara. Stop. Stop shooting." The flashlight had sputtered out when it hit the floor, leaving them alone in the dark. "Mara, where are you?"

Angel froze. She knew that she was facing the general direction of the side door, but wasn't sure exactly where it was. Case was off to her left. Locke was a dead man, but Raven probably not. The shotgun was a fearsome weapon up close, but at a distance more likely to hurt than kill.

Angel reached out with her senses, trying to get some idea of what she was facing. He had to be here somewhere, but was he inside or out? She didn't dare move or speak until she knew. Meanwhile, Case was still calling out to her, his position changing slightly. He was feeling his way around, getting closer. If he got close enough for her to grab, she'd take him down and make him shut up.

Then he kicked the flashlight, which went skittering across the floor, the light winking on and then back off. There was a gunshot, fire lighting up the room, and Angel turned and fired the shotgun in the general direction, but she'd fired all the shells. It clicked loudly and she moved to her right as another shot rang out. She lunged for the light switch and hit it, her left hand already going for the Glock under her arm.

The lights sputtered to life and she had a brief glimpse of Master, but he was moving too, lunging for a stunned Case. By the time Angel could get a good fix on him, Master had ducked behind Case and was using him as a shield.

"Jesus Christ, stop shooting, Mara," Case called out. "You're going to kill somebody. Stop."

"Case, you moron, why did you come here?" She held the Glock out towards him, hoping to get a shot at Master, but he was ducking, keeping the larger Case between them. "Mr. Talley," he said, his voice trembling. "She's snapped. She'll kill me. Make her understand what's happening or she'll kill us both."

"I got this," he whispered over his shoulder. Case put his hands up slowly. "Nobody's is going to hurt you," he said softly. "I need you to put the gun down. Please. Dr. Byrd is here to help you."

"Doctor my ass," Angel spat out. "That's Master."

Master popped his head up over Case's shoulder for just a second. "See," he said. Angel adjusted her aim and he ducked back behind Case. "I told you. It's the voices."

Case nodded solemnly and advanced toward her. "Mara, there is no Master. It's all in your head. I just want to help you get better. That's all both of us want. Now, please put the gun down."

As Case advanced, Angel shifted, hoping to get on his side, but Case matched her move and they danced like that in a wide circle around the room. "He's playing you, Case," she said. "Think. Those guys that came to your cabin, that chased us, they weren't figments of my imagination. You saw those guys. They were very real."

"I know they were," Case said. "Because you killed their boss. You killed a drug dealer, Mara. That's why those men are chasing you."

"Were chasing me," she corrected. "I took care of them. You hear that, *Master*? I took care of them. I never could figure out that second security team. It drove me nuts how I missed them."

"Mara—" Case started.

"That was the one thing I just couldn't reconcile," Angel continued, completely ignoring Case now. "How did I miss that security team? Then I finally woke up and I realized, they weren't a security team. They weren't there for Baca at all. They were there for me. They were a *hit team*."

Master's head popped up on Case's left shoulder and he smiled. "Well, aren't you the clever little girl? Why don't I give you a cookie?"

"Doctor—" Case started, but Byrd silenced him by pressing a gun to the side of his head. "What the...?"

"I told you he wasn't a doctor," Angel snapped. "Damn it, Case." She targeted Master, but again he ducked away.

"Thanks for the intel," Master cackled into his ear. "Of course, I knew she was coming here all along. But, being the fan of true love that I am, I just couldn't pass up a chance to get you two back together. It fills my heart with joy."

"Why don't you let him go and you and me will finish this?" Angel said to Master. "He's got nothing to do with this. I just fell into his lap."

"Oh, he's got everything to do with it now," Master cooed as they kept circling each other. "He knows about me. Now he's seen me. I can't let that slide, Angel. Besides, he's been rubbing up on what's mine, and I don't share my toys. You know that."

"I'm not your toy," Angel snarled. She kept looking, hoping to get a shot at something—his legs, his torso, anything—but Master kept moving. "I'm not your anything. Not anymore. I would've followed you anywhere, done anything you wanted, just like always."

"Don't think I didn't appreciate it," Master said, briefly popping up over one shoulder then ducking away again. "You were my best Angel, so cold and ruthless. It was a pleasure watching you grow and develop. But you got boring, *Jamie*. You didn't like the sex and you quit responding to the pain. What was I supposed to do? You could've been my queen, but I outgrew you. I already have my sights set on my next Angel. Got a couple of real intriguing possibilities."

Angel growled and stepped forward, gun at the ready, determined to line up a shot. Master yanked Case back and tapped the pistol against his temple. "Careful, careful," Master taunted her. "Make a wrong move and Loverboy gets a bloody makeover."

"Mara," Case whispered. "Mara—"

"Shut up, Case," she snapped. "I'm trying to get you out of this. Just shut up. If you'd have just listened to me…."

Master wrapped his left arm around Case's neck and pulled him back. Case grabbed at his arm, trying to pull it fee. "Mara," he whispered hoarsely. "Shoot me. Shoot me."

"Oooh, yes," Master called out. "Please do." He peeked over Case's shoulder again. "Come on, Angel. Show me that nasty streak of yours. Shoot him and let's have some real fun. Or have you gone soft? Don't tell me that you let this pecker get to you."

Angel thought about it for a minute, then shifted her aim, pointing the gun right at Case's face. "I told you," she said. "I told you that I'd kill you if I had to. Why didn't you listen?"

"Because," he gasped. "I loved you too much to let you go." Master pulled tighter, bending Case over slightly. He struggled to keep talking. "Do…what you've…got to do."

Angel shifted her aim again. It should be so easy, she thought. She'd looked how many men in the eyes and pulled the trigger. She'd pushed an innocent girl into the line of fire just to buy herself some time. She'd never hesitated to finish her mission. Now, she stared at Case, saw the hopelessness in his eyes, and she couldn't stop thinking about their night together. He'd remained committed to her, no matter how much she threatened him, no matter how horrible she'd been. He deserved better than to end up like this.

"I'm getting old here, Angel. You gonna shit or get off the pot?"

Angel had to stall, to wait for Master to make a mistake. She circled some more. "Not yet," she said coldly. "No. Before I pull this trigger I want you to tell me why. Why did you turn on me?"

Master giggled in Case's ear. "She's stalling," he said to Case. "You really got to her, didn't you? I didn't think she had a heart, but I guess I was wrong."

In response, Angel fired a shot that just breezed past his ear. "Oh my God," Case cried out, but Master just laughed. "I think you owe me that much," Angel said. "I never failed you. So why?"

Master continued maneuvering Case around in a circle, keeping Case trapped between the two guns. "Well, since inquiring minds want to know...," he teased. "Mr. Reyes made me an offer I couldn't refuse. Get rid of his half-wit son without it tying back to him, and receive a lucrative Midwestern distribution channel as payment. No more running whores or knocking off cheating spouses for insurance money. We're talking about the big time here. I'm going to be a king. I just had to give you up to tie up the last loose end. On a related note, you should've been there the night I killed Mr. Grasso. You wanna talk about one confused motherfucker. He didn't even have a daughter." Master peered over Case's shoulder again. "You were always so careful to research your targets, but you never did think to research your clients. Of course, I knew you wouldn't."

"Son of a bitch," she snarled. "You sold me out to be a lackey for Reyes?"

"No dear, I traded up. Didn't cost me much, though I must

say, you're a damn sight better than those so-called heavy hitters Reyes sent up here. Couldn't take out one little girl when I served her up on a platter. Pathetic."

The ease with which Master had tossed her aside was a knife in Angel's back, stoking the fire of her rage. "That's all I needed to know." She took aim again, sighting the nice, soft tissue of Case's neck. She could envision the hollow point slug punching through Case's neck right into Master, knocking him back, but probably — hopefully — not fatal. That would come in time. Behind Case, Master kept moving, kept bobbing and weaving.

"Come on, Angel," Master taunted her again. "Let's see what you got. Do it, baby."

"Do it," Case whispered as well. When he spoke, Angel found herself looking away from her target, looking up into his kind brown eyes. This man who'd drug her in from the woods when most would have left her for dead. The man who could've taken advantage and didn't. The man who'd given up his entire way of life for her. In that moment, she faltered, her gun hand wavered.

"Ah," Master spat out. "I knew you didn't have it in you. I guess if you want something done...." Master pushed Case forward, toward Angel, and brought his gun to bear. Angel saw what was coming but she was too slow, moving like slow motion as Master raised the gun to the back of Case's head and pulled the trigger.

CHAPTER 21

Case stiffened as Master pulled the trigger. The gun clicked loudly and Master threw his head back and laughed as the two of them froze. Angel gasped for breath, her mind vapor locked. Case was now between the two of them, momentarily free, but only for a moment that neither of them could take advantage of. Master was already moving, grabbing Case by the collar and yanking him backward. He continued to laugh as he made a show of clicking off the safety.

"That's called calling your bluff, dear," Master gloated. "You're way out of your league here, Angel. I know that you think I'm just some sort of bully, but everything you've done, I've done and done it better. Now, let's discuss the terms of your surrender."

Angel finally forced herself to move, but she was beaten and she knew it. Master was right, he'd seen right through her. He'd seen how she had changed, how Case had changed her. "Let him go," she said dejectedly. "I'll come with you. Just let him go."

"Are you dictating terms to me? That sounded like a demand."

Angel sighed. "Please. Please let him go and I will come with you."

239

Master smiled and leaned into Case. "Wow. The Angel of Death, begging for mercy. You must be some kind of man," he said. "You took my best girl, my best Angel, and you gave her a soul. You restored her humanity." Then his expression soured and he gripped his pistol tighter. "Just on principal alone I should kill you for that."

Angel saw Master's trigger finger tightening. In an act of desperation, she tossed her Glock aside and dropped to her knees. "No!" Both sets of eyes moved to her as Angel hit the floor and spread her arms out beside her. The Baretta was still holstered under her other arm if she could just get Master to drop his guard for a moment.

"I'm here. I'm down on my knees for you, Master. All I ask is that you let him go. Just let him walk out the door and I'll do whatever you want me to."

Master snickered at her. "That's not much to offer. You'll do whatever I want you to regardless. I own you. I *made* you. The very thought that you have anything to offer me is an insult. You have nothing to offer that I can't take."

"Then take me," she answered calmly. "Just do it if you're going to. I won't fight you anymore. But I owe this man something. If it's my life, then fine."

"Wow. She never ceases to amaze, does she? I had no idea that she had this level of depth, did you? Well of course you did. What am I saying?" Master's eyes danced from Case to Angel, kneeling in front of him. "My dear, I was just going to kill you, but not now. I see now that there are layers to you I never saw before, and I'm going to enjoy peeling every one of those layers back. I want you to understand, in no uncertain terms, that every remaining moment of your life is going to be filled with pain and misery. You're going to beg me for death, and I won't grant it. You're going to pray to God for release, but he won't hear you, because *I'm your God,* and I'm a vengeful God, and you need to be punished."

Angel knew that every word out of Master's mouth was true. If he took her alive, he would make good on that promise again and again. She closed her eyes to drive the images of her impending doom out of her head. When she opened them again, he was staring down at her expectantly.

Even as a cold shiver ran up her spine, Angel was determined to save Case's life. "Fine. Just let him walk."

Master chuckled again. "Letting him go was never a condition," Master said. "He's a dead man. He's seen my face. He has to die."

"Even if it means losing me?" Angel slowly worked her way back up to her feet. "I know that you're dying to take me apart. I know that it kills you that Case had me." She started circling again, angling for a shot, hoping that Master would make a tiny mistake. "He did things to me you could never imagine," she goaded. "He brought me alive. And what you had to take by force, I gave to him willingly."

She could see the anger building in Master's face as she talked, his grip on the pistol tightening, and he began clenching his jaw. The more it bothered him the more Angel enjoyed herself and the harder she pushed. "What you tried to kill, he brought back to life. You made me a weapon, but he made me a woman, over and over again. And every time he was inside me, you lost. Doesn't it just kill you to know that a man as weak as this could have undone everything you did so easily?"

"You're not helping his case," Master snarled, but Angel could tell that it was a lie. He was shifting his focus. Behind her, there was a clatter as someone, she assumed it was Raven, struggled through the side door. Bad timing. The longer she could go without going for the second gun, the better chance she had. Still, she couldn't have the big lug coming up behind her, so Angel continued to move, going for a position where she could watch them both.

As she slid to the side Master's eyes moved quickly to the door, and he smiled as he saw the wounded Raven make his way inside. "Two on one now, Angel. You took too long to make your move."

Angel risked a glance at the hulking man, his green scrubs splattered with blood as he lumbered toward her. He was moving slowly, struggling with the buckshot in his chest, but still coming. "You want to call him off?"

"Why?" Master asked as Raven slowly began to get his feet under him. "You shot him, I think he deserves a shot at you." He shifted slightly. "Raven?" The wounded man stopped and looked at Master. "Hurt her, just don't kill her. Break a few bones if you want. Spill some blood. Make her hurt."

Raven grunted in response and started moving toward Angel again, gaining speed as he went. Angel looked quickly from Raven to Master and back. "You're really going to let him get to me first?"

"There's plenty of you to go around."

Raven was closing…she had to move. In one fluid motion, she pulled the second gun and fired a series of three shots into the lumbering Raven's chest. His eyes rolled up in his head as he faltered and fell. Angel had to step quickly to the side to avoid the falling body. While she moved away, Master fired a perfect shot through her right bicep. She screamed in pain and dropped the gun as she reached for the wound.

"You think I didn't know you had that second gun? You think that there's anything you can do that I didn't anticipate? I told you, you're out of your league going up against me."

Angel looked at Case, trying hard not to cry. "I'm sorry. I

tried. I really did."

"Mara—" he started, but Master silenced him by pulling back on his shirt collar again.

"Oh, it's not over yet. The three of us, we're going to have all sorts of fun. Since you have such a deep and profound bond, it should be interesting to see how you each handle watching the other suffer for your actions. The pain should be delicious." Angel couldn't help herself, she started to laugh, which angered Master again. "What are you laughing at? I have you both. You have no other cards left to play here."

"You can't take us both alive. Your goons are dead, You're going to have to make a choice."

Master shook his head. "You're probably right. But you know, it's always been you, right? So Loverboy here draws the short stick."

"Yeah, I know." With her left hand, Angel plucked the switchblade out of her waistband. With a tiny click, the blade flipped out and she put the point to her own throat. "And when you kill him, I slit my throat, and you lose us both. More of a moral victory than anything, but denying your pleasure is about all I have left."

"You wouldn't," Master taunted.

"You can let him walk," Angel responded. "And I'll come with you. I need to see him walk out the door."

Master's grip on Case relaxed and he bucked in Master's hands. "Mara, you can't do this. You can't trust him."

"Shut up, Case," Angel barked. "We don't have all day here, Master. How bad do you want me? Case can't hurt you. He knows nothing about you. Even if he goes to the cops, what is he going to say? There are a hundred thousand people in Chicago alone that look like you. What's he going to give them?"

Case continued to struggle against Master's grip, showing

the first sign of fire and fight since the entire ordeal had begun. "Mara, don't. You can't." Yet Angel knew it was too little too late. She did have one last card to play, and she was going to do it.

"For you I can," she said softly. Her eyes locked onto Master's. "For once I'd like to save a life instead of taking one. One of those layers you can't wait to peel back. Come on, isn't his life worth all the torture you get to put me through? I'd think it would be a small price to pay."

Master looked from her to Case, then shoved Case violently forward, sending him tumbling face first into a twisted pile of discarded phones and fax machines. He tumbled into the pile and was promptly buried by the debris. "There," Master said. "But I can still kill him if you don't do exactly as I say."

"I understand," Angel whispered. She tossed the switchblade away. "I'm all yours. Let's go."

"Not yet," Master said, wagging a finger at her. "I don't trust you. Strip. Every last shred. I want to be sure you're not hiding anything."

Over her shoulder, Case was struggling to extricate himself. "No," he cried out. "Don't do it. Don't humiliate yourself for him."

"I want her humiliated," Master thundered at him. "I want her humbled." He turned his glare on Angel. "I want to see how much pride you're willing to swallow for this piece of shit. How far will the Angel of Death fall? Now strip."

All the emotions that Angel had worked so hard to squash threatened to overtake her in that moment. She wanted to cry, she wanted to throw up. She wanted to beg for mercy. Yet in the end she knew she couldn't do any of that. Her only option was to remain as stone cold as she possibly could, to kill the very things Case had brought back to life. Slowly, she peeled away her clothes, piece by agonizing piece, all the time aware that Case was trying to work himself free.

When she was completely nude, she said to Master. "There. Now can we go?"

"Not yet. Crawl over here to me. Heel at your master's feet."

"Don't you dare," Case snapped from the shifting tangle of debris.

"Shut up, Case," Angel snarled over her shoulder. "I'm doing this for you. Shut up. This is almost over. Just shut up." All the fear and sickness were replaced by a burning rage as she dropped to her hands and knees and painfully crawled across the dusty cement floor to Master, and when she was close, he yanked her head back by the hair and snarled at her.

"That's my girl. I'm going to have so much fun with you."

"Let's just go," she struggled to say. "Get me out of here."

Master yanked up to her feet and pressed the pistol into her stomach. "With pleasure, my dear." Across from them, Case had finally managed to get mostly free, but his ankle was still caught in a tangle of cords. "This is your lucky day, Mr. Talley. Angel's selfless act has bought you another day. But be warned, I will have eyes on you. You go to the cops, you come after her, you do anything I don't like, I'll bring you in and feed you her flesh one bite at a time."

Master turned, dragging Angel along with him. She struggled against his grip and twisted her head, looking for one last glance at Case. He pulled his foot free. Her Baretta was still lying where she'd dropped it, just inches away from him. Case lunged for it, but the dirty floor was slick and he stumbled and fell. Still Case kept moving, bear crawling towards the piece.

Master released Angel's hair and pivoted quickly, his gun hand coming up swinging toward Case. He fired once and the bullet slammed into the floor just in front of Case. Case called out in pain as a shard of concrete kicked up and sliced him open just above the eye. The gun was still just beyond his grasp. Master adjusted his aim…and Angel stepped in front of the gun.

"No." He seemed momentarily surprised, and Angel felt a small thrill of victory at this last desperate act of defiance. "I'll take care of him," she said calmly. Without waiting for a response, she turned and walked slowly to Case, who was still on all fours on the ground, eyeing the pistol that was tantalizing close.

Angel saw what he was thinking and shook her head at him. "Don't. He'll kill you before you could even lift the damn thing off the ground." She reached him, bent over, and helped Case to his feet. "Now you start trying to fight. You're a little late." She brushed the dirt off his shirt. "Don't be stupid here, Case," she whispered. With difficulty she managed to look up into his eyes. "Just be happy that you won. You made me a better person than I was. Be content with that."

Case nodded, but his eyes tracked upward, glaring across the distance at Master.

"Don't," Angel chided. "If he's too good for me, you don't stand a chance. Don't waste my sacrifice. I need you to remember what I told you in the hotel. Find someone who deserves your love and make the most of this." She laced her fingers behind Case's head and tilted it down so that he would stop glowered at Master. "Promise me."

"I won't stop looking for you," Case whispered.

"You have to."

"I won't," he responded. "I love you too much to let you go."

"Remember that," Angel said as she let go of Case's head. She saw the question pass across Case's face, but before he had a chance to ask it, she lashed out, kicking violently down on his left ankle. It shattered with the impact and Case crumbled to the ground, calling out in agony.

Without another word she calmly kicked the Baretta away

246

and turned to return to Master, who was howling in delight. "Oh, that was classic. That's my Angel. Oh, that was beautiful."

She ignored him, storming past, heading for the side door. "Come on if you're coming," she said coldly. Master had to jog to catch up, but as they reached the door, Master looked back over his shoulder.

"See you around, Mr. Talley. Have a nice night."

#

Despite the pain that was surging through his broken ankle, Case found a willpower he didn't know he had. As Angel strutted away, he began clawing his way towards the door. All he could see was red. All he felt was rage. In those moments, he thought of his time in the military and the brave men and women he'd tried to help. He thought of the victims of the drug war and the crime war he'd tried to help after that. He remembered every failure, every lost life, and he swore to himself as he inched his way across the dusty floor that for once in his life, he wouldn't fail.

Slowly, Case drug himself to the door. He pulled himself up on the doorknob, balanced himself, then twisted the knob and pushed the door open. He fell out in the humid night air and immediately looked up, scanning the surroundings for any sign of Mara.

She was long gone.

CHAPTER 22

Case awoke in a hospital bed, his ankle in a cast and in traction and his wrist handcuffed to the bed rail. His mind was foggy and his mouth was dry. He had no memory of anything that had happened after he crawled his way out of Safe Haven.

He looked around and eventually found the nurse call button on the bed and pushed it. He heard the ding from out in the hallway, and soon a female voice crackled out of a speaker somewhere behind him. "Can I help you?"

"Could I have some water, please?" Case said hoarsely.

"Yes sir," the pleasant voice said. "One minute."

It kind of sounded like Mara. His eyes went to the door, which was cracked just enough to let in a tiny finger of light. Case stared at the door, waiting. In the movies, this was the part where the heroine would sneak into the hero's room and offer him a clever escape, or at least a reason to hope. He had convinced himself that she was going to walk through the door when it opened.

Instead, a short, bald man in black glasses and a brown suit came in. He was carrying a pink plastic pitcher and a Styrofoam cup. "Mr. Dacus, you're awake," he called out. The man poured some water into the cup, drug a wheeled tray over to the Case's bedside, and set it down. "Here you go."

"Thank you," he croaked as he took the cup. The man in the suit pulled a seat up next to the bed and waited patiently as Case downed three small cups in short order. Case finally smacked his lips and put the cup down.

"Feeling better?" the man asked.

"Yes, thank you."

"Good. Mr. Dacus, my name is Carl Scheer, and I'm with the FBI."

"Oh God," Case said, rolling his eyes.

"Oh God would be correct, Mr. Dacus. You are a man we've been wanting to talk to for a very long time. Drug smuggling, identity theft, fraud, not to mention a host of smaller charges. Of course, the local authorities back in Detroit would like to have a few words with you as well. You're looking at a ton of charges, and probably civil suits after that."

"So I'm screwed. That's what you're telling me."

"Completely. Luckily for you, I don't give two ratshits about all of that. What I care about is The Thunderbird."

Case looked over at Scheer with disdain. "What the fuck is The Thunderbird?"

"Who the fuck is The Thunderbird, to be accurate. He is a mystery. He's a one-man organized crime wave. He started small time, running girls and weed, and moved his way up the ladder. We think that he's been involved in a vast array of things, but more importantly, we think he's moving into wholesale drug running and may be jumping in bed with one of the big Mexican cartels. The thing is, no one knows who he is or what he looks like. Nobody, I believe, except you. I want to know everything you know, everything you saw, in that old shelter."

Case chuckled and turned away. "You're dreaming. Chasing ghosts. People like that don't exist."

Scheer clicked his tongue and sat back in his chair. "I'm sorry to hear that. Then I suppose you're the one responsible for the two dead guys in the Safe Haven shelter. *And* the three guys at the Explorer Inn. *And* the five people at the comic book convention in Albuquerque, which includes Rafael Baca, step son of Ernesto Reyes, one of Mexico's least friendly drug lords. I wonder what he'd think about us catching Rafael's killer."

"I had nothing to do with any of that."

"I believe you. The problem we have...," Scheer said as he stood up, "Is that you were found in said shelter with two dead bodies and the guns used to kill them. Those two guns killed all those other people. Oh, and I think I forgot to mention the three rednecks in a Montana roadhouse, one of whom was killed with said gun."

Case felt the panic filling him up. "Mr. Scheer, please. I can't talk to you."

Scheer leaned over the bed so he could look Case in the eye. "We can protect you, Mr. Dacus. This isn't like the movies, where the bad guys always find the witness. You help us catch The Thunderbird, all of this goes away."

Case met his gaze with one of his own. "You can't protect Mara," Case said. "He'll kill her, in the slowest, most brutal way possible. He told me that. She gave her life for me, I won't waste that. I promised her."

Scheer sighed and stood up. "That's too bad. I was hoping that you'd be smart about this. Federal prison can be a nasty place, Mr. Dacus, especially if the guys inside find out you're a pedophile."

"I'm not," Case answered strongly.

"They won't know that."

Case yanked at the handcuff around his wrist, but freedom was not coming. "You asshole."

"Only if I need to be, Mr. Dacus. I advise that you take my offer under consideration. If The Thunderbird has someone you love in his grasp, she's probably dead already. I would think that letting her killer go would be a greater waste of her sacrifice." Scheer walked slowly to the door of his room. "Think about it, Mr. Dacus."

#

It was worse than she could have possibly imagined. Angel was chained in a small, windowless room. No light came in from the outside, even when someone opened the door. No sound came from the outside. She had no reference point at all.

Angel tried in those early days. She tried to reason with Master or any one of the number of lackeys he might send in his place. She tried to think of ways to break free or to gain some tiny bit of knowledge that might help her. Master was smart and he was careful, and she never had a chance.

Life devolved into a never ending stream of tortures. He beat her, whipped her, and raped her at his discretion. He starved her for days at a time. He deprived her of sleep. He looked for any opportunity to inflict some sort of pain or humiliation, and he made sure that she felt every last bit of it.

After some time, Angel became more like an animal than a person. Life revolved around her sporadic feedings. As she lost touch with her humanity, the tortures became less frequent because Master could no longer obtain pleasure from her pain.

The only thing that kept her tethered were her memories of Case. When Master came to her, she slipped away to her memories and imagined that she was back in the hotel with Case, with the rose petals and the wine and the candles, and she stayed there until long after Master left. She spent more and more time in her fantasy world as she waited for the day when Master would eventually tire of the game and come to slit her throat.

Then the day came. Master threw the door open and brilliant sunshine flooded the room. The bright light blinded and scared Angel, and she turned and thrashed in an effort to shield herself from it. Master strolled into the filth, wearing an expensive, shiny suit and wraparound sunglasses, showing no signs of being disgusted by her squalid living conditions.

Master knelt down beside her, pulled her hair, and looked into her face. "Are you there, Angel? Is anybody home?"

She pulled out of his grasp and he let her go. Angel was pulling up her memories, preparing to escape to Case's loving arms, when Master pulled her back.

"Would you like to get out of here?"

She couldn't help it. Angel looked up at Master expectantly. There was sunlight, and beyond the door she saw dirt and sky and clouds. How long had it been since she'd seen anything at all?

"I think I've got your attention," Master said proudly. He knelt down in front of her again but stayed back. "I need my Angel of Death again. I have a job for you, a very special job, but I need to know that you're back. That we've cured you of your little bout of humanity. Do you think you can do that?"

She didn't speak, but she grunted and looked longingly at the door and the sunshine beyond. All Angel wanted in that moment was to feel the sunshine on her face again, just for one second.

"First, you'll have to pass a test." Master stood and began slowly pacing around the room. "It's pass/fail, and by fail I mean an immediate bullet to the brain stem, so the stakes are high. The target is a sweet, loving family. They've never done anything wrong; they're not involved with anything. They're your basic all-American family. I need you to kill them and I need you to make it messy."

He came back around and bent over Angel. Master placed

a single finger under her chin and lifted her face. "Can you do it? Can you slaughter innocents and walk away? Can you be my Angel of Death again?"

Angel's mind flickered. She imagined it, killing the family, and it turned her stomach. Then, Case came to her. She remembered that night of passion, the night they made love, and in the memory she saw something else that she hadn't seen in ages. She saw hope and opportunity. It would require her to do things that she didn't want to do. Horrible things. She had done it once before, she could do it again. Only this time, she would have something to work towards, a goal to be met.

"What do you say, Angel? Can you do it?"

Angel felt the hardness come back. Her eyes snapped into focus. She could barely speak, but managed to look square at Master and forced out two small words.

"Try me."

To Be Continued....

Donny Hunt has worked as a reporter, sportscaster and photographer. He lives in Amarillo Texas with his wife and four children. He now has three novels, Blessed Poison, The Quest for Aranwa, and now Angel of Death.

Check out the Angel Of Death prequel short story The Recruit on my blog at https://rantsinthekeyofd.wordpress.com/2017/08/11/a-short-story-about-a-girl-at-the-end-of-her-rope-and-a-stranger-who-offers-us-a-way-out/

www.ingramcontent.com/pod-product-compliance
Lightning Source LLC
Chambersburg PA
CBHW050729180626
46814CB00002B/668